This is a work of fiction. Any references to historical events, real people or real places are used fictitiously. Other names, characters, places, and events are products of the author's imagination and any resemblance to actual events, places, or persons living or dead is entirely coincidental.

THE PROPHET
Second Edition, July 27, 2018
Copyright © 2017 Ande Edwards
ISBN: 9781393162407 (Print)
Written by Ande Edwards
Original Cover Design by Matthew David Walling

I0664318

A Note from the Author.
Reader's Guide to the
Demons and Angels Portrayed in this Book:

We tend to think of demons as beady-eyed beings with jagged teeth. So when I sat down to write this book I had to spend some time exploring what the Bible had to say about demons and angels. Taking what was there, I let my imagination take over and create one possible view of the spiritual realm, I hope you find it fascinating but more, I hope it causes you to let your own mind consider how you see the spiritual realm.

This novel functions on the understanding that demon were once glorious creatures. Before their fall they had been powerful and beautiful to behold. At one time, demons shined with the Light of the King, but after the rebellion, their Light was removed. This work suggests that as time went on, they grew darker and darker, further from the angel they had once been. They eventually became black with the evil that filled them.

Throughout the Prophet Series readers will be introduced to a host of different types of angels/demons, each unique, each with their own purpose. In one instant of rebellion, they changed from angel to demon, but the physical transformation from angelic being to cursed demon takes much longer. Lucifer had been beautiful. And he still can be beautiful when the situation calls for it. A demon is not successful at enticing humans to evil if the packaging is not pleasant. Demons still possess most of the same powers they had as angels. In *The Prophet*, the following types of angels/demons are included.

Warriors: All warriors have the sign of the warrior on the left side of their chest. But most of the warrior demons are so far removed from the angels they had once been that the sign has long since been forgotten and no longer visible. Warrior angels fight for the King (God), Warrior demons fight for the Prince of Darkness (Lucifer).

Guardians: Guardian angels cannot communicate with humans. A Guardian Angel that has fallen becomes a Destroyer Demon bringing affliction and disaster to the humans.

Ministering: Ministering angels can speak to humans. A Ministering Angel that has fallen becomes a Tormenting Demon. Whether demon or angel, they can speak only what the human already has inside of them. While Ministering angles use what is inside the person to encourage them and build them up, Tormenting demons use things the person has already heard/experienced to discourage, tempt, and belittle them—thoughts and ideas from movies, books, music, or those around them. Anything the person has fed into their soul can be used. For this reason, the Destroying Demons take great care to assure that the humans have plenty of exposure to things for the Tormenting Demons to use. The media provides a perfect venue to flood human souls with images, words, and ideas that can later be used to torment them.

Both angels and demons can appear to humans in a human form. Occasionally, angels will disguise themselves as humans to test a human or help them in some way. Demons, too, can take on the form of a human for the purposes of testing or tempting. Demons tend to use this ability more often than the angels.

When allowed by the King, humans can see angels or demons in their true form. This is rare, but it happens. The ability to possess a human has always existed, but angels never do it. Demons have possessing humans for thousands of years, but many people have convinced themselves that demon possession no longer happens. This makes it easier on the demons, allowing them to possess someone for years if they want to.

Each of the angels was given a name by the King; their name bares significance and reflects who they are in their purest form. It is a reminder of the beauty and Light that the King sees in them. The King understands the value in a name.

The demons, at one time, had also been given a name by the King, a badge of honor to be worn proudly, but as they transform from the angelic beings they once were into the demons they become, the Prince of Darkness sometimes renames them. He, too, assigns names based on characteristics, but his assignment is branded across their foreheads and sewn into their hearts, a condemnation to forever be connected to that trait. Many tormenting demons wear the same names: Anger, Jealousy, Condemnation—and the list goes on.

As an author, it was interesting to explore how demons and angels may work and what the fall may have looked like. I explore ideas such as, can an angel still fall or was that a one-time event that can no longer happen? Can an angel die? I read all that I could find in the Bible about angels and the different types. I reviewed stories in the Bible about the demons and their behavior and attempted to model my angles and demons after what I found there, but the demons and angels in this series represent my imagination and how I see the spiritual realm interacting with the earthly one. I hope you enjoy the story!

ACKNOWLEDGMENTS

Encounters with angels and demons seem like something out of a science fiction movie, but the Bible mentions both angels and demons hundreds of times, and Ephesians tells us that we battle against the powers of darkness, not flesh and blood. What exactly does that look like? How do they fill their days, and what do their interactions with us look like? This book is a feeble attempt to explore that idea, and I am so thankful to all the people who ventured with me on this incredible journey of faith and discovery.

Thank you to Thea, Nat, Beth, and Melissa for reading, and rereading and reading yet again as I worked on the story and the characters and for engaging with me in endless discussions on angels, demons, and spiritual warfare. Thank you for sharing your experiences and being willing to share your "you're going to think I'm crazy" stories. Your feedback and critique were invaluable to me. This is a better book because of you.

I am so thankful for my Bible study group. You are a fantastic group of people that have inspired and supported me on my journey. You showed me how important it is to have a support system of fellow believers you can entrust with your greatest struggles. You have walked through many fires with me, and I love each of you for allowing me to truly be myself when I am with you. I tried to model the Wednesday night group after our own comradery, and while the characters and their struggles are not reflective of ours, their unity and cohesion are.

I want to thank my husband for supporting the crazy idea that I would write a book. I started down this path with great trepidation, but you have encouraged me every step of the way. I could never have hoped for a better man.

To the college professors I know, at both state and faith-based schools, thank you for sharing your stories and struggles with me. Your wisdom has never been needed more.

To my mom, thank you for making me strong and resilient.

PROLOGUE

To win a war, you must develop a strategy. Titus once again reviewed their battle plan and smiled to himself over the simplicity of it. Some of the greatest military minds on the planet had spent years developing this plan, and it was paying off. The strategy was simple: do not attract the attention of the enemy, be subtle, and pick your targets wisely. It had taken many years to get all the pieces in place for this stage of the battle, but it had been seamless.

The Prince had called in his best, and they had developed a plan so impressive it could not fail. They had lost a great deal of real estate in the process, but some collateral damage was to be expected. Seneca, the most seasoned among them, offered wisdom and cunning. The days of losing ground had not only stopped but had turned around. The transition had been gradual so as not to attract attention—and it seemed to be working.

Titus stood and stretched. It was an unusual practice, but the hairless rats did it so often and with such expressions of comfort that he had adopted the behavior himself. He laughed to think of it. Walking to the long mirror in the Great Hall, Titus looked at himself. He had mastered the mannerisms of the rats. They could not see him for who he was and his study of their behaviors; things like stretching made him blend right in. No one suspected anything.

But this body was growing old, and Titus saw no reason to remain in a decrepit body. When he had taken over this body, it was young, the body of a twenty-year-old, firm, and athletic, and his black hair was thick and wavy. But he had been in the body long enough that it was no longer in its prime. When this battle was over, he would find a new one. He smiled a knowing smile, tucked the manila folder with the latest reports from the field under his arm, and headed into the conference room with Morax. Humans were proving to be a relatively easy target.

Chapter 1

Aegeus strolled toward the meeting spot. He walked as one who had eternity on his side. His hands brushed across the stalks in the wheat field he was ambling through. The grain heads felt soft on his fingers. He closed his eyes briefly as he savored the delicate brush of the plants across his strong hands. He had the hands of a warrior, solid and sure, rough from thousands of years of battle. The gentle touch of the wheat against them was made all the sweeter because of it.

His senses soaked in the glory that was heaven. Light warmed his olive skin; the sweet smell of lilac filled the air; it was his favorite smell. He breathed in deeply, letting it penetrate through him. He turned his face toward the throne room, the light and power of the King washing over him, beckoning to him. For a precious moment, he soaked it all in listening to the voices of a thousand angels singing their praise of the King.

His chestnut-colored hair was loose and blew gently in the breeze. His almond colored eyes reflected the peacefulness he felt. The lite brush of power caressed his skin as if every particle of his being was getting charged. Aegeus savored the rush of love and overwhelming joy that could only come from the King.

In the distance, he could see the glimmer of the city. Reluctantly, he tucked his wings into the compartments on his back where they fit when he did not need them, and headed in the opposite direction, toward a large tree in the center of the field. As he walked, he tried to take in every scent, every color, and every texture along the way. Savoring each precious one for the gift it was because he knew that there were no guarantees he would return.

The tree stood tall and proud where it had stood for all time. The bark of the tree was rough and cracked in a way that was beautiful. If you took the time to look closely, you could see subtle carvings in the bark just below the surface. It whispered secrets of the past and the beauty of the future. It spoke of redemption and hope to all who would listen. Its long, sturdy branches extended in every direction. The leaves fluttering in the breeze sounded like ocean waves, calling out their praise to the King.

As Aegeus reached the tree, he was pleased to see the others were not there yet. He wanted a few minutes to enjoy the quiet stillness of the tree, the peace it brought as you rested near it. He had heard it would provide other feelings as well, but Aegeus had never experienced anything but peace when he was near it. Perhaps because peace was what he desired most.

Warriors tended to be more stoic than other angels. Although there were certainly exceptions to that, Aegeus was not among them. In fact, some considered him the most stoic of them all. But he had not always been that way. There had been a time when Aegeus invested in those he was sent to fight for—when he had fought with his heart, not just his strength. But that was long ago and mostly forgotten, at least by Aegeus.

Pas-Dammim had changed everything for him. After the battle, he had returned to the tree collapsing beneath its limbs and pouring out his anguish. The tree had absorbed it all, replacing it with the peace he so craved. Aegeus's grief was so great that day that the very fruit on the tree had turned gray and dull. The King had heard the call of despair and had come to attend to both Aegeus and to the tree. All of heaven had grieved under the tree with Aegeus, but most especially the King.

Aegeus learned the wrong lesson from Pas-Dammim. He had decided he could not afford to care too deeply. He believed that allowing himself to feel too strongly for any, but the King could prove perilous. Humans were unpredictable. As a warrior, he had to be willing to fight both for and against them. He understood that caring about them could cause clouded judgment, something a warrior could not afford. He had spent thousands of years constructing the wall around his heart.

He was not unkind. To the contrary, underneath, Aegeus's heart was tender. But he was a warrior through and through. He stood tall with broad shoulders and strong, solid muscles. He fought with a ferocity that had moved him quickly through the ranks. The other angels trusted him; if you were going into battle, Aegeus was the warrior you wanted with you.

He didn't allow his detachment from the humans to interfere with his duty. He showed them compassion and kindness, but he did so in a clinical manner that got the job done without risking attachment. For centuries, this had worked wonderfully. After all, warriors were not on the earth for long stretches of time, so he had little opportunity to interact with humans.

Reaching the tree, Aegeus circled it slowly exploring the types of fruit that were on it today. He took his time admiring each option and then selecting a yellow one with small purple dots. This one was new. He smelled the fruit; it had a sweet aroma, like angelo—one of his favorites. Around the tree was a soft grassy knoll greeting all who came to sit beneath its shade and lean against its trunk. Aegeus sank into the lush green grass and leaned back against the tree listening to it whisper.

Sweet nectar burst from the fruit and flowed down his chin when he bit into it. Using the back of his hand, he wiped the juice from his closely cropped beard. There was no end to the King's creativity; Aegeus reveled in the joy of being able to experience it. He retrieved his wineskin and took a swallow of wine that perfectly complemented the fruit. He would miss home.

Chapter 2

"You look like you're in heaven," Kfir said, joining Aegeus under the tree with a quiet swoosh, indicating he had flown there and not walked like Aegeus. It was one of their favorite jokes, although angels were not known for their joke telling.

Kfir tucked his wings away and embraced Aegeus, his brother-in-arms. Kfir's zeal to defend truth had moved him quickly through the ranks and into the elite guard with Aegeus, as signified by the small piercing in the right eyebrow. Like all members of the elite guard, he reported directly to Michael, the head archangel. But unlike Aegeus, whose unit spent most of their time in heaven training, Kfir's unit required him to spend extended periods of time on earth.

"Good to see you, Keef. How are things in Africa?" Aegeus asked.

With a few minor exceptions, Kfir had been working in Africa for more than two thousand years.

"The people are suffering, but they have a love so pure and faith so strong that they suffer not. The enemy is relentless, but the people's prayers are consistent and true. I am strengthened by their passion for the King and their dedication to his service. They suffer tirelessly. It is hard, but I feel honored to fight there." Kfir's love for the King's children poured from him. His bronze eyes gentle and beaming with pride on their behalf. Aegeus did not understand Kfir's affection for the humans, but he admired it.

"And the Spirit?" Aegeus asked.

"The Spirit is ever present, the people treasure the Spirit, and it has not limits," Kfir responded, surveying the tree and the many options the King had created. He chose a green-and-pink striped fruit. Plucking it from the tree, he gingerly stuck his tongue to it for a sample taste. Aegeus laughed at the sight.

"You know it is going to be good. When has it ever not been good?" Aegeus asked, laughing.

"I was in Bethlehem once," Kfir began, which caused deep guttural laughter from Aegeus that drowned out the rest of the story.

"Oh, not the Bethlehem story again!" Lavi said as he joined them under the tree.

Lavi's long black hair was pulled back from his face. His leather tunic, sleeveless and thick to protect his chest and back from the enemy. His massive wings extended a foot above his head and reached to the ground. When they were fully extended, he had a fifteen-foot wingspan.

Lavi's wings did not retract like those of the warrior, as a guardian they were vital to his job. Lavi used his wings to conceal his charge from demons. A demon's talons could not pierce a guardian's wings, nor could their lies penetrate through them. They also served as a shield protecting him from sword blows. In some ways, this made guardians more vulnerable than warriors because severe damage to an angels' wings meant they could never again travel to earth.

"Welcome, brother," Aegeus said as he reached out to Lavi and embraced him. Kfir and Lavi were among the small group of angels Aegeus would consider friends. It had taken thousands of years after Pas-

Dammim for him to allow himself the luxury of close friends. But he had known both Kfir and Lavi since time began, and they had proven themselves strong and true.

Kfir bit into his fruit and found it to be just a little tart and altogether pleasing. It was precisely what his taste buds were looking for.

"The trauma was real," Kfir offered, referring back to the Bethlehem incident as he too embraced Lavi. All three angels laughed at Kfir's misfortune.

"Are you still in Israel?" Kfir asked Lavi as he sat down in the soft grass and leaned against the tree. Lavi sat too. He watched as Aegeus again circled the tree examining its fruit and running his hand over the rough bark. Lavi couldn't help but wonder what news Aegeus delivered that made him choose this place.

"No, my charge came of age; I have been doing special assignments for a while," Lavi answered.

Every family had a guardian angel assigned to them. From birth to twelve, children had their own personal guardian, these guardians had priority with the King. On the child's twelfth birthday, their guardian was reassigned to another charge. As a result, guardians were much more comfortable and familiar with children than other angels were.

Guardians were a tight knit group, and because they rotated families often, most of them knew each other. They were tender hearted and passionate about their charges. The guardians' desire to protect their charge against all threats was sewn into the very fabric of their being. And while they, like all angels, were neither friend nor foe of their charge, serving only the will of the King, that did not prevent them from caring for those they protected.

The three angels spent a few minutes catching up and filling the gaps of time between when they had last seen each other. Lavi glanced toward the city in the distance, and a longing to be in the throne room overcame him. As a guardian angel, he did not get to spend much time in heaven as he would like. His soul yearned to be in the presence of the King.

"We will stop there before we leave," Aegeus offered, understanding the need, and joining Lavi in gazing upon the city. There was nothing equal to standing in the throne room of the King.

"Will it just be us today?" asked Kfir, now eager to move the meeting along. He loved his brothers, but a trip to the throne room was beckoning.

"For now," said Aegeus. Without further delay, Aegeus began to fill them in. "There is a small town in America called Platitude. The King has a great interest in it."

"America? As in the United States?" Kfir had only been to America once. It had been a short assignment, one the other angels referred to as the debacle of 1974.

"Yes," Aegeus continued.

"I did not realize there were small towns in America," Kfir questioned.

"You have much to learn, my friend." Lavi chuckled, remembering Kfir's last visit to America.

"The enemy is planning something for the town," Aegeus continued. "I don't know exactly what, but the King has been moving a small contingent of humans into the town for the last three years. There is a college there that seems to be the center of the enemy's focus. This college is specifically for the King's children. He loves the college and has many children there."

"I always wanted to go to college," Kfir interjected as he smoothed down his corn rows. Lavi and Aegeus laughed and shook their heads at his feeble attempt at humor. Kfir never seemed to fully accept that jokes were not their strong suit. Kfir saw no reason that his status as a mighty warrior meant he had to be serious.

"The King has already moved eleven humans into the town, each with a particular purpose," Aegeus continued. "Each of them currently has a guardian, some also have a warrior." Kfir and Lavi exchanged a glance at this news.

Warriors typically did not serve individual families; in fact, few had ever been assigned to a family. Generally, they were attached to nations and continents, working in military-style units and squadrons to fight against the King's enemies. Occasionally, the King called them to battle against humans; this was particularly true during the time before the Lamb was slain.

But much of their work now was against the dark forces, although they did still march into battle with those human militaries who sought the King's will and direction before going to war. Lucifer had his own army, and he was relentless in his pursuit of the King and his children. To have a warrior pulled from the military and assigned to a family in such a small town was rare indeed, and to have so many pulled out was nearly unprecedented.

"There is one more human who must be moved into place before we are ready," Aegeus continued. "We are to be the guard detail for the Twelfth who will arrive later this week."

"The Twelfth?" Lavi asked with intentional confusion. "That is an odd name." But Lavi knew Aegeus well and understood fully that referring to the humans by number instead of name was one way to keep himself distanced from them. He would refer to each charge by a number. In this case, by the order, they arrived in Platitude. The First arrived first, and so the order went. Despite the oddness of it, the other angels recognized and embraced this as Aegeus's way.

"We would be in trouble if there were to many more," Lavi added with a wink. Aegeus smiled and shook his head, he knew it was odd.

"Two warriors for one family?" asked Kfir, suddenly even more interested in the mission.

"It is unusual, I know, but I confirmed with Michael himself," said Aegeus. In fact, Aegeus had had many long conversations with Michael about it. He had recommended a dozen other angels he felt were more appropriate for the assignment. But Michael had not wavered. He had been insistent that Aegeus was the right one for the job. The King had willed it.

"What do we know about the Twelfth?" Lavi asked.

"Very little. I do know that the King hand-selected each angel in the town. Specifically assigning the three of us to the Twelfth," Aegeus finished.

"And we know nothing of him?"

"Nothing," Aegeus confirmed.

"What then of the other eleven?"

"Where would you like to start?" asked Aegeus.

"Start with the town," Lavi said, glancing longingly at the city inside of which was the throne room. Feeling the King's presence was so much more pronounced here than on the earth, so he savored every second of it.

Aegeus reached up to the tree and pulled a bundle of grapes to share with Kfir and Lavi. It had a wide array of grapes in varying colors and degrees of sweet or tart. He then stretched out in the meadow under the tree before continuing, he wasn't entirely sure how to describe the town.

"This town is difficult?" Kfir asked.

"The town has challenges," Aegeus began. The town had always had a higher-than-normal demon presence because of the college. College students tend to attract demons, but Christian colleges get lots of attention as demons try to side-rail the next generation.

Platitude College had been making strides, and as a result, the Light had been bright there. Because of that, more demons flocked to it in an attempt to stop the tide. Some of the King's children were easily distracted by rules and checklists. When you put so many of them in one place, there became an unspoken expectation to appear "perfect."

They no longer share their struggles—not the real ones, not the ones that grab hold of their souls. They keep those buried for fear of judgment by their peers. Feelings of isolation and shame are one of the enemy's greatest weapons.

Humans seemed to need a pecking order. They had an innate need to belong and yet be distinguished. Sometimes they accomplished that by pointing out the flaws in others. Checklists and legalism helped them feel higher in the pecking order.

Aegeus, however, did not say all this to Kfir and Lavi. He didn't need to. Instead, he focused on more factual information about Platitude.

"Platitude is in the middle of nowhere. It is beautiful, surrounded by the Elpída mountain range. A small brook runs through the center of it, dividing the campus from the town. There are about five thousand students on the campus and roughly eight thousand people in the city. The winters are long and cold, crime is minimal, and many of the King's children are there. Woods line the edge, giving a beautiful display of color in the fall.

"The college has been there for over two hundred years. They specialize in programs of service. Their students are unlikely to grow wealthy, but they will be armed to offer food to the hungry, shoes to the needy, and a drink to those who thirst. They have recently begun a new physician assistant program; our charge has been hired to work for that program.

"They have a single grocery store, a single movie theater, and a single stoplight. In the past, they were making significant strides in understanding and applying the teaching of the Lamb, but over the last year, the demons have strangled that. They have begun moving backward. I fear they will find themselves right fighters."

"Right fighters?" Kfir was not familiar with the term.

"Those who are more concerned about proving they are right than they are about finding the truth," Lavi offered. He had seen it many times on many continents.

Chapter 3

Meir appeared with a gentle whoosh.

"Meir!" They exclaimed in unison. Ministering angels had an aura about them that just made others feel better. It was a by-product of their job.

Aegeus noted that Meir's hair was jet black and her eyes the color of honey, her wings iridescent and reflective of the glorious light of heaven. Knowing they changed with each encounter and reflected her mood and moment, he found himself wondering what color they would be once on earth.

She was clad in a traditional angel robe of glorious white. Her hair was in a simple bun, some of which had come loose and fell softly around her face. Her eyes shone brightly as the other angels stood to greet her. How such delicate angels could carry such tremendous burdens was a mystery to the other angels.

"Meir, how long have you been home?" Lavi wanted to know.

Meir, like Lavi, spent most of her time on earth with only short breaks to come home between assignments. She was rarely assigned to a single family; more often, she worked in neighborhoods and cities, going where she was needed most.

"I have seen four passes of fruit on the tree." She responded.

Angels did not mark time in heaven the same as humans did on earth. There was no night in heaven, there was no end to the days, and time existed in abundance. Who attempted to count the sand in the sea? No one, because there was plenty. One only needed to measure time if time were limited. On the earth, time was a commodity and, therefore, must be measured. In heaven, time was endless; marking time was unnecessary.

But the King loved to create, and regularly he would change the fruit on the trees, the colors of the flowers or sky, and the landscape outside the city. Angels would often refer to how many variations they had been able to see in one of these areas between missions. It was a measurement of the pleasure and joy of watching the King in his creativity. There was no human equivalent.

"You will be joining us on our mission?" Kfir asked with obvious delight. He hugged her in welcome.

"I understand it is of utmost importance to the King and is being overseen by Michael himself," she said in response.

Aegeus also hugged his dear friend.

"I trust you have been briefed on the twelve and that you know about the Fifth and the Eighth?" she asked Aegeus with concern in her eyes. Meir embraced Aegeus's way of referring to the humans. She understood that it was his way of remaining neutral, keeping a degree of separation between them and him.

"I do," he responded. "And I am concerned about the condition of the Sixth."

"We will need extra ministering angels." It was both a statement and a request. Aegeus understood her concerns.

Ministering angels could encourage a human by bringing words of scripture to their mind, or lyrics from a song. They could retrieve words of encouragement and affirmation that someone had once spoken to them, lines from a movie, events, and memories from the past, or even something they had heard during a sermon or speech. But it had to already be inside the person.

But even as the head Ministering angel, Meir could not speak words the human had not first fed into their soul; only the Spirit had the power to do that.

"Recruit all that you need, Meir. Michael has cleared it," Aegeus noted. Having enough ministering angels with them would be critical to the mission.

"I will form a team and meet you in the town," she replied. Meir, like Aegeus, was focused on the mission. She had little time for unnecessary chitchat. She chose her words carefully because she understood their power in a way few others did. Unlike Aegeus, Meir had a profound love of the King's children. Her job had shown her their deepest sorrows; she had seen unimaginable pain and hurt and knew all too well the damage the enemy could do.

It had given her a great appreciation for the kindness they showed each other. She understood the immeasurable value of the little things, those small words of encouragement that could seep into a soul and take root, waiting for just the right moment to be needed. She knew that those simple kind gestures could save a life.

"Meir?" Kfir called to her before she could leave. "What does heaven smell like to you?" he asked seemingly from nowhere.

"Like the King, of course." With that, Meir was gone.

Lavi inhaled deeply and let the sweet smell of heaven fill his nostrils. It smelled like gardenias. He loved the scent of gardenias.

"The Fifth and the Eighth?" he asked, returning his attention to the mission.

"In good time, my friend, in good time. First, let's journey to the throne room and see the King before we go. We will need his power." Aegeus turned to Kfir.

"What does heaven smell like to you, Kfir?"

"Today, it smells like freshly baked bread, I love that smell."

Chapter 4

The sounds of the cherubim singing became louder as they walked. Lavi frequently paused to stand still with his eyes closed and let the Light of God wash over him. He wanted to take his time, savoring every moment and the anticipation of being with the King. Guardians were home so rarely that he treasured every second. Every breath taken in heaven was a precious renewing of his soul.

Aegeus too took his time, understanding the need to savor their remaining time in heaven. He wasn't sure how long it would be before they returned. He had many questions about the mission, and he felt anxious about being assigned to a family. That has not happened since the Lamb was a child, and that was completely different. Aegeus couldn't help but wonder why the King had chosen him for this mission.

As they walked, Kfir noticed a lion resting in the tall grass while a young human child climbed on it. It made him smile. He felt an overwhelming sense of excitement for the humans. Their time on earth was full of trials, but oh, what they had to look forward to. He loved to be near the new arrivals and enjoy the wonder they experienced when they encountered heaven for the first time, experiencing the King in a way they could not on earth. Their eyes finally fully opened. It was beautiful. Kfir snapped a reed off a plant as his hand brushed against it; he put it in his mouth sucking on the nectar. He would miss it.

The power and glory of the King intensified as they drew nearer the city. The closer they came, the less they spoke. Their minds focused only on the King. Aegeus could feel the power surge through him, overwhelming completeness washing over him. Power and energy coursing through his body with an energy unknown to mortal man, as if he were made of electricity.

When they arrived on the streets of gold, Aegeus felt the desire that always filled him when he drew close to the King. The mark of the warrior, a symbol on the left side of each warrior's chest consisting of the tree of life with two flaming swords, glowed in response to being so close. The swords flashed with fire. He forgot all else but the love of the King, and the honor of being in his presence. Michael met them at the door to the throne room.

"He will see you," Michael informed them. He had, of course, been expecting them. Michael swung the large doors open, revealing the glory of the throne room. The Light radiating from inside was so pure, so warm and comforting. It filled the space. You could feel nothing but joy, peace, and love. Not just any love, but the complete and overpowering feeling of being loved.

There was perfect stillness in the throne room. No distractions. When you walked into the presence of the King, you had his full attention. The King had his back turned when they entered. He stood in front of large windows looking out over the city. When he turned toward them, his glory caused Aegeus to stagger. No matter how many times he experienced it, it still overwhelmed him.

"Aegeus." The voice was like honey. The King smiled at him. Aegeus and the others dropped to their knees before their King, bowing their heads in reverence. The Lamb approached and laid his nail-scarred hand gently on Aegeus's shoulder.

"Rise, Aegeus." The Lamb went on to greet each of them in turn. "You are embarking on a critical mission," the King began. "Conditions in Platitude continue to deteriorate. It is critical that you protect the Twelfth. Currently, the enemy does not suspect that we know of their movement. To avoid drawing attention to the Twelfth, Kfir and Aegeus, you are to wear the uniform of a guardian."

Aegeus and Kfir looked at each other, sure they had misheard. Even Michael seemed surprised by the command. "Once the Twelfth has been detected, you may once again wear the uniform of the warrior. Lavi, assist them in understanding how to pass as guardians." The King winked at Lavi as if they shared a secret the others were not part of.

"My King," Aegeus began. The King turned to face him, a smile in his eyes. He knew what was coming, but he waited patiently for Aegeus to say what was in his heart. It was an important act, one the King highly valued.

"Yes, Aegeus."

"This is a most unusual thing you are asking." Aegeus's hesitation was obvious.

"This is a most unusual situation, Aegeus," the King replied. He crossed his arms behind his back and looked down at the beautiful sapphire floor before taking a few paces toward Aegeus. "I imagine that Joshua must have believed marching around Jericho seven times was a most unusual thing. Naaman thought it was a most unusual thing when he was asked to wash in the Jordan River. Certainly, being swallowed by a whale was a most unusual thing. Noah found it most unusual when I asked him to build an ark. Oh, and Moses? Well, Moses thought it most unusual when I told him to stretch his staff out over the Red Sea. Shall I go on?" he asked gently, stopping in front of Aegeus, his point made.

"No, my King." Aegeus's love for the King was second to none, his loyalty unfaltering. He trusted the King. The King was pleased. He smiled at Aegeus and placed his hand on his shoulder, filling him with Light, strength, and courage. From Aegeus, he moved on to Lavi, putting his hand on him as well.

"You are a great guardian, Lavi. I have entrusted many of my children to you. The Twelfth will be unique, unlike any you have protected before. I am proud of all you have done and all you will do."

Lavi nodded slightly to signify he understood.

"Kfir." He stood in front of Kfir and smiled widely. "Aegeus will need you on this mission. You have learned many lessons; do not forget them. You will find the Americans different than those you have served in the past. Learn to value them on their own merit. Oh, and, Kfir . . ." The King paused as a smile crept across his face, "No hot dogs."

Kfir chuckled as did everyone in the room. He nodded in understanding, a slight blush covering his cheeks. The King placed his hand on Kfir, filling him with the Light of God.

The Light of God was the most powerful weapon the angels had. It was their source of energy. The Light of God made them glow radiantly; it provided them strength. The King himself was the source of the Light. When angels went to earth, they relied on the Light. Children of the King also had the Light of God. Exposure to the King kept both the angels and his children filled with the Light of God.

"I have placed the Third there to be a source of power for you. She is a mighty prayer warrior. Seek her out when you need her," the King offered as they prepared to depart. Knowing who the prayer warriors were on any mission was critical. Being on earth, exposed to demons while performing miracles and engaging in battle, would deplete the angels' strength. But prayer and the unsuppressed presence of the Spirit refilled them.

When they had departed, Michael turned to the King.

"You have asked something very difficult of Aegeus." Michael was struggling to understand.

"I have." The King paused. Michael waited for him. "When I create my children, I lay out a path for each one of them, a perfect plan for their life. But they must learn to listen and hear my voice. They must discover that path and align their lives with my plan. Until they do, they are not who they truly are. In many ways, they are disguised. Aegeus has always known exactly who he was. He cannot yet understand the struggle of my children. Until he understands their struggle, he cannot love them."

Michael nodded; it was an unusual situation indeed.

Chapter 5: The Twelfth

The rally point was just over the border between the two states. Aegeus was waiting patiently; he knew how much was at stake. They had agreed to meet at a gas station for the handoff. Sanyi would assure that the twelfth member would be there. Aegeus looked around at the security detail he had chosen for the day.

Most of them were warriors, but today they were each clad to resemble guardians. The uniform of the guardian felt uncomfortable and foreign to Aegeus. He felt exposed and vulnerable in it. As he waited, he became distracted and tugged at the tunic, behaviors unusual for him. But he understood that it was better not to draw attention to their convoy until all twelve were safely inside the town. Kfir paced expectantly. He had not been in America for many years. The customs were foreign to him.

It was a beautiful summer day. The temperature was not too hot yet. The sun shone high in the sky, and a few white fluffy clouds were scattered about. As Sanyi drew closer, Aegeus could feel his presence approaching. "Get ready," he called out to the team. "We do this fast and quiet. Any signs of the enemy?"

"Nothing yet," replied Kfir. "I don't think the Twelfth is on their radar yet."

Just then Sanyi arrived. His dark hair was cropped more closely to his head than Lavi remembered it being the last time they had worked together. Sanyi's facial hair was also shorter and looked more like a light dusting on his face. His eyes were brooding, but he was not. Lavi stepped forward and offered his friend the traditional greeting of the guardian.

Aegeus turned his attention instead to the car. It was an old family car, wholly unremarkable. As the doors opened, soft drink cans and children's toys fell to the ground clanking and announcing the arrival of the occupants. Aegeus watched as people seemed to pour from the car.

"Which one is it?" Kfir asked.

"The woman," Sanyi answered. He had served as the guardian angel of the Twelfth and her family for over a decade.

Aegeus, Kfir, and Lavi exchanged a glance. They weren't sure why, but they hadn't been expecting a woman. As Lavi looked more closely at the family, they seemed familiar.
"I know them," he offered, getting Aegeus's immediate attention.

"Perhaps that is why the King assigned you," Aegeus said more to himself than to Lavi. Aegeus wanted details, but this was not the time, —that could wait until the Twelfth was safely inside the town.

The exchange was uneventful. Lavi checked the car to assure there were no unexpected mechanical issues while the family filled the tank, used the restrooms, and walked the dog. Snacks were replenished, and everyone was settled back into the car for the rest of the journey. The entire stop had only taken thirteen minutes.

Aegeus gave assignments to the security detail, making sure they were close enough to offer immediate assistance but far enough away not to attract the attention of the enemy. "Kfir, take the lead until I catch up. You know what is at stake. No mistakes."

"No mistakes, Captain," Kfir assured him as he took the lead in the convoy and headed east with the Twelfth. Aegeus felt good to be doing something, to be able to return his mind to the task at hand and not his discomfort at the uniform or his thoughts about the humans.

"Sanyi, what is your report?" Aegeus asked when the others had left. Sanyi looked around him and felt the sudden emptiness that always followed handing over your charge. He realized that he missed them already. For many years, he had watched over this family. He had fought battles to protect them through their losses and tragedy. He had grown to love them.

Those were precisely the types of feelings Aegeus worked to avoid. How would Sanyi fight against them should the situation change? Would he be able to destroy those he had grown to love if the King demanded it? Would he be able to put his personal feelings aside to do what must be done if circumstances changed?

Aegeus tried to shake the thoughts from his head. He was glad he had learned to separate from the humans. There was nothing in all of creation more valuable to Aegeus than being in the presence of the King. He did not see any way to reconcile love for the humans with unfaltering devotion to the King.

"The King has been at work, and she is well prepared. She is tough, Aegeus, but she is tender too," Sanyi began and then paused, unsure of how to continue. "Aegeus?"

"Yes?" Aegeus responded with concern in his voice.

"Aegeus, she has seen me." Aegeus was struck silent. He looked at Sanyi, puzzled. This was rare indeed. Humans could not see them unless they allowed it and then only when ordered by the King.

"You allowed this?"

"No, she just did it. He must have allowed it."

"We were in a battle in her room. The enemy was heavy in the neighborhood. One night when the battle was particularly fierce, we ended up in her room. She woke up instantly and saw us."

Aegeus tried to make sense of what Sanyi was telling him. Humans could not see them, not in this form. He could not think of the last time one had been allowed.

"It was just a glance, Aegeus, but it was enough for her to recount the event accurately to her husband the next day. It was as if she could feel our very presence. You should know one more thing." Sanyi paused here because he knew what he was about to tell Aegeus would change everything.

"Yes," Aegeus prompted, wondering what more there could be.

"She has seen the Lamb."

"What do you mean she has seen the Lamb?" Aegeus asked bewildered.

"He came to put the mantle on her, and she woke up and spoke to him." Aegeus felt a rush of power and excitement. This news made Aegeus begin to worry that he had been separated from the convoy too long. Surely the enemy must be aware of her if she had spoken to the Lamb.

"She is a prophet?" was all he managed to say.

"Yes, The King didn't tell you?"

Aegeus shook his head no.

Sanyi paused. "No matter. It's worth mentioning that she doesn't seem to realize it."

Chapter 6

The convoy arrived at the house while the day was still early. The sky was overcast as it was most days in Platitude. The enemy had moved into the town in such large numbers that their presence muted the sun. Aegeus noted that people had arrived to help unload the moving truck.

The humans piled out of their cars and began making an action plan to get the truck unloaded and the house filled. The Light of the Twelfth shined brightly, and the warriors were happy to learn that her husband and those helping unload the truck also had the Light.

Aegeus did not mention to the others that she was a prophet; he needed time to process it first. He wondered why the King had not mentioned that. He watched her closely. She did not seem like a prophet. Perhaps Sanyi had gotten it wrong.

Aegeus circled the perimeter of the house. No sign of the enemy. If the Twelfth were a prophet, it would not be long before the battle began, but for the moment she seemed to have gone undetected. The other warriors also noticed the lack of interest by the enemy, and they relaxed a bit.

After assuring that the family was busy attending to moving matters, Aegeus decided to brief the team on what he had learned.

At the far northern edge of the mountain range encircling Platitude, there was a small salvage yard full of cars and trucks in various states of decay. The salvage yard sat just outside the town and covered about twenty acres. Humans rarely went there, and as a result, the enemy ignored it completely. It provided an excellent source of cover. Aegeus found the decaying vehicles fascinating. Nothing rotted in heaven, and there was no decay. It was something he only saw while on earth. He liked to look at each one and consider its story. How did it end up here, neglected and forgotten?

At the back of the property was an aluminum building that many years ago had faded to a color that almost wasn't a color. Aegeus and his team would be using it for a meeting place. Upon entering the building, he found a small group of warriors and a dozen guardians. Meir and the ministering angels were not there yet. The building was a single room with several huge wooden spools scattered about. Wooden crates also littered the room. The angels were arranging the spools to serve as tables and the crates as seats. Kfir and Lavi had dragged in a bench seat from a 1925 Ford T-bucket that they were using.

Aegeus cleared his throat and began, "As you know, the Twelfth, the final human, arrived in Platitude today. Sanyi tells me that she has had several years of very intense preparation for this task. The training was difficult, but the Spirit is active within her. He also reports that the attacks on the family were powerful and frequent over those years. As a result, she may be worn down.

"Watch for the need to call a comforter. She does not seem to be aware of what is happening or of why she is here. She does know that the King has called her to be here, but it does not appear she has any idea of why or what the task will be. We know that each of the twelve possesses unique gifts that have prepared them for their specific task but, more importantly, we know that together they are an essential part of winning this battle."

Amitiel, a research angel, stood to indicate he wished to speak. Aegeus acknowledged him and turned the floor over to him.

"It is worth noting that many of the Americans view trials as an indication they are doing something wrong," Amitiel began. "It is quite possible that the Twelfth, and perhaps all of them, will see the last years not for what they were —preparation for this task—but as something else. They may see it as an indication they were not in alignment with the King's plan. Many of them tell each other that if you feel a separation from the King, it is you who have wandered away. We should be sensitive to that."

Aegeus did not understand the King's children. Had they not read the Word? Did they not know of Hezekiah? Had they not learned of Job? It baffled him. For the first time, he considered that it may make things simplier if he understood them more, but he dismissed the idea. He was here to do a job; things would go better if he concentrated on the task. Understanding them was not a requirement.

"It is important that you know some basics about the others as well given we will be working closely with their angels. The twelve are all connected, and their failures and successes are intertwined.

"The First has the gift of wisdom and teaching."

"And how does he use them?" asked Lavi. He knew that while all the children were given gifts, many of them either did not recognize them or did not use them for the King.

"He uses them well," Amitiel answered. "The First and his wife settled comfortably into the town, The First has found his position in the counseling department at the college to be fulfilling, allowing him to share wisdom and truth with hundreds of hurting students. His wife started a new career as an art curator. Her ministering angel has been working on her, and most of her wounds are healing nicely. But the arrival of the Strongman will bring unique challenges for them both.

"The Second and the Third work part-time at the college in the department of mission studies. They host visiting missionaries and help organize both foreign and domestic trips for the students and staff. They are acknowledged as people of great faith. They are happy and doing well. They are our primary prayer warriors with the Third being particularly powerful.

"The Fourth has done very well in Platitude. Getting him in was a bit tricky because of his divorce, but the Spirit handled that. He is outspoken, which is needed. He is gifted with knowledge and apostleship, and he has learned to use them very well. His scientific approach to things is welcomed by his colleagues, and he is impervious to many of the demons' tactics because he is not easily swayed by emotion.

"The Fifth has the gift of service. But she does not yet know when to say no. She has not learned to listen to the Spirit regarding which opportunities to pursue and which to leave for others. She often overextends herself." Aegeus was relieved no one had not asked additional questions about the Fifth since there was much about her that was unknown. Her pain ran deep.

Amitiel resumed his report, "The Sixth and the Seventh," but Lavi interrupted before he could finish.

"Did the Seventh see the red-haired woman before coming here?"

"She did not." Amitiel left it simple. "The Sixth has the gift of hospitality and administration. The Seventh has the gift of exhortation, and she uses it very well," he added.

"They make me think of Mary and Martha," Kfir said, smiling at the memory of such dear friends. "Aegeus, have you seen them lately?"

Aegeus grinned, the Sixth and the Seventh were indeed very similar to Mary and Martha. "Mary is precisely where you would expect to find her," he said. "And Martha works in the city. She stays busy—the way she likes it—but she visits the throne room daily."

"I don't like the story of the Sixth and Seventh, Aegeus; something seems missing." Kfir looked at him suspiciously.

Aegeus remained silent—something was missing. The Sixth had a deep secret that she clung to and protected, a source of pain so deep that she had buried it long ago, never daring to even consider it again. But it was not Aegeus's secret to tell, so he remained silent. Amitiel continued.

"The Eighth has the gift of compassion, but he has not learned to use it well. His gift is so powerful he can, in a way, feel the very feelings of those around him. He has had this gift a very long time, but he has not learned to master it. Often, it masters him. His moods are often dictated by the emotions of those around him. It can leave him exhausted.

"He has found Platitude very difficult. Things have not gone as he had hoped, and his family has started to suffer. Both of his children graduated and moved away for college instead of going to school at the college in the town.

"Advanced research has required significantly longer hours and more stress. The stress has come home with him, and he began to neglect his wife. He is away from home more than he is there.

"Both of them regret the decision to move here, and they blame each other. His wife takes frequent trips back to Vermont, where they were from; she stays for longer and longer visits each time.

"The Ninth has the gift of leadership and administration. But she has not yet learned to harness them. If she allows it, the Twelfth will be a great mentor to her in helping her better hone her gifts.

"The Tenth has been given a critical job here. One that will determine the overall success of the mission.

"Because of her personal experiences, the Eleventh, became entirely devoted to women's health issues. She began working in a shelter for battered and abused women. She has cried with many women and shared the love of the Lamb with them in a way only those who have walked the path could understand. Her work with the shelter brought her to the town as a consultant. Once there, they were so impressed they offered her a job."

"Aegeus, can she see us?" Kfir asked. He had developed the habit of standing in front of the Eleventh making silly faces. Lavi could not help but laugh.

"No, only demons." Amitiel answered before he sat down, indicating he was done. Aegeus stood to continue.

"We must work diligently to assure that the twelve encounter each other. Other than that, we are not, as you know, to interfere unless specifically ordered to do so. They must have free will, and they must learn to quiet all voices but the King's."

Aegeus paused briefly before continuing. He knew that each angel had served the King for thousands of years and would fully understand the gravity of his next words. He exhaled, a habit he had developed from his limited time around the humans.

"The Twelfth is believed to be a prophet." Silence and an exchanging of glances followed the statement., as did a long silence that denoted the importance of the moment. Aegeus looked at each angel in turn.

"Are you sure?" asked Lavi, finally breaking the silence.

"Sanyi was part of the mantle ceremony," Aegeus responded.

"Then she must know why she is here," noted Lavi.

"She does not yet know her calling," Aegeus answered. It was unfortunate, but it was the truth. To truly be a prophet, she would have to accept her calling. "There is more," he offered. "She has seen and spoken to the Lamb." That elicited precisely the response he had expected. Excitement rushed into the room, and the electrical charge became palpable. There was to be a great war.

"How can this be possible? What human can see and speak to the Lamb yet not know they are a prophet?" Kfir asked.

It was a fair question. But Aegeus had been in the United States many times, and he knew that as the humans had marked off time, many of them had also convinced themselves that prophets no longer existed. Certainly, they were rare, but to deem them obsolete just proved how disconnected the humans had become. Some among them refused to accept that a woman could be a prophet despite the clear evidence in the Word, which Amitiel noted.

Kfir stood to speak. "This small town is teeming with the enemy. My understanding is that this was previously our territory, but over the last year, the enemy has been steadily streaming in, thinking they are undetected. The King has taken significant steps to assemble the twelve. That has taken nearly three years to complete.

"Today the Twelfth has arrived, and we learn she is a prophet. The enemy will learn that too, and hopefully, she too will figure it out in time. But we all know that means this battle will be more than a mere skirmish, perhaps not part of this mission, but a great battle is certainly coming. We are fighting for more than a simple town. Do we yet know what is happening? Who will be assigned to the post and who will be part of the war?"

"The King did not mention the prophet or a great war. He told me only that we were to protect the Twelfth. I have no word on the plan other than the arrival of a Strongman from the enemy," Aegeus answered. "The Strongman will arrive soon. We are to keep the twelve away from the Strongman unless unavoidable.

"We are to protect the twelve from all threats except those allowed by the King for their continued training to make them battle ready. I want two warriors stationed on the prophet at all times. As long as she doesn't know she is a prophet, the enemy may not notice her. But once they do, it will escalate.

"Lavi, you said you knew her?" Aegeus prompted.

Lavi nodded affirmation. "The Twelfth has many times prayed additional guardians for her youngest child, which was how I came to be among them. It did not take long on the job to see the reason for her prayers. The child is certainly accident prone, at least he was when I was assigned to him. I was an additional guardian to the boy during times of intense prayer from the Twelfth."

Although Lavi found great encouragement in the prayers of the Twelfth, he did not share any of those details. He doubted Aegeus would be interested in them since they did not affect the mission. But they had undoubtedly affected Lavi.

Chapter 7

Titus rose to his feet when Morax entered the room. "Good morning, Titus. I trust everything is moving according to plan?" Titus reached for Morax's hand to offer the customary greeting of the hairless rats. No need to draw attention to themselves.

"Yes, my liege, the Strongman arrives tomorrow." They shook hands and then sat down, Titus on an overstuffed leather chair and Morax in the large executive chair that was behind his oak desk. Titus watched as his commander took a sip of coffee.

"I hate their food," he sneered as he put the cup down in distaste. They are horrible creatures. Just look at this body I am forced to wear," he said as he grabbed the handful of extra fat around his waist. "Do I look like the mighty warrior that I am?" he growled. Titus knew the question was rhetorical and to answer was to risk his position. He waited patiently for the commander to continue.

"Is he one of ours?" Morax asked, returning to the topic of the Strongman.

"Yes, he is a preacher, a graduate of the seminary we control. He trained under one of our best," Titus offered. The commander stood up from the desk chair and walked over to look out his meager window overlooking the campus. The day was warm, and the air in the room was stale with a slight hint of sulfur.

"Will he be detected?" the commander asked. This was a real concern, and one they had spent much time discussing in the past.

"No, my liege. He is close to the truth in many areas. No one will suspect. But he is one of us, and his position on many things will divide them. He will teach them lies cloaked in truth. He will make them feel isolated and ashamed. His yoke will be so heavy that Depression and Anxiety will be able to take over easily," Titus reassured him.

"And Judgment? We cannot sufficiently castrate them without Judgment and Apathy," the commander reminded him.

"Yes. As you know," Titus began, "the council is meeting now to remove all those with Lights that burn brightly. We are also removing a few of our own, those who were the most distant from the truth and draw too much attention. Those terminations will cause people to be cautious and distrustful and will pave the way for him to speak boldly about restoring truth. He will declare that those who do not walk in Light will not be tolerated and must be removed. He will call on the faithful to watch for those among them who do not walk fully in the Light. He will cause divisions and arguing. He will take stands on some of the issues we find so easy with them such as drinking."

Titus smiled at the thought of it. The rats were so easy to control. To imagine that just a year ago, this town and its Christian college was a threat to them. It had been so simple to erode the foundation. Silence those who had the Light shining brightest and convince the rest to follow the rules. Oh, they loved to tell you how Jesus died to set you free as they chained you to the new rules—their rules. He chuckled to think of it.

Yes, this had worked for thousands of years; the rats wanted rules, they lived by the law, and they would die by it.

Morax nodded in agreement with the plan. It was flawless. He had seen lives destroyed over less. He once facilitated the destruction of an entire church using only a disagreement over if they would sit in pews or stadium seats. The memory of it gave him great pleasure. The rats seemed to worship the Bible over the Creator, and yet they appeared to have never actually read it.

The secret, of course, was to start early, teach them the lies as truth, and perpetuate it for generations. Then they wouldn't even question it. It had taken years to get control of some of the seminaries, the Christian universities were proving easier to conquer. One could not argue with the results. Those bearing the title of the King were quick to judge and slow to love, even among themselves. They hid their sins as if they somehow were immune. That served Morax and his team well. Hidden sins festered, they went unchecked, and he and his team were experts at feeding those sins and using them to dim their Lights.

"The Strongman will hire only his own, so the enemy will not be able to bring in anyone else," Titus added.

Before he could elaborate, there was a light knock at the door, and a human opened it as she apologized for the interruption. The council needed the commander. Titus scowled at the rat for the intrusion. Oh, how he hated them. But outwardly he smiled at her and thanked her for letting him know. Her Light was weak, and it pleased him to watch it flicker with uncertainty. He was sure that in time it would go out.

Chapter 8

Aegeus entered the house as Lavi was running through the tricks he had been teaching the dog of the Twelfth during slow times. The dog was a stray the Twelfth, and her husband picked up some years ago. He had been living near a movie theater and would come out at night to eat popcorn and candy that he found in the parking lot. One evening, on a rare night out, the Twelfth and her husband noticed the small black-and-white puppy huddled under their car. Rain poured down on the three of them, and the soaked puppy howled out a desperate cry. He was shaking and wet. They had scooped him up and never looked back. The dog was spoiled and loved, but not particularly well trained.

Aegeus stood just outside the doorway watching as the dog went through all his new tricks: sit, stay, come, roll over, beg, speak. He would even play dead. On command, the dog would drop to the ground, roll onto his back, and stick all four legs straight into the air. After a one-second delay, the dog would stick his tongue out. It was quite comical. Nearly as impressive was that Lavi had taught the dog to freeze in place when commanded, "stop."

Aegeus joined Lavi in the living room, sitting down on the wooden floor beside him. He handed Lavi a cup of wine and a slice of honey bread spread with jam from heaven. Lavi accepted both with a smile. The bread was tender and seemed to disintegrate in his mouth. The jam was sweet and fresh, and the smell teased his taste buds.

It made him think about when he and Aegeus had eaten a similar meal together in Bethlehem. Lavi had been guardian to Mary. The battle around her was fierce once the enemy discovered that she carried the Lamb, and Aegeus had been called in as part of her security detail. Aegeus and Lavi became instant friends. They had been sharing a meal like this while the holy family slept, when suddenly, an archangel, had come to Joseph telling him to take Mary and the Lamb to Egypt. Breakfast had been forgotten.

Today, the two angels enjoyed a quiet morning savoring their meal and reminiscing about old times. After breakfast, they wandered outside and sat in the large wicker chairs on the wraparound porch to watch the sunrise, a sight that never got old. The sun did not rise or set in heaven. In fact, there was no sun; there was no need for such things.

Watching the beauty of a sunrise was something the angels loved. The beauty and artistry of it reminded them of their nearness to the King. He did it twice each day, painting the sky with beautiful colors both at sunrise and sunset—no two ever the same. Here in the town, with the mountains as the backdrop, the sunrise was particularly beautiful. The earth was still and quiet at this hour. The birds were just starting to move about and sing their morning song.

Eventually, the conversation turned to the events scheduled for the day. The Twelfth was to meet the Tenth for lunch. The Tenth was the vice president of human resources, and he wanted to welcome her to the community. The lunch was planned for the one local restaurant. It was a small shop just two blocks from the main street of the town. A jukebox was in the back, and on weekends it was filled with college students. Aegeus and Kfir had done a sweep of the area the day before to get a feel for what it was like. They did not anticipate any problems.

It wasn't long before the family was awake. One of the children was banging on the bathroom door yelling at the other one to hurry up. The dog was barking and jumping about at the sound of knocking. He ran to and from the front door clearly confused as to exactly where the sound was coming from. Lavi and Aegeus stood near the door watching the scene unfold. Aegeus had not spent much time around children, and the chaos of it all was a little unnerving. The amount of activity and noise that came from such small creatures surprised him.

Eventually, the child in the bathroom opened the door and yelled, "stop it," at the younger child. The dog froze in mid-movement. Not so much as a whisker flinched. He stood with one leg off the ground and bent mid-stride. The children stopped as well and looked at the dog, baffled by his stance. "Maybe he's having a seizure," one of them offered. Lavi and Aegeus laughed till they cried

.

Chapter 9

After getting the house settled down and returned to their version of normal, the Twelfth walked to the restaurant. It was about two miles from her home. Her angels walked just behind her. It was strange to be able to walk everywhere, and she tried to appreciate it. She truly valued the time alone, the peace and tranquility of the walk. She wore her earbuds and put the music on her iPhone on shuffle. It gave her time to think, to plan for her upcoming classes, and to pray. And, it discouraged well-intentioned strangers from talking to her. Today, she found she had a lot to discuss with God, so she prayed nearly all the way there.

When she arrived at the restaurant, her Light was burning brightly and radiated from her. The restaurant was cozy with a large stone fireplace on the wall directly to the right when you entered. The building had high-angled ceilings that came to a steep peak at the top. The entire backside was windowed overlooking the brook that ran through the town. The back faced a drop-off, giving the distinct impression that the restaurant was floating.

The floors were wooden, and large oriental rugs adorned them, making the place feel like a mountain lodge. Large oversized chairs were scattered about, and the tables looked like they had been made from wooden barrels. One side had traditional restaurant-style tables and chairs while the other half had the oversized chairs. On the front wall, there was a small stage for live entertainment or poetry readings. The Twelfth loved it instantly.

The Tenth had already selected seats on the side with oversized chairs. The Twelfth was pleased; it was what she would have picked. The Tenth stood to attract her attention, and she joined him at the table, shaking his hand before sitting down. The chair was painfully comfortable, and she had to fight the urge to take off her shoes and curl up in it. As she settled in, her Light flared brightly, filling the room. Kfir closed his eyes and soaked in the power of the King.

"Aegeus?" he then asked, the obvious question left unspoken.

"I don't know." Aegeus hated that he didn't know. He was not accustomed to not knowing. The Twelfth shifted uncomfortably in her chair, but otherwise, she gave no indication that anything had happened. She chatted with the Tenth easily about moving, preparing for classes, and their families. Lavi leaned in close; he could tell that she struggled. He wanted to get a greater sense of her, of what was happening within her. He wanted to know her.

Aegeus watched. The Light again flared in her. Something was happening. She squirmed in her seat and sent a glance toward heaven, but her conversation did not falter.

Kfir stepped closer. He looked around the room to see if the flares of Light had brought additional demons. So far, it had not. He felt a sense of excitement, the type of feeling you get when riding a roller coaster and you get to the top of a big incline. You know the drop is coming, and of course, the drop is the whole reason you rode the coaster, but those few seconds in anticipation of something great just before you start the descent are precious and not to be overlooked.

The Twelfth seemed to grow more distracted, but outwardly she smiled and nodded as the Tenth spoke. Finally, as if giving in to a highly distasteful task, the Twelfth took a deep breath and began. The angels leaned in with anticipation. Aegeus caught himself holding his breath and waiting. He chastised himself for getting so drawn in and started the process of trying to distance himself, once again focusing solely on the mission.

"Sometimes, God tells me things. And right now, he is telling me to tell you something." She paused so as not to say it so quickly that she looked like more of a freak than she was sure she already did. He was the head of human resources for goodness' sake, and she had only met him one other time during one of her interviews. She was sure he would think she was certifiable.

"Okay, well let's have it," he said. The Twelfth was stunned by his nonchalance. She wasn't sure what she was expecting, perhaps something more like him backing from the room with eyes wide and finger-pointing. She sighed.

"I don't think you are going to like it. It doesn't seem positive," she explained.
He sat quietly, looking at her expectantly. She sighed again.

"You are embedded with a holy passion like Phinehas, son of Eleazar. And like Phinehas, you will need courage and strength to intervene, but so far you have taken the safe route. You must be bold, not just for your own purpose but for God's. You have a sin that has mastered you, but you must master it; otherwise, you will never confront the plague that is spreading."

With the message delivered, she sat there uncomfortably staring down at her lap. Her Light caused the air to crackle with the power of heaven. The angels looked at each other pleased.

The Light of the Tenth burned brightly. On the outside, he sat calmly, looking at the Twelfth. She was utterly unimpressive to look at. Her hair was a dull shade of brown. She was not particularly attractive. She was the type of person you would walk right past and never notice. She was smart, but not brilliant. There was nothing remarkable about her with one small exception. She had a quality that made you immediately feel comfortable with her. He couldn't explain it, but he certainly had noticed it during her interview.

During the interview, she had been honest and sincere. She was polished without seeming practiced. She had no sense of pretense, and she spoke to the interview team as if they had all been friends for years, and they were merely having lunch together—all while maintaining a professionalism that could not be questioned. He had been impressed; all of them had been captivated by it, lured in. Some of them shared personal information with her that had not been shared before. It alarmed him, and thus, he secretly feared her.

A power such as that—something that made people feel comfortable enough with you to share their secrets—could be dangerous. What if he slipped? He decided right then to avoid her as much as possible. He could not afford for his secret to be out. He was making a fresh start; things were going so well. People wouldn't understand; he would be fired, and his family humiliated. Thankfully, her office would be far from his, and there was no reason for their paths to ever cross, other than this one obligatory lunch.

Now here they were, sitting in this restaurant, and she knew things she should not. He had not even had to reveal his secrets for her to know them. He pondered the idea that God had told her this message then concluded that there was no other explanation. How else could she have known about the Phinehas thing? She looked very uncomfortable as she waited for him to respond. He felt sorry for her, but he also felt like he wanted to get away from her—and quickly.

"Who is my Goliath?" he asked her.

She looked up startled and a little confused. "Your Goliath?"

"Yes, who is my Goliath? You know, the person I will stand against. And who will stand with me?" He was genuinely disappointed that she didn't seem to know. She appeared equally disappointed.

"I don't know," she paused to consider his question. "But I do know that Phinehas stood alone. I don't know what it means, but I believe you do."

He did indeed know exactly what it meant, but he was not going to tell her that.

She sat painfully still, clearly still feeling uncomfortable. The Tenth eased the conversation back to safer ground until he could end the lunch when it was no longer awkward to do so. When the time came, the Twelfth put her earbuds in and started the long walk home, arguing with God all the way there.

Kfir was ecstatic. Aegeus was cautious. He scanned their surroundings for any signs that demons had seen the exchange. Lavi walked beside her, beaming with pride.

Chapter 10: The Tenth

The Tenth leaned over the edge of the bed feeling sick. He honestly thought he might vomit. He looked back over his shoulder at the woman in the bed. She was beautiful. Even with her hair disheveled and her makeup smeared, she was a beautiful woman. They all were. That was the problem. He stood up and gathered his clothes from around the room, dressing as quickly as he could. He suddenly felt the need to escape, to run from the room and never look back. She woke up as he turned the knob to leave.

"You're leaving," she muttered in a still mostly asleep voice.

"I have to; I have a meeting." He smiled at her to cover the regret.

"When will I see you again?" she asked, concern starting to pepper her voice.

"Soon," was all he could muster as he left the room and headed to his van. When he pulled into his parking space at work, his wife was there waiting. She did not greet him; she merely launched into complaining about the traffic, a strange sound the car was making, and something their son had done that morning.

He wasn't sure he had heard her correctly, but if so, their son had eaten his cereal with Coke in the bowl instead of milk. He wanted to laugh, but he knew that his wife would not see the humor in it. She didn't see the humor in anything these days. He looked at her as they walked together across the parking lot toward his office. He had no idea what she was talking about, but he let her prattle on because it required less of him.

They had met when he was in graduate school at Cornell working on his MBA in human resources. She was one of the few women in the engineering program. They dated for two years before he proposed. One night, when they were celebrating the end of finals, things had gotten a bit out of control. They were already engaged, so he didn't see the big deal in having sex a few months early. At the time, she had agreed.

But the next day her heart had changed. She regretted what they had done, and she blamed him for it. She was angry—angrier than he had ever seen her. She cried, she screamed, she threw things, she called him names. He sat, naked on the bed, too shocked to speak. Eventually, he tried to comfort her, but there was no comfort to be had. She was so ashamed and filled with regret that she did not want a wedding. They went away for a long weekend and eloped. That was twenty-five years ago.

His wife had never gotten over what she considered to be a betrayal. She had become someone different than who he knew and had fallen in love with. They had one child, whom she adored. But after she had their son, marital relations had ended. She had gained weight with the pregnancy, and she just didn't feel beautiful or desired anymore. He agreed. The affairs began five years later.

Each time, he hated himself for what he had done. He didn't want to want other women. He didn't want to have affairs. He wanted his wife to be the woman he had met and fallen in love with, but that woman was long gone. He told himself he deserved an award for all the women he had not had an affair with but could have. In his darkest moments, he told himself he was justified. But if he was justified, why did he feel so sick?

For many years, his shame had kept him from the church. He just couldn't bring himself to sit among the righteous. What if they learned of his secret? His wife did not understand why he wouldn't go to church with her, but she continued to go faithfully. He often wondered why.

But his heart yearned for communion with the saints. He never ceased communing with God. He prayed fervently, repeatedly asking for forgiveness, and yet never felt forgiven. He begged God to remove these desires from him, to help him desire his wife. Sometimes it worked; sometimes he would make it years before slipping again. Then, his guilt and shame would be renewed. But never, in all those years had his relationship with his wife improved. He stayed with her only to fulfill his commitment to God. He didn't like her, and he was no longer attracted to her.

When they arrived at his desk, he turned to look at her. For just a moment his eyes were opened to see her for who she was. She looked sad. Rejected. Like a woman who was trying not to notice that her husband had affairs. She looked like a woman unloved by her husband. The truth of it was overwhelming.

"Let's move," he blurted out before he realized what he was saying.

"What?" Understandably, the suggestion shocked her.

"Let's move; start over. It would be nice to get a fresh start." He pushed on. At that moment, he wanted nothing more than a fresh start. A place where none of their history existed. Where they could be new. He knew he sounded crazy, perhaps even frantic, but he wanted so desperately to be free of his past, of their past. His eyes looked at her longingly.

"Sure, let's move; that will fix everything." The sarcasm dripped from her lips. Hatred stained her face, but in her eyes, he saw hope. Her eyes reflected all the sadness of the years and yearning for things to be better. In her eyes, he saw his own feelings. He walked toward her and took her hands in his. Shock registered on her face; it was the first time he had touched her in years.

"I think this would work. We could start over." He was sincere, his eyes pleading with her.

"I just came here to trade cars with you. I need the van. As far as moving, you do what you think is best." She pulled her hands from his and stepped back from him, suppressing the sudden flood of emotions that she felt. She did not trust him. She hadn't trusted him in many years, and she doubted he would do what was best for her. She couldn't remember the last time he had.

He understood, but it hurt just the same. She extended her hand for the keys. He handed her the van keys, and she left.

"Are you coming to the meeting?" his secretary stuck her head in his door.

"Yes, sorry I'm running late." He forced a smile and followed her into the conference room. He entered the room to find it full of middle-aged men in suits and one woman. The woman had wild red hair pulled into a tight bun, giving her the look of a librarian. She wore stylish glasses that almost hid her green eyes. Being the only woman in the room was enough to make her stand out. The red hair sealed the deal.

He greeted everyone and sat down to begin the meeting. The woman did not speak, but she looked at him in a way that made him feel uncomfortable as if she knew him as if she knew the secrets that he hid. It was not condemning. To the contrary, she exuded a gentle warm feeling. But it was as if she could see his very soul. As the meeting was nearing its end, she finally spoke.

"The landscape is shifting around us. Continuing to do the same thing you have done will not bring new results—only disappointment. You have been given very specific gifts that should be used wisely. But like Phinehas, to stop the plague, you must first have courage, you must stand up and intervene. You must confront Goliath. Identify your Goliath. Then you can begin to make progress. Like Moses, you will need help. Your Aaron will meet you along the path, but when the time comes, you must stand alone."

She spoke with such authority that it made the Tenth question everything that had been said during the meeting. It made him question himself and his very direction in life. He felt a sense of joy to have even heard her words as if they were spun from gold. But the context was so odd, he needed a moment to consider it, to delve into the philosophy behind it. He felt like she was speaking directly to him. No one else in the room even looked at her as she spoke. They did not respond. The meeting ended.

The woman rose from her chair and walked purposefully from the room. The Tenth tried to follow her, but one of the men in the meeting stopped him to ask a question. The delay was just long enough that she was gone by the time he left the room.

"How did he end up in Platitude?" Lavi was curious about the Tenth, the one who was to challenge the Strongman.

"His cousin is the Eighth. When the position for VP came open, the Spirit led the Eighth to recommend him. The timing was right, and he readily accepted." Kfir answered.

"I see the sin the enemy has found for him. What is his gift?" Kfir asked.

"Knowledge and teaching. He has excellent insight into the Word. But Shame covers him, and so he rarely shares his knowledge. Lust has been with him since adolescence. He clings to it, both despising it and keeping it close.

"I once had a charge in Persia who found a baby tiger. The tiger did not know its own strength and often would hurt him. The man clung to the tiger. It grew, and his injuries became greater, and yet he would not let it go. Eventually, famine came to the land, and the tiger devoured him." Lavi looked at the others with a sense of understanding.

"You let your charge get eaten by a tiger? What kind of guardian are you?" Kfir laughed a deep roaring laughter that made Aegeus laugh too.

"You miss my point!" Lavi laughed, giving Kfir a gentle brotherly shove.

"Oh, I heard your point; the Twelfth is doomed!"

"Only if she gets a tiger," Lavi countered.

"Only if she gets a tiger," Lavi countered.

Chapter 11

Summer in Platitude was beautiful. The sweet smell of honeysuckle filled the air. Days were warm, and nights were cool, perfect for lightning bugs and crickets. The old Victorian house was filled with boxes and chaos. The children had no friends yet, and everything they owned was somewhere in a box, so they were full of energy with no outlet.

The house was old and in desperate need of renovation, but a fresh coat of paint would have to do for now. She awoke early, determined to get the youngest child's room unpacked. She washed her face, brushed her teeth, and threw on grungy clothes that would be okay if she got paint on them. She haphazardly pulled her hair into a ridiculous excuse of a bun with random pieces sticking out in most directions. The kids had camped out in the den, the only room that wasn't giving birth to boxes. She decided to let them sleep in.

"Coffee?" her husband asked, handing her a hot cup as she stood in the doorway to the youngest child's room.

"You are so good to me." She let out a sigh as she took the cup from him. *How did I ever get so lucky?* She thought as she gently sipped the steaming coffee.

"What's on your list for today?" he asked. The Twelfth was a list keeper. But she didn't let the list rule her; it was more of a suggestion. She loved crossing things off the list but often found she got to the end of a day and had to add her actual tasks to the list, so she had something to cross off.

Nevertheless, she loved the list, and it kept her moving in the right direction.

"I thought we would paint this room and get it unpacked. The boxes are driving me crazy. I can't stand it." She took another sip of the coffee. "I am so thankful that God saw fit to make the coffee bean. Specifically, the ones used to brew this very cup," she added, smiling.

Aegeus and Lavi looked at one another in amusement. Aegeus could not recall ever having encountered a charge quite like her; of course, he had never been assigned to a prophet before. He thought fleetingly that if she were a prophet, there would be little chance he would ever have to fight against her. But he shook the thought from his mind almost immediately—there was great danger in becoming connected to the humans.

"Let me go get a drop cloth and the painting supplies. You work on moving these boxes out of here so we can get in the room," her husband directed, then left to retrieve the necessary supplies.

"Where am I supposed to move these boxes? The whole house is overrun!" she called after him.

"You'll figure it out!" he called back. Before she had moved many boxes, her husband returned without any painting supplies.

"The welcoming committee is here," he whispered to her.

"What?" she whispered back, not knowing why she was whispering.

"Neighbors. Come on." He had that desperate look he got. Meeting new people was not one of his favorite things to do.

"Look at me!" she whispered, gesturing to her disheveled appearance. He shrugged, pushing her toward the back door and laughing.

The Twelfth was pleased to find an older couple at the door. They had brought a packed picnic basket with everything the family would need for lunch, snacks, and dinner that evening. They greeted each other warmly, offering introductions and handshakes all around.

Kfir had gone to do a patrol, but Aegeus and Lavi followed the Twelfth to the door. Aegeus dressed in the traditional uniform of the guardians—mostly leather coverings and arm guards—arrived first.

"Voog, guardian of the King sent to the earth to oversee his children." Voog, the guardian of the Second and the Third stepped forward, extending his hand to Aegeus, and offering the traditional greeting of the guardians. Aegeus stood befuddled for a moment.

"You are not a guardian; you have no ring," Voog assessed quickly.

All guardians wore a signet ring made of osmium and emblazoned with a Celtic cross on the middle finger of their left hand. The King fashioned each one for the guardian who wore it. Their name was inscribed on the inside, a constant reminder of who they were.

"Lavi, Holy is the King." Lavi stepped forward, extending his hand to complete the traditional greeting.

Voog accepted the greeting from Lavi but looked more closely at Aegeus. "You are a warrior," he said both in astonishment and confusion. Aegeus shifted in discomfort.

"Aegeus?" Voog questioned after a moment more. Upon recognizing Aegeus, he erupted in laughter. "Aegeus, if you are to pass as a guardian, we must work on your greeting. And your uniform—look at you," he chuckled. While Aegeus and Voog had not previously met, Voog knew of Aegeus—most angels did.

"You should see Kfir," Aegeus offered in a desperate attempt to deflect the attention from himself.

"Kfir? As a guardian?" The thought made Voog laugh more heartily. Voog had served in Africa many times and knew Kfir well.

"He is on patrol, but you must be sure to see him as a guardian when he returns." Aegeus smiled. Voog was right: warriors did not make good guardians. Even the uniform was uncomfortable; it felt binding to Aegeus.

Pretending to be something he was not made him feel ill at ease, as if he were an imposter. As others discovered the truth, he felt embarrassed and awkward. The King had created him to be a warrior. Anything else was an identity that was not his own. It was confining both physically and mentally.

The Lights in the humans had been gradually burning more brightly. The Light in the Twelfth now burned bright enough that the angels could feel the power of the King. Aegeus looked at her. She smiled kindly at the Third, laughing and chatting comfortably. Her husband and the Second wandered off to the garage and were discussing power tools and yard-waste pickup. Aegeus suspected the Twelfth must be offering praise to the King—that would explain the Light.

"I hear she is a prophet?" Voog asked, hope tainting the question.

"We hear that as well, but we have not seen evidence ourselves." Aegeus tried to sound matter of fact; he was not yet ready to declare the prophet. One message was not enough for Aegeus to be sure. Besides, she was not truly a prophet until she realized it herself. He wondered how long she would wear the wrong uniform before the discomfort of it caused her to be who she truly was.

"We would love to have you stop by," the Third said. The dog, who had been sniffing the Third with a great deal of interest, suddenly froze. The Twelfth noticed immediately. She tried not to be distracted from the conversation, but the sight of the dog standing there frozen was bizarre.

"We should be going, dear," the Second offered as the men rejoined the Third and Twelfth. He too noticed the dog, but he tried not to draw attention to the bizarre sight. "They have lots to do; we don't want to keep them." He gently placed his hand on her lower back, directing her toward the door. His wife had never met a stranger. He knew her well, and she would

undoubtedly spend the day communing with the Twelfth if left to her own devices.

The Second and Third returned to their home, and the Twelfth and her husband climbed the stairs to begin painting.

"I loved them." The Twelfth had a smile on her face and a prayer of thanksgiving in her heart as she climbed the stairs.

"I could tell," her husband offered, pleased to see her happy again after the trials of the last two years.

"How incredibly kind of them to bring that basket." She was a bit overwhelmed by it. "I am never going to fit in here," she lamented.

"You just did," he offered in reassurance.

"No, I mean, I am not that thoughtful. If everyone here is that 'good,' I will stand out as not belonging."

Doubt attracted to the home by the Light of the Twelfth, swooped up through the floor and grabbed her ankle. He began clamoring his way up her leg, moving like a lizard toward her head before he noticed Aegeus and Lavi. When he saw them, he froze, a bit startled.

Aegeus drew his weapon. Lavi shot him a look that said, *that is not how guardians do it.*

The husband of the Twelfth walked over to her and wrapped her in his arms, trapping the demon between them. He leaned down and kissed the top of her head.

"They are going to love you. You'll see." He kissed her gently again. "Now, let's get this painting done." The Twelfth smiled, grabbed a paint roller, said a quick prayer, and sent the demon flying from her.

Aegeus laughed at the sight of the demon being shot from her body by a burst of the Light.

"Aegeus, if you are to pass as a guardian, you must act as a guardian," Lavi offered in gentle correction. Aegeus did not want to pass as a guardian—it was not who he was—but he accepted the correction, acknowledging it was the task the King had given him.

Just then Kfir returned from patrol. "What did I miss?"

"The Second and the Third dropped by," Lavi offered.

"And I think they discovered the dog," Aegeus added, laughing.

"What do we know of the Second and Third?" Lavi asked. Aegeus filled them in.

Chapter 12: The Second and the Third

The Second and Third arrived at the town together. They had met and fallen in love in the sixties. They were married in 1969 and left for the mission field in 1972. They had traveled to more than seventy countries in their work. The Third gave birth to three children, two sons, and a daughter.

Over the years their children grew up and moved back to the States, pursuing their own lives, and having their own children. Their oldest son became an architect, the second son was a linguist, and their daughter had heard the call to ministry. She began speaking in churches in her twenties and was now regularly invited to speak to those of faith around the world. She was not a preacher—she did not shepherd a church— but her choice to speak in churches was often met with criticism and reprimand. She knew that she had been called to this path, but it was not an easy one. She often prayed that God would call someone else, but she had a love for his people, a longing to encourage them with his words.

Four years before moving to Platitude, the Second and the Third were serving in the Middle East. Terrorists raided their village one night to rid it of all Christians. They were dragged from their home, and the Third was shot in front of her husband and left for dead. The Second was bound and taken into captivity.

The Third had been found in a mass grave, clinging to life. She was stabilized and flown back to the United States where she spent a year recovering. She prayed that her husband would be found alive. Four months into her recovery, the first video of him emerged. He was blindfolded and wearing an orange jumpsuit—beaten, frail, and thin, but he was alive.

She began to pray more diligently for his protection and God's provision. When she had recovered enough to move around the hospital, she made regular visits to the chapel and organized prayer warriors who would each commit to praying five minutes each day. Soon she had enough people that someone was praying for the Second every minute of every day.

After eighteen months, on a beautiful spring day, while working in her garden, the Third heard a knock on the door. There had been a raid on the captors to rescue several hostages, including her husband. During the attack one of the attackers had attempted to kill the Second, slicing his throat. First responders had been able to save his life, but they were not sure of his prognosis.

Waiting for his return to American soil had been difficult. She was not allowed to see the Second for some time after his arrival. He required numerous surgeries. His condition was critical, and he was not expected to live. But the Third had come too far to give up hope now. She would stand outside his room and, placing her hand on his door, she would pray until God saw fit to let her in the room. Day and night, she prayed. She thanked God for getting them both this far. She thanked him for bringing her husband home even if he had been brought home to die.

The day finally came when she was allowed in to see him. The Third stood over his frail body, and her foundation was shaken. He weighed just ninety-eight pounds. He had bruises and scars all over, and his head looked as if it had been cut off and sewn back on to his body. She placed her hand over his and prayed for forgiveness for the hatred she felt for those who had done this. She prayed for their souls. When she had finished praying, she stepped out of the room and let herself cry.

Months passed, and the Second began to regain his strength. Shortly before he was released, he and the Third planned a short visit down to the hospital garden for some fresh air.

The Third had pushed his wheelchair all around the hospital, and they had been laughing at their apparent state of going in circles.

"Do you need some help?" a woman asked, her wild red hair escaping from the clasp she had used to pull it back.

"We're trying to find the garden," said the Second.

"Ah, yes, so many are searching for the garden. I'm going that way; I am happy to show you," she offered, her green eyes sparkling. The three of them chatted as they made their way to the garden. The Second and the Third talked easily with her about their experiences.

"Our histories are so interesting," observed the woman. "But more important is where we are and where we are going. What will you do now?" she asked, her hair further slipping from the clip.

"Oh, we're retiring," offered the Third. "We are headed to Florida as soon as he is released."

After settling them in the garden, the woman went farther into a more secluded spot, and they did not see her again. They sat comfortably in the garden enjoying the sun and each other. As the warmth of day gave way to the cool of night, they began their journey back inside to the Second's room. As the Third pushed the wheelchair back toward the hospital doors, she ran over something, and the wheel stuck. Bending down, she picked up a small broken hairclip engraved with the name of a college that was hidden in the mountains, in the middle of nowhere.

Chapter 13

Summer was moving much more quickly than the boxes and painting. The Twelfth was flustered and discouraged by the lack of progress and was quickly learning that nothing they had moved from their previous home worked in this one. So many times, over the last few weeks, she wished she had just sold everything and started over when they got here.

She sat on the floor in what would one day be the living room, surrounded by boxes and covered in random dirt she couldn't quite identify. Her husband had already started his new job, so she was on her own to get the house put back together. Perhaps trying to paint before unpacking was a bad idea. She had lost her steam, so she poured herself a large cup of coffee and plopped down on the floor. She sat thinking about nothing in particular.

"Aegeus, she has been sitting on the floor for over an hour. We are warriors; where is the battle?" Kfir lamented. "Lavi, how do you do this?"

Lavi had been leaning against the wall, staring out the window and dreaming of heaven. He looked over at Kfir and smiled. He could only imagine how difficult this must be for Aegeus and Kfir. They were accustomed to more action.

"We have done our job well," Aegeus answered.

"Is there nothing we can do to get her moving? What would Meir do?" Kfir pondered.

"Meir would walk in, put her hands on her, and the Twelfth would get up and solve world hunger," Aegeus offered with a chuckle.

"That's true, that's true." Kfir nodded consent.

"Why don't you get her husband? Bring him home, and we will see if we can get her going again," Lavi suggested to Kfir.

"How am I supposed to get him here?" Kfir questioned.

"Be creative." Lavi smiled at him.

Kfir looked to Aegeus, his eyebrows raised in question. Aegeus nodded his agreement. Kfir flew from the room happy to have a task. Aegeus busied himself with once again patrolling the perimeter. Lavi sat down next to the Twelfth, studying her.

It had been several years since he first met her. She had changed. Age had been kind to her skin, but her hair was streaked with hints of gray, and the texture was a little coarser. The years had added a few pounds to her. But there was something else, something more profound. When Lavi had met her before, she had had such fire, such passion. Now she seemed worn, tired. She wore it like an undergarment, something no one was meant to see but that was there all the same. Lavi wished that he could be a ministering angel to see what was inside of her.

"What happened?" he asked her as if she could hear him. She sighed deeply in response.

"God, where are you?" she spoke into the room. The suddenness of it startled Lavi. "Why aren't you here?" She leaned back against the wall.

Lavi laid his hand on hers. He wanted so desperately to let her know that the King was there; he was always there. He wanted her to know that the King had sent an entire team to care for her. He hated that she felt alone. At the same time, he was glad that Aegeus and Kfir were not here to hear her, it would discourage them to know her thoughts.

"I felt so sure you were sending us here, but since we got here, I can no longer feel you. Did we do the wrong thing? Did I bring my family here outside of your will?" She spoke into the room. The room filled with her prayer crackling in power and Lavi soaked it in. If only she knew how much the King was with her if only she could understand how many were working together for her good.

"Looks like you are getting a lot done." Her husband entered the room unexpectedly.

She was pleasantly surprised. "You're home!" She got up from the floor and hugged him. Reality struck her, and she stepped back, perplexed, "Why are you home?"

"Some kind of fluke power outage. The whole block lost power, so they sent us home."

"That's great! You can help me paint." As she finished the sentence, her face fell at the thought of it.

He took her hands in his and smiled. "I got a free pass; let's not paint. Let's sit out on the back porch and barbecue."

"I like the way you think."

"Power outage?" Lavi asked Kfir.

"He's here isn't he?" Kfir said with a smile. Aegeus returned from the perimeter sweep.

"She's up." He was pleased.

"They are having something called a barbecue," Kfir offered. "The Twelfth seemed pleased by this."

"Excellent. Now, see if you can get the First here" Aegeus directed Kfir. Kfir raised his eyes in alarm.

"You know I'm a warrior, right?" Kfir asked, a sly smile on his face.

"You'll do fine." Aegeus smiled at the thought of it. Kfir started from the room.

"Keef," Lavi called. Kfir looked back over his shoulder. "No electricity." He winked as Kfir left.

Aegeus was sure he didn't want to know what that was about.

Chapter 14

The Twelfth and her family were playing Frisbee in the backyard while their lunch cooked on the grill. The smell wafting toward heaven made the angels think of burnt offerings, a scent pleasing to both the King and the angels.

A small dog came running into the yard, followed by a slightly flustered woman. The Twelfth positioned herself in the dog's path, stooping down to stop him when he got to her. He rushed toward her, and she reached out to grab his collar. But she didn't have to catch him. Kfir stopped right in front of the Twelfth and knelt, placing his hands over hers. The dog stopped directly in front of her and sat down. He licked her hands and squirmed as she picked him up to give him back to his owner.

"Thank you," the woman offered, out of breath from the run. "I don't know what spooked him; he just freaked out and started running."

"Seriously?" Lavi laughed at Kfir. "You tricked a dog into chasing you here?"

"I made myself smell like bacon," Kfir admitted. "Then I ran just far enough ahead of him that he couldn't get me. It was all I could think of." Lavi and Aegeus laughed.

"This is the First?" Lavi asked, looking at the woman who carried so much hidden pain.

"No, this is his wife. He is on his way, he got tangled in the leash as the dog ran by. His guardian was not thrilled," Kfir added, making a face.

"Leave it to Kfir, winning friends," Lavi chuckled. Aegeus looked at the women talking in the yard.

"Would you like to join us for lunch?" the Twelfth offered the wife of the First.

"Kfir, fan the smell of the barbecue over here; no one can resist it. They'll stay for sure," Aegeus called. Kfir rolled his eyes but fluttered over to the grill and blew gently on the smoke, sending the smell directly toward the wife of the First. She agreed to stay. Shortly after, the First arrived with bandages on his knee and elbow from the fall. Otherwise, he was unharmed. Aegeus and Lavi looked at Kfir, who shrugged.

"Feel free to leave that part out of the report, Aegeus," Kfir joked.

The Twelfth brought out extra place settings, and they all sat at the table talking easily. They had much in common, and conversation flowed effortlessly between the two couples.

Suddenly the Spirit within the Twelfth flared brightly. The angels looked, but she gave no outward indication of what had happened. She looked at the wife of the First, and compassion flooded her eyes, causing them to water for just an instant. Still, she said nothing. The afternoon turned to early evening, and the First and his wife got up to head home.

"Did she get a message?" Lavi wanted to know.

"What happened, Aegeus? That was a very bright flare. Did you see how she looked at the wife? What was that?" Kfir was very interested.

Aegeus walked closer to the couples. He said nothing.

"We are planning to start a small group once a week. Just a few families getting together each week to fellowship. Have you met your neighbors?" the First asked as they were leaving.

"We have; they're great" the husband of the Twelfth answered.

"Oh good, they're part of the group; it will actually be at their house, so you wouldn't have to go far. If you would like to come, we would love to have you join us." The Spirit again shined brightly within the Twelfth.

"We would love to," she answered.

"Great, we'll see you then." And he and his wife left.

"We'd love to?" her husband asked when they were back inside, and there was no risk of the First and his wife hearing.

"I don't know why I said it; it just came out." She smiled up at him. He sighed in response and smiled at her, shaking his head in disbelief. Maybe it would be great, but he doubted it.

Aegeus was pleased with the development. "What happened, Aegeus? What is it she knows about the wife of the First?" Kfir asked. Aegeus shared the story of the First and his wife.

Chapter 15: The First

The First had such high hopes when he graduated from medical school. He was going to find a wonderful medical practice eager for a soft-spoken psychiatrist, and he and his wife would settle into a lovely coastal town. His wife had waited patiently for him to finish school so they could fill their home with children. All she had ever wanted was to be a mother.

But God had other thoughts. As his classmates moved away to begin their careers or ministries, his opportunity came in a different form. A small clinic that provided counseling to low-income families asked him to join them. The pay was minimal and the hours long, but the mission was noble. After considerable prayer and many discussions with his wife, they agreed that the clinic was where God was directing them. The coastal town would wait.

Instead, they moved to a small Alabama town. The First and his wife bought an old antebellum home in need of considerable work. But it was within their price range, and they began to plan for their family.

His wife began pouring herself into repairing the house. But children were apparently not part of God's plan for them either. The First watched helplessly as month after agonizing month his wife wept to discover that she was not pregnant. After a year of trying, they conceded that something might be wrong. She went to the doctor and received a clean bill of health; there was no reason she could not get pregnant. And so, they continued trying, until it was no longer enjoyable to do so.

He watched as his wife began to age before his eyes. Her once beautiful smile faded. The shine in her eyes replaced with the glistening of tears. Her once patient and gracious manner was overcome with sadness and frustration. Daily, he went to God on her behalf, begging that she would become pregnant—worried that she never would.

Five years passed and their home, once so perfect with such promise for a beautiful family, now seemed vast and empty. The empty rooms seemed to scream reminders to them constantly. Instead of nestling children in their bosom, they were used to host visiting missionaries or guests as they came to the church. But even that seemed to be a reminder of her failure.

The First watched as his wife painted a smile on her face and poured her energy into caring for others. She became heavily involved in their church, serving on numerous committees and missions. But in private moments, her anguish was real. She wanted to be a mother.

And then the fateful day had come. The grant that had funded his job at the clinic was not renewed; the clinic would be closing. The same day they received news that the fertility issue was his. He was unable to give his wife the children she had so earnestly sought.

That night they cried together late into the night. He poured out apologies to her that he was not able to give her what she wanted. His anguish poured out over her suffering, and he begged her forgiveness. And then, something happened. A strength he had not seen in her in years filled her. She wiped the tears from his eyes even as her own continued down her cheeks.

"You are the love of my life," she began. "God has given me all that I ever needed. He has given me his son, and he has given me you." She kissed him gently. "I wanted so badly to be a mother. But that is not what God has planned for me. Now that we know, we can move on, together."

Two days later the First was carrying a box from his office to his car when the bottom gave way, sending books toppling out. A woman with wild red hair was passing by and stopped to help.

"Need help?" she said, stooping to help him retrieve the books.

You have no idea how much help I need, the First thought, but "thanks" was what he managed to say. There was a genuine kindness and warmth about her that was comforting, and the First found himself telling her about his position there at the clinic and how they had lost their funding.

She listened intently with wide green eyes that seemed to peer into his soul. As he gathered the books, she managed to repair the box. After the books were secure, the woman with the wild red hair picked up the box as if to carry it.

"I'll take that," said the First, attempting poorly to reach for the box, his own arms already full of other items.

"I'll help; I'm heading that way," she said smiling. "If you don't mind, I can walk with you."

They chatted as they walked across the parking lot. Her kindness disarmed him a little, and he felt himself wondering when the last time was he had stopped to help a stranger. He learned that she was just passing through on her way to a conference at a small college. There was someone in his office building that she had stopped to meet along the way. *A college, now that would be a great place to work*, the First thought. He decided he would explore options at universities. The Light within him burned a little brighter.

Over the next few months, the First noticed that his wife seemed to be walking straighter, with a small skip in her step. A smile returned to her face for the first time in years, and she set about packing their home as he searched for a new job. A burden had been lifted from her heart.

Moving day arrived, and they stood together on the lawn of their home, looking at it for the last time. The First slid his arm around his wife and kissed her gently on the cheek. He was pleased to be leaving, starting fresh. They had found a modest house in their new location. Something small that would not be a reminder that they would never fill it. He felt this place would be right for them both, a place where they could start over. With one parting glance, he led his wife to the car, and they drove away to start a new life at a small Christian college hidden in the mountains.

Chapter 16

Wednesday morning was rainy. The Twelfth hit the snooze alarm and rolled back over, snuggling further into the bed. They had finally gotten the frame assembled for their bed—no more sleeping on just the box springs and mattress on the floor. She had enjoyed her first night of proper sleep in their new home.

The idea of getting out of bed and facing another day of unpacking and painting had no appeal; her bed did. She had concluded that she had been foolish to insist on painting each room before they unpacked it. That made no sense. *What was I thinking?* She mused. She stilled her mind and drifted back to sleep.

She stood in a field of amber-colored wheat. The stalks were soft like silk to her hands. The air smelled clean with a hint of lilac. Birds, somewhere in the distance, sang a song that was beautiful. Her heart felt as if it knew the words. Her soul struggled to break free from her humanity and sing along with them. An abundance of love washed over her. She was at peace. There was no rush, no hurry. Slightly in front of her was an enormous tree. The tree stood with a majesty she could not explain. It seemed to beckon to her, inviting her in with whispers of hope.

As she got closer to the tree, she noticed there were three men under it. One of them had beautiful wings that glistened in the light. They were not made of feathers like those of a bird; instead, they were made of a nearly translucent material that captured and reflected the light. It was stunning.

They seemed to know each other well. From where she was, she could not hear what they were saying, but she could see them picking fruit from the tree. Each time one of them would select fruit and pull it from the tree, the tree would emit lights that reminded her of the aurora borealis. It was as if the tree itself celebrated the act of providing for them. It was so beautiful and captivating that she willed them to eat more. A deep guttural laughter erupted from one of the men, a laugh so contagious that she laughed with him—the stress and anxiety of her life all but forgotten.

Her alarm went off again abruptly pulling her back to reality. She stretched lazily, not ready to release the dream. It had given her such peace and seemed so real. She wanted it to be real. And she longed to return to that place. The smell of coffee hit her nose and made her smile. She rolled over and found a steaming hot cup next to the bed.

The Twelfth pulled herself up to a sitting position and reached for her Bible. She had started one of those "read the Bible through in a year" programs when she moved here. It was interesting. She had read it all before, but she found a new layer of God every time. It was her favorite time of the day.

Currently, she was reading Leviticus, and she had to admit it was not her favorite. Nevertheless, each day she found a small nugget of something beautiful, a treasure God had left just for her. Today she read about the sacrificial system and the law regarding one being unclean after bearing a child. This did not sit well with her, so she took it to her father.

"God, how come you think women are dirty?" she spoke out into the empty room. The woman with the wild red hair sat, unseen, on the end of her bed.

"Where do you get that idea?" she asked back.

"Right here, in your word. Give birth to a male child, and you are unclean for thirty days, but give birth to a girl, and you are unclean for sixty days." She spoke out again, looking toward heaven. The woman with the red hair could not contain her joy at the comment.

"And if today, you received thirty days of parental leave for birthing a son and sixty days when you birthed a daughter, would you still feel like girls were devalued?" she asked the Twelfth. The Twelfth had never considered it that way.

"What about the animals?" she asked. "To atone for sin, it normally had to be a male animal sacrificed. Doesn't that make them more valuable?"

"How many animals were sacrificed in what you read today," the woman asked her.

"Thousands."

"What would happen to the herd if we killed thousands of the females in one day?"

The Twelfth sat frozen, her Light blazing with new understanding.

"But you make most male animals the beautiful ones, and the females are normally dull, like the peacock for example or the duck."

The woman with the red hair could not contain her laughter. "Which duck is easier for the hunter to see?"

"The male." Realization began to dawn on her.

"And if a female duck had the colorful plumage of the male, how would she protect her nest?" And just like that, the matter was settled.

The day passed swiftly, and before they knew it, it was time to go to the Wednesday night gathering. The group members had decided to each bring a covered dish to share. The Twelfth was not much of a cook and had spent most of the day reviewing recipes and comparing the ingredients list to what she had in the pantry. Options were limited. She eventually settled on a Mexican dish that she hoped would be well received.

The Twelfth and her husband made their way to the neighbors' house. Aegeus, Kfir, and Lavi joined them. The group hit it off immediately. The home of the Second and Third was lovely. The Third had a refined taste that was elegant and upscale without seeming stuffy. She had used warm colors and lighting to bring an inviting feel to the home. The décor was classic but had pieces from all the countries they had been to during their travels.

The First and his wife, the Second, the Third, the Eleventh and her husband, and the Twelfth and her husband were all there. Each family brought a dinner item so that combined they had an entire meal. They put the dishes on the table and then served themselves buffet style, gathering in the large living room to eat.

The room had beautiful chairs around a rustic wooden table made from a boat that had sunk off the coast of Sierra Leone. The Second had been onboard at the time. The table was beautiful, but the story was better and listening to him tell it captivated the group, drawing them into the circle. There was something about the Second, something distinguished that made you feel important.

The angels watched as the King's children laughed and enjoyed one another's company. Aegeus was pleased to see them bonding. He knew the group was not quite complete, and a few more would be added over the next several months, but tonight's gathering was important. It was small and intimate, and the Twelfth would leave tonight with a support system, something she hadn't had when she woke up that morning. In this place, she was surrounded by those more experienced and wiser. Those who could mentor and support her. People, she would call friends.

Aegeus looked around at them and knew they would all benefit from being together. Tonight, a bond would begin that would become a lifelong connection between them. But of course, they did not know any of that yet. All they knew was that they felt the King in this place and they had enjoyed being together and breaking bread.

The Third had a natural talent for hosting, and she kept the conversation flowing smoothly. They laughed together and shared stories to get to know one another. The conversation eased gently into a discussion on their faith, which tended to happen when a group of the King's children was together for long.

The angels relished the Light as it poured from the group and filled the house with the Light of God. They felt almost drunk with its power. They watched as the lights intermingled, making glorious colors before melding together into one. The angels seemed to be enjoying the evening as much as the humans.

Aegeus had been distracted sharing stories of old with the other angels when he noticed that the King's children were discussing demons. This got his undivided attention.

The King's children were discussing their thoughts on demons and if they thought "the devil made me do it" was a clever ploy or if demons actually roamed the earth. It was fascinating to Aegeus to listen to them discuss the spiritual realm.

The angels positioned themselves around the room and listened intently to the discussion. The Eleventh was adamant that demons did indeed exist, but she gave no proof for her strong conviction. The Twelfth suggested that if you believed the Word regarding demons, then you would have to conclude that demons did indeed roam the earth.

Aegeus wasn't sure which of them brought up the question of angels. The angels shifted in their seats both uneasy and amused. It was a strange sensation to listen to someone debate if you existed while you were sitting right there. Soon, Aegeus realized that he and the other angels were wholly engaged in the discussion the King's children were having.

He noticed the other angels were answering questions that were being posed and cheering when one of the humans said something correct—almost as if they were watching a sporting event.

For just a moment, as Aegeus watched, it was as if they really were all in the room together. He had never felt so connected to the humans. But of course, he knew that was not the situation. He tried to pull back—to separate himself—but the experience was so powerful, the King's love so overwhelming in the room, that he struggled to disengage.

The evening ran late, and the families made plans to meet again the following week. They each bid their good-nights and headed out toward their own homes. As they were walking out, the Twelfth asked the Eleventh, "How are you so sure there are demons?"

"You are going to think I am crazy, but...," the Eleventh hesitated. She had had such a great time that evening, and she liked the group, so she didn't want to say anything that would make them avoid her. The Twelfth looked at her with anticipation, waiting for the end of the sentence. In her experience, sentences that started that way were the start of a great story. The Eleventh plunged on, "I have seen them."

Kfir and Lavi looked at Aegeus with raised eyebrows. Aegeus smiled.

Chapter 17: The Eleventh

The Eleventh sat on the side of the tub, the cold porcelain serving as a witness that she was awake. She stared at the pregnancy test. This could not possibly be right; why would God let this happen? She closed her eyes tightly, willing it to be a mistake. She picked up the box the test had come in and once again read the directions. She had followed them, and it was hard to misread the word "pregnant" on the digital display.

Nausea overwhelmed her. Not the nausea of pregnancy, but the kind of nausea that hits you when you find yourself in an unbearable situation. Something so horrible that you have only one course of action, throwing up. She dropped to the floor in front of the toilet and threw up until she thought her very insides were coming up. Tears poured down her cheeks, wails of sorrow flooding her and filling the room. She collapsed on the floor sobbing and begging God to undo this thing that had been done to her. She fell asleep on the floor in front of the toilet.

When the Eleventh woke up, she was slightly disoriented—not quite sure where she was for just a moment. The room had grown dark. Then, it all came flooding back as she looked at the pregnancy test still clutched in her hand. Her eyes and throat were sore from crying, her nose stuffy. She stood to her feet, her legs unsteady. She left her hope on the floor.

The Eleventh made her way to the sink and ran cold water to rinse her face. The water felt refreshing. She looked up into the mirror as it dripped down her face and back into the sink. Her eye was black, her mouth busted, and the bruises on her cheek and on her forehead were still there. They had transitioned from the black/purple they had started as to a green/yellow mix. How could this have happened? Wasn't it enough that God let her be raped; must she be pregnant too?

Fresh tears ran down her face. How could she ever survive this? She had one more semester of graduate school after this one. Walking into class beaten and bruised had been hard enough. All the questions, all the prying eyes. How many times had she been asked what happened? She had created a vague story about being in a car accident. No one questioned it when she couldn't remember the details.

But she had not been in a car accident. She had been beaten and raped in her own home. She had gone over it a thousand times in just the short time since it happened. Coming home from her run to find two strangers in her apartment. They wore masks, but they knew her name. They had left her bleeding on the floor. Her first instinct, whether right or wrong, was to shower—she felt so dirty.

She just wanted it to be over. She wanted to forget. She wanted to scrub the smell of them, the touch of them from her body. Perhaps, if she scrubbed hard enough, she could reverse it. She had clawed and scrubbed at her skin until the water ran cold. Then she sat down and cried until she had no tears left. But life didn't stop just because she had cried herself out.

She supposed she told people she was in a car accident because she didn't want to have to admit out loud what had happened. She didn't want to say it over and over again. She didn't want their looks of pity. She didn't want it to be real. It was embarrassing, and she felt great shame. She lived in constant fear since the incident. Someone she knew—someone who knew her name—had done this. Who? Every man she encountered was a potential suspect. She no longer felt safe in her own home. She was angry with God. And now? Now she was pregnant.

After another hot shower, she double -checked the locks on the door, making sure the chair she had wedged under the knob was still secure. She triple-checked the windows and then made it to her bed exhausted physically, emotionally, and mentally. She crawled into bed and cried. But sleep was elusive. Eventually, she gave up and got out of bed; she felt too vulnerable. She took her pillow and a light blanket and went to the back corner of her closet. With the closet door closed and her back against the wall, she was finally able to doze off; it wasn't long before the nightmares began.

Two months passed. During that time, the Eleventh moved from her apartment into a smaller apartment off the back of an old woman's home. It was much smaller, and she felt safer there. Her visible bruises and cuts had almost healed, but it was still evident that something tragic had happened to her.

For the first month, she had ignored that she was pregnant. She just couldn't deal with that on top of the rape. But over the last month, she had been forced to acknowledge it. You couldn't say that she decided on an abortion. She didn't think about it. She wouldn't allow herself to think about it. She merely acted as if it were the natural course of things. It wasn't a baby; it was a reminder. It was like having the rapist inside of her still.

The drive to the clinic was uneventful. They had told her to have someone drive her, but she didn't. She couldn't, who could she tell? She came from a very devout Christian family. Her friends were all believers. How could she tell them? And so, she drove alone, not sure what she would do afterward, except finally be free.

When she arrived at the clinic, there were protesters out front. She thought about times she had gone and protested, holding signs, and pleading with women not to commit murder. Now, as she walked the long sidewalk from her car to the clinic and they yelled similar things at her, it didn't seem very loving.

What did she know of her pain? Which of them had bothered to know anything about her at all? How could they stand in judgment of her? She walked with her head down, not looking to the left or right. Had she bothered to look, either way, she might have seen the woman with the wild red hair and beautiful green eyes holding the door for her. The woman's hand gently brushed her own as she walked in.

She walked past the woman into the waiting room. That's when she saw them. Demons. The waiting room was dark; a thin black smoke filled the room. Not enough to choke you, but enough to cloud your vision. The smell of sulfur hung thick in the air. Demons were hanging about in the waiting room, clinging to the other women there. Their red eyes fixed on her horror-stricken face when she walked in. She stood frozen where she was, her eyes wide in horror.

The woman with the red hair and green eyes that seemed to look straight through you walked up from behind and stood beside her, looking at the demons too.

"Do you see them?" the Eleventh finally whispered.

"Oh yes, I see them," the woman answered, her voice bringing comfort and peace, something the Eleventh hadn't known in quite some time.

"What are they?" she whispered again, not moving from her spot.

"They are tormenting demons," the woman said with confidence.

"What are they doing here?"

"They are everywhere. Anywhere people are, they go." The answer seemed so simple.

"How come I can see them?" the Eleventh wanted to know.

"Perhaps you needed to be able to see them," the woman answered. She stepped slightly closer to the Eleventh so that their arms barely touched. "Do not be afraid, I am with you," the woman said gently. A surge of power and electricity pulsed through the Eleventh. Her fear was gone.

The demons were standing very still, anxious, and unsure of what to do now that the woman with the red hair had entered the building.

"Let's leave here," the woman suggested. Nodding in agreement, the Eleventh turned and walked from the clinic with the red-haired woman. From that day on, the Eleventh was able, on occasion, to see demons. In many ways, it was terrifying, but in some ways, it was also liberating. She found it easier to fight what she could see.

Chapter 18

Aegeus called a meeting of the team covering the Twelfth. They met once again in the old salvage yard. He wanted to lay out a plan.

Now that the twelve were all in place, he didn't think it would be long before the enemy detected them. The sky over the small town had darkened even more over the last two days, which could only mean one thing: the arrival of the Strongman.

The demons swarmed the sky, forming a canopy of evil and deception over the town. The streets were clogged with them, but nowhere was their presence more noticeable than at the college.

Aegeus knew that his small fleet was grossly outnumbered and his warriors posing as guardians would not be able to wear their disguises much longer. Soon the demons would know they were there, and they would understand why. The King had begun to call other angels to the battle, and Aegeus looked forward to their arrival. But getting through the swarm to the town would not be easy, and it could delay them. The demons had become confident in their position, and as their confidence grew, their activity grew.

Lavi arrived at the meeting first. Kfir and Adiel entered next with a nearly silent swoosh. Adiel a warrior, like Kfir and Aegeus, had fought alongside King David in many battles. She was a highly-decorated warrior. Aegeus was pleased she had joined the team. Adiel did not care for the uniform of the guardians and found the leather to be constricting. She preferred her own combat gear. She tugged at the tunic since it did not provide for the same range of movement or protection that her armor provided. She worried about how much good the guardian uniform would be if the demons discovered them.

Adiel wore her hair in a long braid down her back. She had the dark hair and eyes of the Greeks, whom she had protected for many years. Her skin was olive colored and flawless, but she had many physical reminders of each combat and one thin but distinct scar under her right eye.

Aegeus looked at the three angels assigned to the Twelfth. Like Kfir and Adiel, he was eager to engage in battle. Seeing the gathering of the demons and not engaging them was a test of their patience. But the King had been clear in his instructions.

"Comrades," he began, "as you know, all twelve are now in position inside the town. Based on the increasing number of demons over the last forty-eight hours, a Strongman must have arrived. We will need to join our efforts to those assigned to the rest of the twelve. Each family has a warrior and at least one guardian. Meir and Adiel arrived last night, and Ayo and Berhanu will be joining us over the next few days after they finish an assignment in Africa. We are hopeful to get them into the town without having to fight and reveal our positions."

The other angels nodded in understanding. Meir, Ayo, and Berhanu were ministering angels.

"Make sure all twelve are feeding truth into their soul so that Meir, Ayo, and Berhanu will have something to work with. This can come from reading the Bible, listening to music, or interacting with others of positive influence, particularly those that love them and are kind."

Aegeus continued, "This nation was once founded on the basis of freedom of religion. It was once a holy nation that trusted in our King. They prayed and remembered the one True God."

At the very mention of his name, the angels began to emit a strong electrical energy and to shine ever more brightly.

"But the nation has lost its way, and those who follow the King have become silent. In place of the love he called them to, judgment, fear, and lies have filled their hearts. They have become meek and afraid to speak the truth. When they try to speak the truth, they do not do so in love, but out of fear and ignorance. The Lights of many have dimmed, and they have resorted to the same hypocrisy as the Pharisees.

"The truth is being lost. The enemy is quickly gaining this nation, and this battle signifies the beginning of what may be the end of them. You have been assembled here to preserve what is left. If we lose this town, Lucifer will send deception, hatred, and judgment out from this place cloaked in the lie of being the truth. The twelve will be the key to reigniting truth and love in this place. As you know," Aegeus concluded, "victory does not always look like the humans expect it to."

"Kfir, survey the town and find the Strongman. We need to know where and who he is. Adiel, try to find the meeting place of the demons. Find out anything you can, we need to know their plans. Lavi, visit the church and the coffee shops; get a measure of where the people are spiritually. We need to know what we're up against and who, other than the Third, we can count on for prayer cover."

The meeting ended, and the angels headed out of the salvage yard each to complete the assigned task. Lavi headed for the coffee shop that was on the way to the church. The smell of freshly roasted coffee beans flooded from inside the shop and spilled out into the street, welcoming Lavi as he got closer.

The smell of the coffee beans made him long for home. He reminded himself that after this assignment, he would spend time in heaven renewing his strength before the next one. Unlike the warriors, guardians spent more time on earth than in heaven. Time on earth was draining.

After each assignment, guardians were given respite in heaven to renew. It was a time to rest and a time to spend in the presence of the King. Energy flowed freely, and his senses were fed in a way they could never be on earth. But the distinct aroma of freshly ground coffee beans was one of the small pleasures that Lavi had on earth. He found the smell aromatic and a reminder of the comforts of home.

The coffee shop, Perks, was overflowing with college students, professors, and some high school students. Demons stood in the doorway of the coffee shop, sliding their hands over each person as they entered. Lavi knew it was one way for them to determine who was worth further attention. The smell of sulfur quickly overpowered the smell of the coffee beans.

A young couple walked into the coffee shop just ahead of Lavi. One of the demons ran his hands over the girl's long hair, lingering only a moment before letting out a hideous hissing sound, and holding his hand as if it had been burned. The girl's Light exploded in intensity because of the unwanted touch. She seemed to shiver imperceptibly and looked in the direction of the demon. She could not have felt him, and yet the Spirit inside her had given a clear message to the demon.

The boy did not have a Light, and the demon found him to be a more willing host. Very quickly, in the time it took the boy to open the door for the young lady, the demon used one of his long talons and pierced it through the boy's head. A black stream of evil thoughts and desires passed from the demon to the boy. The demon laughed in glee as the boy moved into the coffee shop.

Lavi put one hand on his sword as he approached the doorway where the demons were standing. While angels served at the pleasure of the King, they were always free to defend themselves from attack.

"Easy there; you know the rules. This is common ground," said the demon who had just retracted his talon from the boy.

"I know the rules," Lavi said grudgingly. The temptation to engage in battle was strong, but his love of the King was stronger. He would not defy the rules of the King to satisfy his own desires. Lucifer had done that once and look what had come of it.

Lavi knew the end that was in store for the demons. The demons knew as well, and it fed their hatred for the humans. Lucifer had desired to usurp the King. He had revolted and taken around a third of the angels with him in his rebellion. They had been cast from heaven. The King had created a prison for them, a prison the humans referred to as hell. The King had specially designed hell to contain the demons, those who rebelled against him. But then Lucifer tricked Adam and Eve into disobeying the King. Man's fate had been sealed to share in the destruction and punishment intended for Lucifer.

But the King offered a solution. He provided a way for the humans to avoid hell. He knew the road would not be easy, but for those who would persist, death would bring about eternal life. The King's son volunteered to take the punishment intended for humanity. He would be killed to pay their debt. The King had not made a similar provision for Lucifer and his followers. For this reason, Lucifer declared war on the humans. He could not touch the King, but he was committed to doing all he could to destroy those created in the King's image, those he called children.

The coffee shop had all brick walls inside with large rounded windows. The walls were decorated with antique coffee vestiges sparsely placed along the walls throughout. The six baristas stood behind a long black counter with a solid marble top.

A huge chalkboard hung behind them with the menu written on it. Someone had put a considerable amount of time into writing it, complete with chalk drawings of the different coffees randomly throughout.

Bistro tables were scattered around the shop, each having a marble top with either two or four bistro chairs. A small bakery case on the side wall contained a selection of baked goods like scones, bagels, or fresh quiche. According to the sign stuck to the front of the case, everything was baked fresh daily by the local bakery. The coffee was served in plain white coffee cups on plain white saucers. For those in a hurry, there were traditional to-go cups.

Lavi scanned the room quickly. Many of those present, had the Light of God, although some of their Lights were very dim. There were only five tormenting demons in the coffee shop making their way from table to table and whispering suggestions or feeding thoughts to the occupants. Sometimes the unwanted thoughts and ideas would be met with a flash of Light that would burn the demon or send him flying backward, depending on how active the Spirit was within the person.

But for those who did not have the Spirit, the human had to fight the thoughts themselves. Some of the humans embraced the thoughts and ideas offered by the demons while others struggled against them. The demons were relentless and continued to feed their poison into the crowd.

There were three guardians already in the coffee shop. Two of them were in the back-corner chatting. Lavi assumed they knew each other. The third guardian stood very close to his charge. He was protecting a college student from the demons. The guardian had wrapped his wings around the young man so that the demons could not touch him. The demons were not foolish; they knew they could not break through the wings of the guardian, so they directed their taunts to the angel himself.

The guardian stood firm without even blinking. A look at the young man would never reveal the sorrow that was in his heart. But as Lavi walked closer to him, he could see that the boy had considerable pain. He wore a smile on his face and laughed at all the right times, but his soul felt great sadness. As Lavi moved closer, he could feel the depth of the boy's sorrow reach out to him.

The proximity of two guardians made the demons move farther away and redirect their attention to other patrons. Lavi noticed them latching on to a high school girl who did not have the Light.

As they began to pour darkness into her, she accepted it willingly; she did not have the strength to fight. Her soul cried out as she embraced the lies they fed her—lies of her worthlessness.

Lavi felt his anger begin to rise at the sight. But angels were neither friend nor foe of the humans—they served the King. They defended those the King told them to and fought those whom the King declared enemies. More than once the King had directed the angels to fight against his chosen people, Israel. Long term, it had always worked to the advantage of the Israelites, but Lavi was sure they had not seen it that way at the time. Humans did not tend to understand.

Lavi looked up to see that the guardian had not taken his wings from around his charge.

"Lavi, guardian of the King, sent to the earth to oversee his children," stated Lavi in the tradition of the guardians.

"Octar, holy is the King," responded Octar, finishing the traditional greeting.

"Have you been assigned to him long?" asked Lavi.

"Only since he went home for Easter," Octar replied. "His mother became worried and prayed me here."

"And she has maintained you since?" Lavi asked the obvious. Human mothers were powerful beings. Their prayers were some of Lavi's favorites to hear. Many of his assignments over the years had been at the request of a mother. But humans were impatient and keeping a guardian on a special assignment required daily prayer.

Usually, the humans lost heart too quickly and gave up. Because they could not see that the King was responding to them, they assumed he was not. The mother who had kept a guardian assigned to her son for two months was an impressive being.

"She is an extraordinary prayer warrior," Octar replied. "She has even sent a second on occasion." Guardians could be given individual assignments based on the prayers of that day. For this charge to have had a guardian for months meant his mother had been praying for her son diligently every day. To send a second guardian would require numerous prayers throughout the day. Typically, it was from multiple people praying.

"What is the boy's condition?" Lavi asked.

Just then the demons erupted in laughter. Lavi turned to see the situation, and he noticed the girl without the Light was now crying. Her face had grown red, and she jumped from her chair, sending it crashing to the ground. The metal bistro chair colliding with the well-polished stone floor made a tremendous sound, attracting all the patrons in the shop.

The outburst brought more demons streaming into the coffee shop, and Lavi realized he and the other guardians were now outnumbered four to one. Demons continued to pile in. The girl did not have the Light, and she had no guardian. She had little to defend herself with.

The demons had climbed onto her and wrapped their arms around her throat. Anger had sunk his talons into her temple, and Worthlessness had grabbed her heart. Insecurity had covered her mouth and was spewing dark thoughts through her open mouth and nose. Spittle flew from her mouth as tears streamed down her cheeks. She was yelling things at her tablemate that made no sense to Lavi and didn't seem to make much sense to the tablemate.

The girl at the table with her—her sister from what Lavi could tell—was trying to calm her. Her face flushed from the scene developing around her. Everyone in the coffee shop watched. She spoke words of apology and encouragement to the girl, but they were met by demons who refused to let them in.

Patrons in the coffee shop began to grow increasingly uncomfortable, and the demons grew increasingly jubilant. Lavi felt anger rising within him, but he was severely outnumbered, and he had not gotten the order to protect the girl.

Increasingly demons swarmed the coffee shop, piling onto the girl. Her anger and despondency becoming greater and greater. The smell of sulfur became so overwhelming that Lavi wondered how the humans could not smell it.

The guardians in the room began to move strategically around the room to position themselves for the best possible attack should the order come. Except for Octar. He remained steadfast, wrapping his wings even tighter around his charge.

Lavi surveyed the room and found that as the demons had piled in, they had launched full attacks against many of the patrons. He fidgeted in his position as the demons bumped and shoved him in their eagerness to get closer to the girl.

Where was the prayer? Why was no one praying for this girl? Did they not realize the signal was powered by their prayer? Lavi searched the room for those with the Light. He had to believe that one of them would plead with the King for this girl. Did they not know they had the very power of the King inside of them?

In the corner sat the girl with the long hair who had deflected the demon upon entering. Her Light began to burn more brightly. Her eyes were open, but she prayed. Her Light got stronger, more powerful. She closed her eyes and bowed her head—even more fully committed to her purpose. As the Light grew, others in the room joined her until finally, the room was full of the Light. And then the signal came.

The guardians drew their swords simultaneously in one swift and silent motion. Lavi grabbed the demon closest to him and thrust the sword straight through his back. The demon let out a scream of pain, and an electrical surge left his body as his corpse dropped to the ground.

Lavi ducked just in time to miss a poorly aimed sword being wielded by an untrained demon. He grabbed the sword, spinning around, and stabbing the demon with his own sword. The air crackled with the released power of the demon as he fell to his death.

A long-haired warrior demon with a deep scar moved to position himself between Lavi and the girl. Lavi could see the other two guardians slashing their way through the demons toward the girl, but they were not yet close. Lavi knew that he was little match for a well-trained warrior.

The girl, oblivious to the battle around her, knew only of the battle that raged within her. Her anger had reached a fevered pitch, and her sense of hopelessness and worthlessness had overwhelmed any sense of propriety.

She raged on, having thrown her hot coffee from the table; she was now ranting at other clients, hurling accusations that made little sense. Her eyes had taken on a frantic look of pain, anguish, and not understanding her own actions. Her hair flew about in the unkempt manner of an animal. Lavi thrust his sword at the long-haired demon with the scar, who easily dodged it. The long-haired demon smiled a knowing smile as if he were part of some elaborate secret, then tipped his head slightly to Lavi and vanished just as another demon thrust his sword deep into Lavi's stomach.

The remaining demons outnumbered the guardians. But they were not warriors—they were tormenting demons untrained in the art of real combat. Guardians had some combat training, although they were by no means warriors. But all angels had a weapon that demons did not. They had the Light of God. Demons had lost this during the rebellion.

Lavi spread his wings as wide as they would go, and mustering all the strength he had left, he emitted the Holy Light of God, which shot the demons from their feet and through the walls of the shop. Only one remained. A small tormenting demon had dug his claws into the girl, and just as Lavi reached for him, he darted inside the girl, where he was protected from Lavi. The girl had no defense now.

The smell of burnt demons lingered in the air. Lavi collapsed to the floor, golden blood pouring from his wound.

Chapter 19

The blast of the Light of God did not go unnoticed by Morax. He summoned his leadership team to his office at the college. Titus brought one of the tormenting demons with him to testify to the situation at the coffee shop. Morax glared at the demon and demanded an explanation.

"You have evoked the Light of God in this place!" he yelled, sulfur pouring from his mouth and filling the room.

"Don't worry, Lord," the demon responded without fear. "It was only a few guardians. No real cause for concern."

"Just a few guardians? Just a few guardians!" Morax railed, grabbing the demon by the throat. "Those guardians just blew a hundred demons from a stronghold!" Morax screamed.

The room had grown dark with sulfur, and Morax found his human eyes starting to burn from his own essence. "You have given away our numbers; do you not realize they will wonder why there are so many of us here? They will have reinforcements by morning," he snarled.

"But . . . but—" the demon sputtered, realizing his position was perilous. "We destroyed one," he blurted out, hoping to help his situation.

"You have destroyed one?" Morax asked, an uneasy calm coming over him. His eyes became glassy and his stare cold. The rage from only a moment before was instantly gone, and the hand clutched around the tormenting demon's throat began to tremble.

"Yes, Lord; I saw him collapse in his own blood," the demon added, his confidence returning. "And, we took possession of a girl," he added, sure that he was advancing his position.

Morax released the demon, shoving him as he did so. "You are an idiot," he snarled with a cold hatred that was shocking even to the demon. "Kill him," he said to Titus. Titus, without hesitation, drew his sword and decapitated the tormenting demon in one swift motion. The demon's body jerked slightly and then collapsed to the ground, dissipating into black smoke.

Morax stood in front of his office window looking out over the campus. His office was large and spacious, precisely the type of office a man in his position at the college would warrant. But his window was much too small for his liking.

He stood silent for a long moment as he watched the demons darting in and out of buildings around campus. Tormenting demons were common. They were the most common type of demon, and their presence on a college campus would be expected. They had taken control of this campus, being careful not to attract attention. The demons had controlled the hiring, and only a short time ago had fired a large number of faculty members who posed a problem to their plan.

They had sought zealots, those who loved the Word more than the Creator—those who would adhere to rules above clinging to love. Those who were timid and would not speak up or sacrifice their own comfort to defend the truth. Those who knew of the King but did not actually know him. But these things had to be done over time.

While the strongest among them had been eliminated, there were still many who had the Light. And thousands of years had taught Morax that those with the Light were unpredictable. If the guardians attacked the demons in the coffee shop, it was because they had been given orders to do so. The death of a guardian would bring many angels to the town. Morax walked from the window to his desk and sat down, looking across at Titus and his team.

"I believe we all know what is at stake here," Morax began. "This small college is our ticket to taking over America. We will defeat this town using the Strongman, and we will send false religion under the cloak of truth out into this nation. We are so close to destroying this generation. The Strongman will rise in notoriety, and we will progress to phase two of our plan." He looked at each of them in turn.

"In mere days, the students will begin classes, and the last of the new faculty will be in place. We have brought in all new faculty for the Bible department, all from our seminary. We will control all that these students learn about truth.

"We will flood the campus with Depression, Anxiety, Guilt, Distrust, Worthlessness, and Shame. Suicides will rise, breakdowns will rise, and they will feel despondent over their sin, but they will not repent because we will convince them they are not worthy. They need not repent if they read the Word more. That will save them, we will say.

"We will teach them to say the right things while understanding those things the wrong way. We will strangle them with rules and checklists of what 'good Christians' do. They will lie and heap judgment upon each other.

"We will enervate the faculty members who contain the Light. They will not know who to trust, and so they will remain silent. We will fill them with the fear of losing their jobs and convince them that they will not ever work again. Our version of the truth will be close to the truth, and they will wonder if they are the ones who are wrong. We will shame them if they speak of the Spirit. We will fill their days with what is good to keep them from doing what is best."

The demons in the room smiled at the thought of it. It was a brilliant plan.

"We have done our research," Morax continued. "The Strongman is getting settled and acclimated. He is preparing opening remarks that will stir their hearts and confuse them greatly. It will divide them and make it easy for us to determine who will be trouble. But we need more time. We must not attract unnecessary attention. The angels will flock to the town over the death of their own. So, we will pull back, all of us. Everyone is to leave for three days.

"Titus, gather all the tormenting demons and move them to neighboring cities. Leave only a few, less than would be expected. Move our warriors too. In three days, return. Then focus over the summer on building up our warriors; make sure we are at full capacity by the time school resumes."

Titus nodded his head at the command and stood to signal to his team that it was time to depart.

Chapter 20

The Light of God was a powerful tool that every angel possessed. But emitting it like Lavi had required a great deal of power and energy. Angels reserved it for rare occasions, and often, after such a battle, they had to return to the King to bathe in his presence and recharge.

Lavi's decision to use the Light of God to defend the girl and his fellow guardians did indeed draw the attention of all the angels—just as Morax had predicted.

All the guardians and warriors in the town flooded to Perks when they saw the Light. Upon entering the building, Aegeus immediately saw Lavi's lifeless body lying on the floor, unseen by the humans. Lavi was covered in the gold that was the lifeblood of angels. Aegeus scooped up his friend's body and headed for heaven.

Aegeus stood under the tree where he and Lavi had first stood with Kfir and discussed the mission. He could feel the tree celebrating the life and service of Lavi. Streams of golden light poured from the tree's branches. Aegeus laid his hand against the tree and walked around its base. The rough bark rubbed against his hand, and thousands of years of memories with Lavi filled Aegeus's mind. He held each one tightly.

All of heaven would stand at this tree and honor Lavi. But for now, Aegeus stood alone. He needed the solace. Aegeus carefully selected a variety of fruits from the tree and placed them in a wooden pestle. He sat quietly under the tree and crushed the fruit, making juice. The simple act brought him comfort and peace.

Angels do not have bodies like humans; they have celestial bodies. But those bodies require food and drink. They require the Light of God. There is no death in heaven, but that doesn't mean nothing in heaven can die. Angels could die. They do not die in the sense that humans die, but they died nonetheless.

Only demons could kill angels, and the death of an angel was something all of heaven mourned. Before Lavi, only four angels had ever died. The King had said that only seven angels would ever die before the day of wrath. They were to see each death as a signal that the day of wrath was drawing nearer. The King's children referred to it as the tribulation.

Aegeus leaned against the tree; he could feel Lavi. When the day of wrath was upon them—Lavi would again walk the streets of heaven. Knowing that encouraged Aegeus, but it did not remove his pain. He missed his friend.

He felt Michael arrive behind him. Michael stood silently a few paces behind Aegeus, waiting on Aegeus to initiate. Aegeus rose to his feet but did not turn around to face Michael.

"Do we lose this battle?" It was all Aegeus wanted to know.

"According to human standards or heavenly standards?" Michael asked, placing his hand on Aegeus's shoulder.

Chapter 21

The fall of Lavi left a large hole in the team and in their hearts. Aegeus knew the toll for this mission would be high, but Lavi had been one of his closest friends.

He entered the abandoned building in the salvage yard where the other angels sat quietly. They looked to him for leadership. He cleared his throat unnecessarily. At that moment, Aegeus felt an overwhelming love for them. He stood silently looking at each one of them in turn, remembering battles fought together, moments shared.

Angels were comfortable with silence; they sat very still, meeting Aegeus's gaze. He took out a glass decanter etched with a Celtic cross, the sign of the guardian. Aegeus poured himself a glass from the decanter. It was the juice he had made in heaven. The liquid sparkled in the decanter. It had an iridescent quality, highlighting the colors from each of the fruits he had used to make it. He passed the decanter around, and each angel poured a glass. Aegeus held his glass up.

"We have lost one of our brothers." His voice cracked slightly with emotion. "But Lavi gave his life in service of the King; there is no more noble honor. He fell fighting to protect a human girl, a girl who does not yet have the Light. If she were to be lost, her suffering would know no end. But because of Lavi's sacrifice, she will live to have another chance. The King loves his children. He has sent us to defend and protect them. The journey will continue to be difficult, but we will not waiver from our path. We will not turn our heads to the right or the left but will run the race set before us."

The other angels nodded in agreement. They drank the sweet nectar of heaven in honor of Lavi. Eventually, Lavi would have to be replaced, but Aegeus was not yet ready.

Chapter 22

The Twelfth was relieved to be headed to campus for her first official day. It was a warm summer day, but she decided to walk anyway. The college was close enough that walking was reasonable. As she made her way toward the school, she listened to music and prayed. The last two years had been especially difficult. She had worked in a pressure cooker for a man she often thought was the devil himself.

Walking along the path toward her the school, she felt both excited and nervous to be starting something new. It would be nice to work in a Christian environment where people weren't lying and looking out only for themselves. But she worried that she wouldn't be good enough to fit in. How would she stack up? If they found out how flawed she was, she had no doubt they would fire her.

Aegeus walked beside her dressed as her guardian. He scanned the streets for any sign of demons, but the town seemed quiet. The Twelfth turned her face toward the sun and closed her eyes for a moment as she walked. Aegeus couldn't help but think how much stronger the light was in heaven and how one day she would have the honor of feeling real light upon her face.

He also found himself hoping that she would not trip and fall because he wasn't actually a guardian and he was ill-equipped to serve as one. She needed a proper guardian, not a warrior disguised as one.

Her Light flickered quietly as she prayed. Aegeus thought about how much easier it would all be if he could hear her prayers. But of course, prayers were not meant for him.

The red-haired woman arrived quite suddenly, as she usually did. She placed her hand gently on Aegeus's back and smiled at him. Then she moved so that she walked just behind the Twelfth, out of sight. She laid her hand on the Twelfth's shoulder and kept it there as they walked toward the campus.

Aegeus looked at her and smiled. Things were always better when she was here. As they rounded a corner, Aegeus saw the Fifth approaching with Haywood. In a matter of seconds, the Fifth and the Twelfth had converged and were walking side by side, but not speaking. The red-haired woman laid her other hand on the shoulder of both women. Their Lights flared, but neither woman spoke. Aegeus and Haywood greeted each other as they too walked toward the campus. It did not take long before the two women were also chatting.

"It is strange to see you dressed as a guardian," Haywood chuckled to Aegeus.

"It is strange to be dressed as such," Aegeus said, looking down at himself and smiling.

"How is the Fifth holding up?" Aegeus asked, real concern in his voice. He knew her past.

"She carries a heavy burden, but she resists any ministering angel that comes to her. It is as if she does not want to release it. Her body carries the effect of her soul. She prays often, but because we have had to battle to get in and out of the town our response has been delayed, this has caused her to feel distant and unheard. In her darkest days, she feels abandoned by the King and alone."

Aegeus sighed. This was such a common attack from the enemy. He again thought of Lavi, who had just given his life in battle to protect a child of the King. His mind wandered over the other brothers he had lost over the centuries. All the battles, the time away from heaven, all in service to the King for his children, who didn't even know they were there. Children who cried out, feeling abandoned and alone when Aegeus and those like him were there fighting and dying. Then, he remembered the Lamb and how he too had felt abandoned in his darkest hour.

"Aegeus?" Haywood's voice broke through his own thoughts.

"Yes?"

Haywood hesitated. "I think she believes she deserves to be abandoned by the King. It is why she fights the ministering angels so strongly."

Aegeus could not understand this; he made a mental note to discuss it with Michael. The two women were engrossed in whatever it was human women talked about, as they all approached their building. From the outside, there was no indication of the anguish that was within the Fifth. The King's children were good at concealing their pain. Perhaps this developing friendship would help both women. The women parted ways inside the building, each heading to her own office. Hayward and Aegeus did the same.

When Aegeus was satisfied the Twelfth was settled safely in her office, he decided to walk the perimeter of the building. Low-level demons were darting about in the halls, looking for people to torment or taunt. Usually, they would just reach out and touch a person, leaving a stream of black smoke behind and the thoughts that went with it.

Aegeus watched as the Light would flair in some of them, rejecting the thoughts immediately and sending the demon howling in pain. It made Aegeus chuckle to see. But occasionally, a demon would land on a target that had not been feeding their soul. The demons would latch on to those and dig their talons deep into their minds, feeding them messages from the enemy. The other demons would cheer at their success and rush to join in.

He witnessed one such attack on a student who had stayed on campus for the summer to work on research—or so that was the story she was telling people. She was walking out of the bathroom when Aegeus first saw her, and she was covered in demons. Despair had the firmest hold on her, but she was covered in Self-doubt, Worthlessness, Lies, and Shame. Additional demons latched on to her as she walked the halls silently, wearing a smile that said everything was great. But Aegeus knew the damage demons could do. Intrigued, he followed the girl at a distance.

The Twelfth came around the corner and stopped suddenly when she saw the student. The Twelfth's Light flared brightly. She was carrying an empty coffee cup in her hand. The Twelfth smiled at the girl.

"Am I heading in the right direction for coffee?"

"The faculty break room is that way." The student gestured down the hall, smiling as she did. She gave no outward indication of her demons.

"Thanks." The Twelfth started in the direction the girl had pointed and then paused and stood very still. Aegeus watched; he loved to see the Spirit at work. The Light in the Twelfth was burning brightly, but he could see her face was wrestling with what she knew to do. The girl had already turned and started the other way. The Twelfth turned back toward her suddenly.

"Hey," she called, "would you like to get a cup of coffee with me?"

The girl was several paces away, but she stopped and looked back at the Twelfth briefly before answering.

Aegeus watched as she too struggled. Her Light flickered and flared until finally she answered, "Sure."

The two of them walked together to the faculty break room. Aegeus followed. Their initial conversation was superficial. They introduced themselves and shared safe things such as where they were from. But as Aegeus watched, the Spirit arrived and whispered to the Twelfth. Her Light filled the room with warmth and power. Aegeus lifted his face to soak it in. He thought of her doing the same this morning as she walked, and he again wished she could know how much greater this was than the sun. The power of the King surged through him, strengthening him. His wings began to unfurl just slightly.

And then, without warning and with a boldness Aegeus had not seen in her before, the Twelfth spoke a message from the King. "God wants you to know that you are not alone. He has not abandoned you. He sees your pain, He knows what happened to you as a child, what is happening to you now. But what man has meant for evil, he will use for good." The Twelfth paused, full of the Spirit and a little anxious at the same time. She nervously waited for the girl to say something, anything.

"Who are you?" the girl asked, looking nervous. The demons that clung to her also grew still and silent as they stared at the Twelfth. Aegeus moved into position. He could not allow the demons to leave and alert others to the prophet.

"I'm nobody. I'm new here," the Twelfth stammered.

"Who told you those things?"

"God. He tells me things sometimes." This was the part where she expected the girl to reach the conclusion she was crazy and excuse herself from the room. That was usually what happened; the Twelfth couldn't blame people for thinking it.

The demons, who had been silent and were still staring at the Twelfth, suddenly realized the situation. Their eyes met Aegeus's for a moment, and then the room erupted into motion. The demons each scurried for a way out. Aegeus sprang into action, grabbing them as they tried to escape. Sword drawn, he managed to get Lies and Shame with the same blow. Kfir arrived, drawn in by the Light. He dropped from the roof of the building onto the table where the Twelfth sat drinking coffee with the girl.

Worthlessness was squirming in Kfir's hand. Black smoke spewed from Worthlessness as he fought to escape. Aegeus thrust his sword into Worthlessness and turned his attention to Self-doubt. Self-doubt had a talon caught in the girl and could not break free. Aegeus walked slowly forward.

"You must have been with her quite some time." Aegeus said as he slid his sword back into its sheath.

"You are no guardian," the demon accused as he squirmed to break free of the girl. Kfir jumped down from the table and positioned himself behind the girl and the demon. Self-doubt twisted around trying to see what Kfir was doing. Free of the other demons, the girl's Light began to burn brighter—bright enough to start burning the demon. He started to squeal in pain, tugging the stuck talon. He put both feet on her face and pulled with all his might, but he could not free himself.

"I am Aegeus, warrior of the King, protector of his children." Aegeus walked closer.

"She is a prophet," the demon spit the words from his mouth as if they were poison.

Kfir grabbed the demon and destroyed him with his bare hands. The demon dissipated into black smoke, all except his talon, it dangled from the head of the girl, making it appear as if she had a horn.

"I saved you," Kfir teased.

"What? I totally had this." Aegeus smiled at his friend.

"How long will she have that horn?" Kfir couldn't help but chuckle. Aegeus walked over to the girl and tugged on the talon. It was stuck deep inside her head.

"No telling."

"I am Aegeus, warrior of the King," Kfir said in his best Aegeus voice. He puffed his chest out and strutted forward a few steps before being overcome with laughter at his own joke.

Aegeus shook his head and playfully shoved his friend.

The Twelfth finished her coffee with the girl, who interestingly didn't run from her. Instead, the girl was quite intrigued by the whole thing. She was not entirely convinced that what the Twelfth spoke was true, but there was something about the experience that gave her hope and left her feeling a little lighter.

What if it were true? What if God did see her, did know what was happening? What if he hadn't forgotten her as she had told herself for so many years? What if he did have a plan to use all her pain and sorrow for good? Well, that would change everything, wouldn't it? The idea was powerful. The girl was not sure she was ready to believe it, but she was at least interested enough to sit with this strange new professor and consider it.

After coffee, the Twelfth returned to her office and unpacked the few items she had brought with her then she began the process of figuring out the computer system. She checked e-mails, set up her voicemail, and then poured herself into creating her courses. She wanted them to be great. She had been working for several hours when a light knock on the door snapped her from her concentration. Her head popped up.

"Am I disturbing you?" the Fifth asked sheepishly.

"No, please, come in." The Twelfth gestured toward one of the chairs in her office.

"I didn't bring lunch; I thought you might want to walk over to the cafeteria with me?"

"I would love to." It was hard being the new person; she was grateful the Fifth had thought to invite her to lunch.

Haywood, the guardian of the Fifth, joined Aegeus and Kfir for the walk to the cafeteria.

"You are in for a treat, boys," he teased as they got closer. "The smell in this place is not soon forgotten." He shook his head in disgust. A few taunting demons fluttered about the campus, but overall things seemed quiet.

Suddenly, out of the corner of his eye, Aegeus saw a quick movement. He stopped and looked in the direction of the clock tower. Nothing moved, but he could feel someone watching him.

"Aegeus?" Kfir stopped too.

"Someone is there," Aegeus offered. "A warrior."

"One of ours?" Kfir asked.

"No." An ominous feeling settled over him.

Chapter 23: The Fifth

The Fifth stared at her reflection in the mirror. These pep talks were becoming increasingly necessary. She looked deep into her own watery eyes and let out a slow, deep breath.

"You are a smart woman. You know what you're doing. You have managed this lab through hundreds of research projects. You can do this."

The speech was simple, and it usually worked. Today she wasn't so sure. Another deep breath.

The chemicals from the morning research project caused her eyes to sting and demand a cry to flush them out, but she refused. There was not time for that.

The ministering angel leaned closer. "It is all meaningless, a chasing after the wind." The Fifth shook her head at the thought as one might shake something sticky from their finger. Where did that come from? She asked herself.

She stared at her reflection, feeling the urge to cry slipping away and the frustration returning, which seemed to be her new normal.

She would walk into this meeting and show them why she should be selected for this promotion. She stood up straight and walked confidently from the bathroom to the conference room. The ministering angel shook his head. *They will have ears but will not hear*, he thought.

The board was convened around the large conference table, and they rose when she walked in, a tradition that was nearly lost but one she appreciated.

"Gentlemen," she said in greeting as she took her seat.

"Thank you for joining us," the chairman began. And so, the interview started. The Fifth enjoyed interviewing; she thought she excelled at it. She had been interim director of the lab for more than two years, the very job she was applying for. There was nothing they could ask her about the job or their research that she would not know. She had worked with these men, and they knew her; they already knew her strengths and weaknesses. This should have been a formality—and yet it wasn't.

"How is your daughter?" The question would have been reasonable had they been walking down the hall or standing over a set of microscopes, but during an interview, it was out of place. The Fifth paused for a moment.

"She is doing well, thank you." She sat up even straighter in her chair, glad that she had chosen the black suit today and worn her hair up in a strict bun.

"And how does she feel about you getting this promotion?" the board member continued.

The Fifth tried to imagine how this line of questioning had anything to do with the interview. How was this appropriate? And yet, she hesitated to say anything. Let it play out; see where they are going, she told herself.

"Are you concerned, being a single mother, that she will be alone for too long each day if you get this job?" the board member pressed. The Fifth sat stunned as if she had been slapped. She would have preferred to be slapped.

"I have been doing this job for more than two years. Being granted the official title of the position will not change my schedule nor should it impact my personal life." She tried to answer the question without mentioning her daughter. Her daughter was not their business.

Although she answered the professional questions flawlessly, she did not get the position. Instead, they selected a recruit, fresh from medical school. Someone she had hired—someone she had been training. He would become her boss, and she would step back to the job she'd had two years ago. The board requested she continue to teach him. Train her own boss? For the very job she wanted? She thought not.

And so, the days dragged on. She tried not to think about why she had not gotten the position. She began to pour herself into church activities. She would serve others to help her forget about her own pain. She tried to look at the bright side, to focus outwardly.

One year after she had been told she would not be given the title for the job she was doing, the US Office of Research Integrity showed up. The trainee they had promoted instead of her, was missing, along with millions of dollars in grant funding. A formal investigation was launched, and the lab was under considerable scrutiny. The Fifth was once again asked to step in as interim research director.

The records were disastrous and the investigation grueling. The Fifth worked tirelessly with the investigators to restore order. Early mornings and late nights became her new norm. When she wasn't in the lab, she was serving in her church. Sleep became a commodity she could not afford.

After six months, the investigation was complete, and the Fifth had restored order to the lab. She had written reports on every project and accounted for all the spending. All except, of course, what her boss had embezzled. The board requested to see her.

This time she walked into the conference room in her scrubs and lab coat. She hadn't given herself a pep talk—she didn't need it. She had worked tirelessly to prove to the Office of Research Integrity that it was one rogue researcher that had falsified data and stolen funds.

But an hour later she emerged from the conference room without the title of director. She had once again been asked to train someone to do the job. The Fifth walked purposefully from the room, picked up her keys, and headed out the front door. She spoke to no one. She was numb. The ministering angel sat in the car beside her and laid his hand on her shoulder.

"It is a chasing after the wind; it's all meaningless unless it is for the King." He spoke gently but distinctly. Her Light flickered. She didn't know where she was going—she just drove. She drove until the numbness became rage. She drove through the rage until the pain surfaced, and then she drove until the tears ended and she returned to numbness. Night had fallen, and her phone had rung many times. She had ignored it.

As she began to regain clarity and the realization that she had neglected all her responsibilities flooded over her, she also realized the car was losing speed. Pulling to the side of the road, the Fifth looked around. She had no gas, she was lost, and her cell phone battery had finally died.

Night had settled in, and she began to feel foolish. She decided to approach it the way a scientist would. There was nothing she could do about her dead phone, she hadn't brought a charger. No phone meant the cavalry was not coming. Opening the trunk, she found a small gas can, and she uttered a silent prayer of thanks. She wrapped her lab coat around her to block out the chill of the evening, and she started walking.

Walking helped her clear her head, and she found herself singing worship songs as she made her way mile after mile. Just when she felt her feet might refuse to take her another step, a small car pulled up beside her. The Fifth tensed involuntarily. The window of the car rolled down, and a woman with wild red hair leaned over from the driver's seat.

"Need help?" she asked with a voice that was soft and warm.

"I ran out of gas," the Fifth offered, holding up the gas can as unnecessary proof.

"I'm heading that way," the woman said. "I would be happy to help."

The Fifth hesitated. Everyone knew not to get in the car with a stranger. And yet the woman had a presence about her that made the Fifth feel comfortable and safe. Her options were limited.

"Thank you, I would appreciate that," she said, easing into the woman's car. They drove several miles to the gas station. The two women made small talk on the way to the station. When they arrived, the Fifth got out of the car and thanked her for the ride.

"You will need a ride back to your car," the woman offered. "I am happy to help you get where you need to go." Her kindness was radiant, and the Fifth could not seem to say, "no, thank you." The truth was, she did need a ride. She looked at the woman and was struck by how willing she was to help. She didn't seem rushed or flustered. In reflecting on the drive to the gas station, the Fifth would have to admit the same was true. The woman had been wholly present in the moment.

"Thank you," was all she managed in response. She filled the small gas can and got back in the car. As they were driving back, the woman asked her, "How did you find yourself in this predicament?"

The Fifth shared the heartache of the last few years. She vented her frustration over not getting the position she wanted, and she shared how much it had hurt her to feel rejected by the very people she had worked so hard for.

And then, she did something she never thought she would do. She told the woman about her daughter. Tears flowed freely down her cheeks as she shared the story—her story, her most precious and protected story. She shared her feelings of failure, inadequacy, and loss. Her Light began to burn more brightly. The woman with the wild red hair said nothing. She simply drove the car, allowing the Fifth to pour out her heart uninterrupted.

When they arrived back at the Fifth's car, the woman pulled to the shoulder and stopped. She looked at the Fifth and smiled. That was not the response the Fifth was expecting.

"What has all your work and sacrifice accomplished?" asked the woman.

The Fifth sat there a little stunned. She took a deep breath and whispered the words she had not been willing to admit to herself. "Nothing. It has been meaningless." She said it more to herself than to the woman. The truth was that the last five years of her life had been the hardest she had ever endured. She had carried an enormous burden, and she had used work as a way to lighten it. But it left her feeling empty. Work could not return her love; it only took from her and left her feeling empty.

The woman looked at the Fifth and smiled. As she pushed a stray hair away from her face, she said, "It is meaningless—unless it is not. When you work for more than yourself—when it is lasting, when it is eternal—then you find meaning and fulfillment."

The Fifth felt the words sink into her soul. She knew these words to be the truth. There was something about the woman that made the Fifth want to stay there with her, but they were back at her car, and she knew that she needed to go. She thanked the woman for the ride and got out, her Light burning brightly, filling her with hope.

The Fifth did not return to working in the lab. Instead, she spent time in prayer and fasting, seeking out the King's will. In time, she found a teaching position at a small Christian college hidden in the mountains. There, she believed, she would find meaning in her work, and it would have eternal consequences.

Chapter 24

Aegeus was pleased to see that the Twelfth was settling into the town, making friends, and feeding her soul. She walked to the college most days, praying along the way. Often, she prayed aloud, allowing Aegeus the opportunity to hear her heart. But her prayers were around hiding her Light. She asked daily that the King would silence her, allowing her to blend in. She prayed fervently for this.

"Doesn't she know that salt that is merely called salt is worthless? You must actually be salt to be beneficial to the kingdom," Kfir observed one day as she made her plea. But Aegeus did not think she knew. Like many of the people in the town, she put on a smile and went to work and tried to ignore her humanity. She felt like she wasn't enough—not good enough, not holy enough, not righteous enough. This was one of the great weapons used by the enemy, and it worked well.

Multiple times over the summer the King had given her messages to deliver. In each instance, she had wrestled with the message. She had argued and protested and questioned, and then she had delivered the message exactly as the King had required. Yet during a conversation with the Fifth and the Eighth about spiritual gifts, she declared she had none. Aegeus had searched her face for an indication of false humility, but it was not there. She didn't know. Aegeus twice had gone to the King out of frustration with her, but the King had smiled and answered, "Be patient, my good and faithful servant." Despite his numerous requests, the King would not reassign him.

In resignation to the King's will, Aegeus returned to the salvage yard for the shift change. He arrived in the abandoned building they were using as a meeting area to find that Kfir already had breakfast laid out. Manna was one of Aegeus's favorites. He picked up a bagel-shaped piece of manna and carefully spread a light coating of honey on it. Kfir handed Aegeus his wineskin, and Aegeus poured himself a glass of wine to go with the manna. He surveyed the room where the next shift was finishing their own breakfasts.

Amitiel, engrossed in a novel, was sitting in the corner on an old wooden crate. Aegeus took a long swig of his wine and walked over to him.

"What are you reading?" he asked as he tapped the book with his free hand.

"This Present Darkness."

"Ahh, Peretti, one of my favorites," Aegeus said, smiling. "What have you learned?" he asked.

"About Peretti or about the twelve?"

"About the twelve," Aegeus answered.

"They are not holding up well, Aegeus," he said, "but I have researched their backgrounds extensively, and I believe we will be able to break through to them. It just takes time."

"Indeed," noted Aegeus.

Aegeus walked to the head of the room and cleared his throat. The other angels stopped chatting and waited for him to give them the morning report.

"We had another quiet night. The college has a meeting today that is required for all employees. So, all twelve will be in the same room for the first time. The Strongman will be there as well, so this will be our first real look at him. Kfir, stay close to the Twelfth and see if you can tell if she recognizes his for what he is..."

"Has she carried any messages?" interrupted Adiel.

"Yes. She has delivered messages for the King this summer," answered Aegeus. "She knows they are from the King, and she has told the recipients they were from the King, but she still does not recognize she is a prophet."

"This makes no sense," Paki, a guardian angel recently joining the team from Africa, interjected. "How can she carry a message from the King and not realize she is a prophet?"

Amitiel, as the specialist on researching customs and cultures, jumped in to help. "Paki, in America, many of the shepherds have convinced the people that prophecy is no longer one of the spiritual gifts. Furthermore, among many denominations, even if it were a gift, it would never be given to a woman. The Twelfth has been told this her entire life. She does not even consider that prophecy is an option. Someone will have to tell her this is her gift. She will not believe them, but it will plant a seed, and the Spirit will water that seed until she is forced to see what is there."

Paki nodded his head, but he did not truly understand. How could anyone read the Word and conclude that prophecy was no longer a gift? Was it not listed in the lists of spiritual gifts? Were there not multiple places that spoke of it? Did the King not say that he was the same yesterday, today, and tomorrow? But Paki knew that generations of misinformation could indeed lead people astray. It was hard to ignore what you had been taught to believe and even harder to use untainted eyes to see what was in the Word.

"The Eighth is struggling; we may lose him," Aegeus continued. "He is essential to encouraging the other eleven, but he is so discouraged he is of limited use. Understanding the history of each of the twelve will be important. Amitiel, prepare a file on each of them for tomorrow's briefing. Keep it to the essentials. Our reinforcements will be here by then, and we can get everyone caught up at the same time. For now, we will focus on the encounter with the Strongman. The demons are returning to the town, causing the sun to be muted, and many of the humans are impacted by the lack of sunshine."

"I have heard them refer to the demon cover as 'the dome,'" Kfir added. "They know it is there even if they don't fully understand what it is."

"Dome sounds less ominous than demons," chuckled Paki, still trying to understand the Americans and their view on spiritual things.

"I do not know what the Strongman will say in today's meeting," continued Aegeus, "but we must be prepared for anything. The King is sending the army, and they will arrive when the time is right. A squadron will come as part of the advance party. He is sending in additional ministering angels, guardians, and common angels. They will begin arriving today during the speech. The demons will be distracted then, and we expect a good deal of them to be in the Great Hall when the Strongman gives his speech. That should allow the angels to arrive with little notice. We will do all we can to remain undetected until that is no longer possible." Aegeus finished his wine and licked a small trace of honey from his fingers. Oh, how he missed home.

Chapter 25

The Great Hall was teeming with demons, mostly low-level demons whispering anxious thoughts and doubts into the people. Aegeus and Kfir watched as the Twelfth entered the hall. She was accompanied by the Eighth—their friendship was developing quite nicely. The Strongman was mingling about the hall as people entered. He was shaking hands and offering conciliatory introductions, smiling, and laughing. He referenced the King repeatedly and how grateful he was to be in the service of the King. He told person by person how he was so pleased the King had brought him here and provided this opportunity for him to further the kingdom. It made Aegeus's skin crawl, but the humans seemed to believe him.

The Twelfth and the Eighth drew near the Strongman. They were positioned to greet him next when Aegeus noticed the Light in the Twelfth suddenly erupt. Her skin became covered in what she would describe as goosebumps coming from the inside. Both the Twelfth and Aegeus recognized it as the Spirit. She stepped back from the Strongman and stared at him, her eyes opened wide in horror or shock—Aegeus could not tell which. He was mesmerized to watch the Spirit work in her, and a bit caught up in the surge of power he felt from heaven as it happened. Kfir elbowed him, breaking the moment.

"Look," Kfir whispered. Directing Aegeus's attention to the Strongman and away from the Twelfth. The demon inside the Strongman was raging. He fought against the flesh and blood body that contained him and reached for the Twelfth. The Strongman recognized her for what she was, a prophet of the Most High.

While the demon struggled to reach her, sulfur roaring from his mouth, his arms reaching for the Twelfth, the human body of the Strongman continued the charade of greeting each new person as they entered the room, reciting his speech about advancing the kingdom.

The Twelfth stood still just looking at him, unable to see his true form but sure that something was wrong. The Spirit whispered to her, "It is not God's kingdom he is here to advance." She heard the message and accepted it, taking another step back from him. Aegeus moved closer to her, positioning himself between her and the Strongman.

"Do you smell that?" asked the Eighth. "Smells like someone farted." He chuckled as the sulfur reached his nose. "That's awful; we should get out of here." And he and the Twelfth moved on to find seats. They found a place with the Fifth to sit. The Twelfth couldn't help but wonder why the Fifth had come alone. Aegeus looked over at Kfir, who was snickering like a child.

"What is so funny?" he asked, starting to chuckle just from the sight of it.

"He thought the demon smelled like farts," Kfir laughed. Aegeus just shook his head and took his position near the Twelfth.

The Strongman took the stage, positioning himself in front of the large cross that served as a backdrop to the pulpit. The Great Hall had many purposes at the college, but once a week the students, staff, and faculty gathered in it to worship the King.

In years past this had been a beautiful time, and angels would gather on the roof of the building to hear the songs of praise coming from the hall. Five thousand voices strong singing songs of worship was a beautiful sound to the angels and the King alike.

"Let us open with prayer," said the Strongman, kneeling in front of the group. Prayer was normally a source of power for the angels. But the Strongman's prayer was not to the King, but to the Prince of this world. The angels in the room became antsy to be in the presence of such darkness. The warriors had been in this situation before, but the guardians and ministering angels did not typically get exposed to such forms of evil. They shifted uneasily, feeling the full burden of being close to such filth. For an angel to stand in the presence of such evil and listen to a prayer to the Dark One was a true test of their self-control.

Aegeus looked around the Great Hall to see how well they were handling it. Paki was horror-stricken and shaking with rage; he had unknowingly gripped his sword. He appeared as if he would vomit—if angels did that sort of thing.

Aegeus sent calm and peace to Paki, who feeling the gift, lifted his eyes searching the room for the source. His eyes met Aegeus's and he nodded to acknowledge the gift. Aegeus looked around at the humans who had all bowed their heads and closed their eyes, a tradition the Americans had when praying. But the Twelfth did not have her head bowed or her eyes closed. She was staring at the Strongman with the same look of disgust that Paki had displayed only seconds before. Aegeus smiled feeling pleased with her.

The Strongman concluded his prayer, which had consisted of a mini-sermon for the sake of convincing those present of his piousness and dedication to the King. He had worked up tears and allowed them to pour down his face and strangle his voice, so he seemed wrought with emotion over his passion for the King. The problem was that it was not the King he was passionate about. He stood from his kneeling position and made a show of wiping the tears from his face. Then he turned to the crowd and began his well-rehearsed speech.

"My family and I are so honored to be here," he began. "I feel God has blessed me in innumerable ways by giving me my dream job. I love that we are a community of faith and that we are pouring into the next generation to send them out on fire for the kingdom."

He put his hands in his pockets and looked down at the ground as he began to pace a few steps on the stage. The pause was dramatic enough to cause a short moment of silence and create the effect he was after without being too long. "Now I understand you have had some trouble here," he continued. "The board brought me in to clean house and remove those among us who were not true to the faith—radicals who had strayed from the truth."

He paused again to let that sink in, then he removed his hands from his pockets and stared out at the four hundred faces looking at him. "It was not easy terminating people, but I am committed to keeping our mission pure and our path straight. If any of you are not in agreement with our beliefs, I will remove you as well." The threat lingered in the air and seemed to have the effect he was looking for.

The tormenting demons squealed with pleasure at that comment and began to flit about the room spreading fear. Lights all over the room started to flicker and dim. But the Twelfth's Light began to shine more brightly, her righteous anger beginning to simmer as she shifted uncomfortably in her seat.

"In two days, five thousand young college students will descend on us, and we have the great privilege of shaping their futures. I take this responsibility very seriously. We will pour into them; we will saturate their minds and souls with the truth. We will not let them be swayed by the lies of the culture. We will teach them to stand firm for the faith, to oppose what our culture is telling them and fight for religious freedom!"

This statement elicited applause from the crowd, although Aegeus noticed that a few did not join in.

"We will put God first in all that we do, and we will teach the students to do that as well. We will restore this institution by setting things right and removing the cultural creep that has set in. I have great plans, and I am hopeful that you are the right team to come on this great journey with me."

More applause.

"I want us to trust each other. So, I would like to open things up for questions," he continued.

Early questions were silly things about where he had moved from and what types of things he liked to do in his spare time. He answered each question graciously and tried to seem likable in the process. A small woman in her early fifties rose from her seat, her Light burning brightly as she made her way to the microphone. She was flanked on both sides by ministering angels giving her courage and offering affirmation. The Spirit was ablaze inside her.

The demons, seeing her Light, became nervous and repositioned themselves throughout the crowd. But the Strongman seemed to know what was coming, and he smiled at her widely, inviting the question. He signaled almost imperceptibly to the demons who moved to try to silence her. This woman had not been part of the plan. Morax sat in the back of the room and shifted in his seat; he did not like this at all.

"In researching your background," she started, "it looks like there is a considerable amount of controversy surrounding your position on women. Could you clarify your view of women?" she asked.

"Of course," he answered. "I like women; they are great cooks! I even have one of my own," he said, laughing at his own joke. Chuckles filled the room. "But seriously, I value the soft perspective a good woman brings to a situation. I want to be sure we have women involved in all appropriate areas of the college. We need them to mentor the young women on campus and teach them about becoming godly women. The Word tells us that our older women need to teach the younger women how to be good wives and mothers. I fully support that as should you all."

"And when you say, 'all appropriate areas,' what does that mean to you?" the woman asked as a follow-up.

"Well, we all agree that God created men and women differently. Women were designed to complement men, to be their helpers. Paul tells us that it is not appropriate for women to be over men or to teach them. Now culture would tell us that is not right. Culture would have you believe in this whole feminist movement. But as believers, we know that God has established order, a hierarchy if you will and that he has told women to submit to the leadership of men.

"It is crucial that we hold tight to those truths and not let Satan draw our young women away from the truth and God's divine plan for them. In accordance with God's law, we will not have women speak in chapel, we will not have women preach—nor will we have women in leadership positions that could cause them to violate any of the aforementioned rules.

"We will make sure our young women hear that God has a great calling for them, the greatest calling a woman could ever hope for, the call to be a good mother and wife. When you get a dog, it is not truly yours until you name it. But once you name that dog, you have dominion over it, you are given authority over the dog. In the Bible, you see that Adam named Eve, giving him dominion and authority over her. These are not my rules; they are God's rules, and we will honor them. Now, in the past, there have, unfortunately, been some Corinthian women among us, but they have been removed. There is no place for that here."

A murmur settled over the room as people looked at each other and commented to their neighbor. The demons giggled with glee, the plan was working exactly as they had hoped.

"But those are rules for the church, and we are not the church," she countered.

"The church is the body of believers, those who join to worship God. It is not a building; surely you know that" he responded with a slight sneer.

"One last question," the woman said, her Light burning bright and her rage causing her hands to tremble slightly.

"Of course," the Strongman replied.

"One report I saw said that you advised an abused woman to go back to her husband and simply pray more. You reportedly told her that if she would just submit more, her husband would not beat her. Is there any truth to that?"

The room went silent; the demons even paused in their glee to look to the Strongman. Morax was not pleased that things had gone this direction. This was not the subtle plan they had discussed. This was too much; he feared they would be undone by this woman in the very first day. Everyone waited for the Strongman's response. A smile spread wide across his face.

"That is one of my favorite stories. There is nothing simple about praying. Is there anything better than a story of redemption? The Word tells us that the shepherd will leave the sheep to go search for the one that is lost. And this is a story of him finding and redeeming a lost sheep.

"We are taught to turn the other cheek when someone strikes us, to pray for those who do evil to us. To love those who persecute us. And that was what I advised that woman. Her husband's very soul was on the line. And what is more important, salvation by grace, or a few rough nights?

"God had put that woman under the authority of her husband, and she had the incredible privilege of showing her husband God's unfailing love by following God's command for her to stay under her husband's authority and submit to him.

"God never says to obey his commands only when it is easy or when we like the results. He commands us to turn over our lives to him, take up our cross, and follow him. Sometimes that means making sacrifices. Now I am not condoning violence against women; I don't want you to hear something I am not saying. I abhor violence against women. We are not called to violence. But I lift that woman up for staying in a situation that was hard and following the command of the Lord."

The Strongman ended the discussion and then closed the meeting with another kneeling prayer. He thanked God for a group of people who loved the Lord enough to sacrifice their own comfort to take the gospel to the ends of the earth. He thanked God for a people so dedicated to doing his will and so unified in mind. He thanked God for ridding them of those who would tell lies and divert the path in honor of the ways of the culture, and he asked God to give him discernment so that any other distractions among them could be found and eliminated.

Aegeus looked around the room and noticed that the Twelfth was not the only one who did not bow her head and pretend to pray. Now at least, they knew his hand.

Chapter 26

As the faculty and staff made their way back to their offices, many did not speak about what they had just heard for fear of being labeled as a rebel. The demons flew about assuring that the men were not overly concerned given it did not apply to them. Most of them had tuned it out and couldn't even tell you exactly what was said. Those who had listened dismissed it immediately as something that would not make any difference to the everyday functioning of the college, so there was no need to get worked up.

The women were reeling from the comments but did not want to be seen as "Corinthian women," so most of them remained silent, wrestling internally with the remarks and concerns for what this meant for them and their jobs. What he had spoken was so close to the truth, perhaps it was the truth. Maybe they were the ones that were mistaken? What if they were being rebellious; after all, the abused woman's husband did get saved, and wasn't that the most important thing? Divorce was a sin unless your spouse was unfaithful.

The Strongman was an ordained preacher; he had been to seminary and earned a Master of Divinity degree. He had overseen numerous churches. He was a man of God. Who were they to argue with him? And yet, something didn't feel right. Most of them tried to stifle it as their own pride and rebellion.

The Fifth said she had to go across campus for something, and she left them. The Twelfth and the Eighth walked back to their building. Upon entering the Great Hall and encountering the Strongman, the Twelfth had been sure he was not of God. After hearing him speak, she felt even more certain. And yet, she too feared this was her own selfish pride. Didn't Paul say those things that the Strongman had quoted? Didn't the Word tell women to submit to their husbands?

The Word was clear about the qualifications to be a shepherd. She did not want to be rebellious, and yet the thought that the God whom she loved so much would love her less than another just because she was a woman was a sickening thought.

The idea that her Creator had made her to be second class was something she was not prepared to digest just yet. Was she a rebellious woman? She agreed that the Bible said a woman was not to shepherd a church, but this was not a church; it was a college. Could a woman not speak? Were those same rules of leadership applicable outside the church structure? Despite what he had said about the church being the body, weren't those rules for organized church meetings? Was a woman forbidden from preaching? What about Anne Graham Lotz or Beth Moore? She just couldn't believe those women were violating God's law.

The Eighth, whom the King had adorned with intuition and an abundance of compassion, could feel the conflicting emotions of the Twelfth. He had spent several weeks getting to know her over the summer, and they had bonded as friends. He slowed his pace slightly as they grew closer to their building.

"I don't think he should have advised that woman to stay with her husband," he said, hoping to gently open the topic. The Twelfth had come to trust the Eighth over the last couple of months. The Spirit had told her that he was safe. He was "normal," and she liked that about him. He was honest and real and imperfect. He got angry, he struggled, and he hadn't always done the right things—he still didn't—all things that made the Twelfth more comfortable around him. He seemed to understand her, and he seemed to know what to say to make her feel better. Gifts the King had given him. But this subject was so raw for her, so intimate that she was not quite ready to talk about it.

"I don't either. I would never advise my daughter that way. But maybe that is because I am a woman; perhaps I should go home and ask my husband what to think," she quipped, trying to sound like she wasn't struggling. She knew it was snarky, but she felt incapable of responding any other way. The Eighth could feel her pain. He could feel all of their sadness and anger. Sometimes it served him well to know the feelings of those around him, but sometimes, it was an overwhelming burden. As the anger and sorrow grew around the town, he felt their burdens; he carried them in his soul. He and the Twelfth walked the rest of the way in silence until their paths separated each to their own office. Normally, he would have said a silent prayer for her, but things were not anywhere close to normal for him.

Chapter 27: The Eighth

The Eighth looked around at the small campus as he walked from his car to the building whose address he had scribbled on the notepad. It wasn't a bad campus—it was immaculate and relatively new compared to his own. But he was used to a much larger school; this one felt too small and suffocating. He flipped over the paper he had been carrying with information about the ribbon-cutting ceremony and saw that the college boasted five thousand students. He couldn't help but feel a little superior.

The college was opening a new physician's assistant program, and he had been invited, along with hundreds of others, to the ribbon-cutting for their new building. As he walked toward the building, he wasn't sure why he had even agreed to come. No one had ever heard of this school. It was in the middle of nowhere, hidden in the mountains, and it was a competitor to his own program. Well, if you could even call it that. As he walked toward the building, he once again wished that his wife would have been able to come with him, and even as the thought entered his mind, he wondered what had brought it on.

He reached the door of the building, and a woman with wild red hair was coming out. She smiled at him and held the door. "Need any help finding your way?" she asked, clearly detecting that he was a visitor.

"I'm here for the ribbon-cutting," the Eighth said, noting that no one had ever held the door for him at his own campus. He could feel the warmth and genuine kindness radiating from the woman. It disarmed him a little.

"Oh, that's right around the corner," she said, gesturing in the direction he should go, which was not the way he was headed. "I'm headed that way, too; if you would like, I can walk with you."

"That would be great." The Eighth felt an urge to stand up a little straighter and straighten his tie. He wasn't used to such courtesies. That never happened on his campus. The Light within him began to burn more brightly.

The ceremony was simple yet elegant. Much nicer than the Eighth had expected, and the people were so sincere in their joy over the new building. They had been working for years to start the school and having a new building of their own just seemed something tangible they could point to. Everything was state of the art, a small pang of jealousy swept over him as he thought about how much research he could do in a lab like that.

Several months passed, and the Eighth had long since put the visit to the small school behind him. His days were once again filled with his own students, his own school, and his own research. He was happy; things were going well.

One evening, as he was leaving the office, the phone rang. He hesitated; if he answered it, he might be stuck there for much longer than he wanted to be, and he had promised his wife a night out. Reluctantly he reached his hand out, saying a silent prayer that it would not take too long.

"How was your day?" his wife asked as they sat across from each other in the restaurant later. They had been to a movie and were having dessert after, a tradition they had started in college.

"Something strange happened," he offered, easing into the conversation that had ended his day. He told her about the call from the small school hidden in the mountains. The dean had called and offered him a job. He would be able to do more advanced research and would have a reduced teaching load, but the pay wouldn't be quite as good. They discussed the offer and what an honor it was, but they also agreed they weren't interested in moving, and so he would decline.

They finished their ice cream without thinking any more of the offer. They chatted about the movie, their children, and their dreams. And then they walked hand in hand to the car for the drive home. The Eighth leaned down, kissing his wife on the head. Things were good. He was happy just the way they were; there was no reason to change anything. The small school was forgotten.

They arrived home late, and both of them were ready for bed. The Eighth was waiting in the bedroom for his wife to finish her nightly routine.

"Perhaps this night may end with my tie on the doorknob," he chuckled to the empty room. His wife walked into the room, her toothbrush still hanging from her mouth, toothpaste starting to drip from her lips. She reached up with her left hand to catch it as it fell.

"Maybe you should consider the job," she garbled through the toothpaste.

"What?" He understood the words, but he was surprised. She held up a finger to give him the "wait a second" sign as she went to spit out the toothpaste and rinse her mouth.

"I've been thinking about that offer since we discussed it," she continued when she got back in the room. He had not thought about it again.

"Maybe it would be fun to move and start over," she said as she climbed into the bed next to him. "I mean, the kids are old enough to adjust well. And if you are teaching less, you would have more time at home. We're adventurous, aren't we?" she said, smiling at him. He was struck by her beauty. She had aged so well, and he reached up to stroke her face without thinking about it.

"Next time, we don't go to an adventure movie," he said, teasing her. She laughed easily at his joke.

"I just think we should pray about it before we discount it completely. There's something about it I like," she said, putting the topic to rest for the time being.

Chapter 28

The next day, the campus was transformed from a virtual ghost town into a bustling community filled with young energy. The students flowed into the dorms and filled classrooms. They were full of hope for a new year and dreams of a future.

As was the college's tradition, opening day involved a worship service as part of the convocation ceremony. The ceremony was held in the Great Hall. Every student, staff member, and faculty member was required to attend the midday service.

The demon presence was thick, and the day overcast with a haze that could only be explained by the sulfur oozing from them. Thousands of tormenting demons filled the rafters of the Great Hall. Several hundred warrior demons were also present, some of Titus's best.

Aegeus and his men found themselves severely outnumbered once again. The ministering angels had been busy encouraging parents to pray for their children as they dropped them off. This had led to the arrival of more guardians, which pleased Aegeus. But the arrival of the guardians had raised alarms for Titus, and he had doubled his warriors swarming over the town, completely sealing it in a dome of demons. All of them were destroying demons. Now every angel that arrived would have to battle their way in. The demons far outnumbered the prayers that were calling the guardians in.

The faculty, donned in their academic regalia, filed into the Great Hall behind the mace, as was the tradition. The service started with singing to the King. Their voices filled the room with the sweet sound of praise. It overwhelmed the space and charged the angels. The demons screamed in protest, covering their ears, and swarming the room as they worked desperately to distract the humans.

"Wow, that girl is way off key," one whispered to an unsuspecting male who could then only hear the off-pitch sounds coming from behind him. The distraction would keep him from focusing on the King and draw all his attention to wishing that the off-key girl would stop singing.

"Look at what he is wearing," another demon suggested to a girl. "Were his eyes shut when he got dressed?" This, of course, led her to check out what others were wearing and even rethinking her own choice for the day.

"Check her out," another enticed. It would draw the eye to a girl he found attractive. "Imagine what her skin must feel like," the demon offered. "Imagine touching her hair, gripping it in your hands, and breathing in her smell," was all that was required to start his mind down a path of lust. The demon could then leave him and attend to another.

But as the tormenting demons approached some and reached toward them, the Light would burn the demons, sending them scampering to find someone else to tempt and torment. The warrior-demons found this particularly amusing and laughed riotously from their posts. The warriors were there for one reason only: to fight. They did not bother with petty tormenting; they were bred for war. At one time, they had fought for the King, under the command of archangels. But now, they fought only for the Prince.

As the singing ended, the Strongman walked confidently to the podium and called those assembled to prayer. He knelt on one knee. "Lord, we are so honored to be in your house with the freedom to worship you. We are so thankful that you sent your son to die so that we may live. We ask, Lord, that you guard our hearts and minds as we begin this academic year. We know how tempting sex can be. We know how tempting it is to rebel against your plan. We know that the call of alcohol can be loud, but we ask, Father, that you deliver us from these evils. Please don't let us be tricked by those who would speak against your words or try to twist them for their own purposes. Give us discernment when we encounter those who have sacrificed your truth for a modern culture so that we may rid them from our midst." The subtle threats and warnings of his position wrapped in righteous packaging and delivered, he rose and began his first address to the students.

"I know that for some of you this is your last year here at the institution, and some of you are just beginning. But I am so thrilled for all of you to have the opportunity to be here. I wish I had had this type of experience. I did not go to a faith-based school. I had my priorities all wrong. I went to a secular school, and you know how those are—everyone is doing drugs and drinking and having sex. There are no morals or values, and it is easy to get pulled into that. We are called, as you know, to be in the world but not of it. We must engage culture to show them where they have gone wrong, but we must not embrace it. We must fight against the lies that we are being taught about marriage and family and the new normal. But the good news of the gospel will free you from those temptations. I was very blessed that God delivered me from those evils and preserved righteousness in me.

"You are in a wonderful position here to find a spouse from among this impressive collection of believers." Applause erupted from the students.

"Seniors, if you haven't been blessed with the gift of singleness, you only have one more year to find a spouse. After this, you will be searching for diamonds among thorns.

"Ladies, you need to find yourself a good God-fearing man to lead you before you graduate. A man who will love you as Christ loved the church and will lead you and your family.

"Men look around at these ladies. They are good Christ-loving women who will honor you. They understand the biblical role of women is to submit to their husband's authority and care for your children.

"You will not find that outside of here. Women in the world are feminist. They will tell you that women can have it all. They have convinced the culture that women should put off marriage and pursue their careers. We see that happening across the nation.

"An education is a good thing—look where we are—but it is not a woman's highest calling. Bearing children and caring for her family is her highest calling. Good Christian women, those in this room, recognize that. They know how to show respect to their husband; they understand that they should not make more money than their husbands. Doing so is a blatant sign of disrespecting your husband.

"Ladies, you must guard your bodies and not lead men into temptation by wearing provocative clothes; yoga pants and sleeveless tops have no place in the Christian woman's wardrobe. Now I know the devil will tempt you this year. He will tempt you with the desire for sex. But for you to have any hope of a successful marriage, it is vital that you are a virgin when you marry. Don't let Satan destroy your chances of finding a mate and getting married by giving away the most precious gift you have to offer your husband.

"Gentlemen, if the cow will offer you the milk before the wedding night, it is not the right cow."

Laughter filled the room. These were teachings most of them had heard many times. But a select few sat stunned, offended even.

"I was fortunate to find a beautiful Christian woman when I went to seminary. She is a strong woman, and she does a great job of caring for our children and home. Now I don't think she will mind me telling you that she went through a bit of a rebellious stage about two years after we got married. We had just had our son. He was not sleeping much, and my wife was getting up with him about every hour all night. This had been going on for about two months, and as you can imagine, she was tired. When you get too tired, you become vulnerable to the temptations of Satan, and she fell prey to his tricks. Selfishly she asked me to alternate getting up with her, so she could get up once and then I would get up the next time. Now don't judge her —don't judge her—she is a good woman. But the devil got her while she was weak.

"But, men, I knew my calling to love my wife and my responsibilities to lead her. I pointed out her selfishness and reminded her that God had given me a brand-new church to disciple and I had to be fresh and rested to do his work. And at the same time, God had given her a family to care for. How beautiful that he had chosen her to bear our son and care for him, this precious gift from God. I loved her, and I would never deprive her of fulfilling her divine calling, nor would I expect her to try to keep me from fulfilling mine.

"We each have our God-assigned roles. She recognized the truth in it and apologized to me, asking my forgiveness for her selfishness. Men, you need to offer your forgiveness to your wife; don't withhold it. Well, years passed, and God saw fit to bless us with six more children. After they all started school, my wife once again fell victim to temptation. That time it took a little longer for her to repent; the devil had his talons in her deep. But we are out of time today so I will save that story for next week. Let's close in prayer."

When the Strongman was done praying, he dismissed the congregation and sent them out to their educational pursuits. The tormenting demons immediately latched on to any student without a guardian. There was so much material from the Strongman's speech for them to work with. But Aegeus noticed that it was not just the students. The tormenting demons also grabbed the faculty and staff who had attended. The Twelfth was among those leaving the Great Hall. Her rage burned bright, but her Light grew dim.

Chapter 29

The Twelfth, the Fifth, and the Eighth had attended the service together. They remained silent as they exited the Great Hall and were relatively clear of students' ears. Then the Twelfth eased into the subject.

"I went to a secular school. It wasn't evil," she started.

"That was your takeaway from this?" the Fifth asked, a little shocked. It wasn't, but it seemed to the Twelfth like a safe place to start.

"I did too," the Eighth and Fifth both agreed. It was trite to suggest that secular schools were nothing but evil. Having found a small slice of common ground, the Twelfth ventured out to more dangerous territory.

"Do you think God created women to be second class?" she asked hesitantly, secretly desperate for them not to agree with the Strongman's statements. Desperate for affirmation that she wasn't a rebellious woman who didn't know her "place."

"That isn't exactly what he said," offered the Eighth cautiously. He could sense how delicate this situation was. "He didn't say God made you second class, just that God made men to lead."

"So, women can't lead?" asked the Fifth, not pleased with the answer. Aegeus watched as tormenting demons swooped in beside the Twelfth and began whispering to her. But Aegeus had been warned this test was necessary, and he did not interfere. The Twelfth would have to learn to listen to only one voice. Learning to silence the lies and hold to the truth was valuable training. And so, he stood at a distance watching the situation unfold.

"No, that's not what I'm saying," said the Eighth, immediately regretting that he had said anything at all. Did anyone ever win this discussion? He could feel their anger, but mostly he could feel their pain. The comments of the Strongman had damaged their souls, leaving them feeling underloved by a God who loved them dearly.

"I am not saying I agree with him," he continued. "And certainly not with the way he put things. But he didn't say that women were loved less or held less status or importance with God. He just said there is a hierarchy in the family and church and in that hierarchy, men are the leaders." He paused there because he knew they both already knew that.

"Yes," said the Fifth, "but what he said wasn't that simple. It was offensive and degrading. He likened us to cows!" She felt repulsed at the idea. If all she had to offer a man was servitude and virginity, she was in trouble. The idea that her sole purpose was to be a good wife and mother dug deep into wounds she thought had finally scarred over. But with only a few distasteful words, they were ripped open, and anguish poured from them.

"It was indeed offensive, but I think what he was trying to say was biblical—his delivery was just poorly executed. I don't think he was trying to be offensive."

"You can't be equal if there is a hierarchy. If the two are to become one, how can one of them be over the other? You would have to still be two," The Twelfth noted.

"And yoga pants are evil? Seriously?" The Fifth wanted to move the conversation toward safer ground—something they could more easily agree on.

"And the whole idea that what a woman brings to a marriage is virginity is awful. Why was that directed to the women anyway and not to both?" The Twelfth wanted to hash this out. She needed to discuss it, to hear other perspectives, to be challenged or affirmed.

"I think you might be taking that out of context." The Eighth just didn't hear it the same way they had.

Neither woman was convinced. The Twelfth began to doubt herself even more. The tormenting demons jumped onto her back and dug their talons into her head, leaning close and whispering in her ear.

"You are not a good woman," they told her. "You are violating God's will for women. You are selfish and think you should have an equal say in your family. God hates your rebellion against him. Your husband wishes you were more submissive. God created you to be led."

The demons stayed attached to her throughout the day, continually feeding her messages of anger and despair. "You have no more say in your life, you have gotten married, therefore giving up your freedom. You are like a child who needs a man to tell you what to do." They badgered her throughout the day, leaving her distracted and grouchy.

If this school promoted those types of beliefs, perhaps she was in the wrong place. Her soul ached to have answers, reassurance. She sat at her desk, trying to focus on preparing for class. There was only an hour before she was to stand before her students, and she believed firmly that the first day set the tone for the entire semester. She wanted it to go well, but she just couldn't quite get her head straight.

"You have a second?" The Fourth stuck his head in her door. He was the head of her department; she stood and welcomed him in. There was something about the Fourth that she liked. He was a massive man, the kind you would expect to find on the football field, not in the classroom. He was no-nonsense and shot straight from the hip, both characteristics she valued. But more important, she could feel the presence of God when he was around.

He walked into her office and took the seat directly across from her. He paused a moment, taking time to see her, to read the concern in her eyes. She sat a little uncomfortably with the silence and the intensity of his gaze.

"What did you think about the message this morning?" he asked without any conversational cushioning. She sat frozen, trying not to let her face reveal her sheer panic at the question. She said a quick prayer before she started. Aegeus smiled to see her turn to the King.

"As a woman, I suppose it is only appropriate that I defer to you to tell me what I should think of it," she said gently. The sarcasm was obvious but conveyed hurt, not anger. The Fourth understood the statement for precisely what it was.

"And the rest of the female faculty in the department? They too are waiting for us mighty males to tell them what to think?" he asked, playing along.

"Those who have spoken. Many remain silent—after all, we want to adhere to Paul's rules." She winked at him. He leaned forward in the chair that suddenly seemed much too small for him.

"You know we are not a church. We are a school. I have no desire to get into this conversation, but I want it very clear that here—in this place—there is no male or female. We are all here working toward the same goal. What happens in your home, between you and your husband, is between you, your husband, and God. It has nothing to do with me, and I want to keep it that way." He peered at her over the top of his glasses.

"Understood." She left it at that. He rose from the chair, considering the matter completely settled. "Good, I don't want any distractions." He walked to the door, his shoulders sagging just slightly. Over half the department was women; he had a lot of offices to visit.

Chapter 30: The Fourth

The sunshine was bright, and the little umbrella in his drink almost made the Fourth forget the week he had had. He closed his eyes, letting his other senses soak in the feel of the warm sun on his skin and the sound of the waves lapping against the shore. The smell of the beach wafted through his nostrils, bringing him a soothing feeling of nostalgia. He hadn't been to the beach in years—not since before the divorce when things with his wife had been good. He shook the thought from his mind and refocused on not thinking at all.

The week had been tough; he deserved the break. Lounging here at the beach, listening to the ocean almost allowed him to forget that he had changed the course of a life this week. He let his mind wander to days gone by, but it insisted on landing on unpleasant memories, memories of dropping his son off at rehab—again. Memories of his wife telling him she was having an affair. Memories of his son being arrested. Memories of his wife refusing to go to counseling and insisting on the divorce. He took a sip of his drink; this mini-vacation wasn't working out.

The week had started with a summons to the dean's office. Never good. A female student had reported an unwanted advance from one of her professors. At large state schools, this was not unheard of—not okay, but not unheard of. The student had declined the professor's advances; the professor had failed her. This was medical school. Failing could be a death sentence. But for the college, it meant a possible lawsuit. The accusation had to be investigated.

The Fourth had heard all sorts of accusations over the years. Many were found to be things students said to get better grades. A few were founded in truth. But all of them were investigated. The faculty member accused was one of their best. He was a top-notch cancer researcher receiving millions in funding every year. His research was innovative and could one day save millions of lives. He had been at the institution for years, married, with grown children.

But something in the girl's eyes had told the Fourth this was not going to end well for the professor. The Fourth was not driven by emotion. He was a man of science, and he moved methodically. He was fair and unbiased and searched out the facts of the situation.

When the week was over, the faculty member had been escorted from campus by security. Apparently, he had had inappropriate relationships with many students over the years in exchange for grades. The Fourth had been made to resign as well. As the chair of the department, he was told he should have known what was happening.

The Fourth left campus Friday and drove east until he hit the ocean. He just needed some fresh air and time to think. He began to wonder if he should leave academia and go back into full-time practice. But getting up from his lounge chair reminded him why he had gone into academia in the first place—an old football injury. College football had taken a toll on his body, and age had magnified that toll. Full-time practice was no longer an option, but a swim in the ocean might be just what the doctor ordered. He chuckled at his own joke as he eased into the warm ocean water.

After what seemed like a very short swim, evening started to set in. The Fourth remembered having once heard on Shark Week that sharks came close to shore around sunset looking for dinner. As tiring as the week had been, he decided dancing with a shark was not how he wanted to end it.

He made his way back to gather his things and find a hotel. He rubbed his knee as he struggled to get his chair folded and his towel back into the small drawstring bag he had brought with him. Getting things gathered up was easy; carrying all of it across the sand was a little less easy with his knee acting up.

The Fourth was fumbling with the chair, shoes, and bag when the bag slipped off his arm, hit the shoes, and sent them flying in two different directions. A woman in sunglasses and a big sun hat appeared like a wisp of air, her wild red hair blowing in the ocean breeze.

"Let me help you," she offered. Her smile was so radiant and warm it brought with it a sense of peace and belonging.

"Thanks," said the Fourth, accepting her help. He reached for the shoes she carried over to him.

"You seem to have your hands full," she said. "I'll carry this for you," she offered as she fell into step with him.

"Oh, that's okay; I can get it," he said, not wanting this woman to carry his shoes.

"Don't be silly; I'm going that way," she said with a confidence that settled the topic.

"Are you a local?" the Fourth asked, knowing from her pale skin that she probably wasn't.

"No, I just made a quick stop here on my way to Platitude College, a small little school hidden in the mountains," she said.

"Oh, are you a professor?" the Fourth asked, happy that he would perhaps have something to discuss with her as they walked. Small talk was not a skill he was good at; in fact, it exhausted him.

"The people there are of great interest to me," she offered. They reached the car of the Fourth, and he put his chair, bag, and towel in the trunk. The woman handed him his shoes and smiled. The Fourth thanked her and turned to get in his car. He turned back to wish her luck with her interview, and she was gone. He scanned the parking lot, but she was gone.

His interest piqued, the Fourth found a hotel room and, once settled in, he looked Platitude College. Much to his surprise, they were hiring. *Why would you ever name a college Platitude?* He wondered.

Chapter 31

The Twelfth put on her lab coat and headed to class. It was her first class, and she had prepared carefully. She was teaching first years about the transmission of infectious disease and had gone into the room early to put germ powder on the doorknobs and all the table surfaces.

Germ powder glowed under a UV light. You could put it on surfaces, and without people knowing, the dust got on them as they touched those surfaces. Once it was on them, they would pass it on to everything they touched. It was an excellent tool for teaching disease transmission and hand-washing.

She had positioned posters of the different stages of the disease cycle around the room with QR codes that would take them to short, interactive games on each topic. She planned to start by asking the students to get vitals from five students not sitting near them. Then they were to peruse the posters to gather the lesson information and group back up. She would do the grand reveal, showing them how contaminated they had become during the short class session. Then she planned to cover proper hand-washing for the clinic and finish the class by going over the syllabus.

Aegeus and Adiel went to class with her while Kfir patrolled the hall. Tormenting demons clung to the students and swarmed about the room. When she began class, the Twelfth called on a small blond-haired girl in the front to pray.

"Wouldn't you rather ask a boy?" the Ninth quipped. A demon clung tightly to her throat. The Twelfth was a bit taken aback.

"Why would I do that?" she asked.

The girl went from looking angry to looking tearful in an instant.

"Men are here to lead us, so have them pray." She was angry. The Twelfth did not like the direction this was going, and yet she instantly admired the girl's spunk and courage. Adiel looked up at Aegeus, shock on her face at the idea.

The demons in the room howled with laughter, flitting about the place, whispering in the ears of students, stroking their hair, or brushing against their hands. Occasionally, one of them would have a Light that would flash and send the demon scurrying away.

"Yeah, but they can't seem to be responsible for anything when you're dating. During that phase, we are the ones who must be in charge. But say 'I do' and forget it," another girl in the back chimed in.

"What do you mean?" the Twelfth asked.

"Oh, you know, girls have to be the ones to say no all the time. We are responsible for protecting our honor. A boy can't be trusted to do that. You can't trust him not to 'try to milk the cow' because you are wearing yoga pants, but he should be in complete control of you once you're married. How does that make sense?"

She put the stress on the Strongman's own words, air-quoting them, so there was no question. The girls were hurt, and their pain was seeping out as anger and resentment. But the Twelfth knew that is was not about the boys. It was not about anger. She looked at the males in the room.

"Gentlemen? What say you?" she asked, her lesson for the day temporarily forgotten.

"I'd say today is not a good day to be a guy thinking about asking someone out on this campus," a young man with a full thick beard said, eliciting laughs from the entire class.

"I don't care what a girl is wearing. If I think she's hot, she could be wearing a potato sack, I'm still going to think she's hot. If I don't, she could be naked, and I am not going to be interested," one brave guy in the back of the room offered. Others nodded in agreement.

"Do they teach you how to deal with lust?" the Twelfth asked sincerely.

The males all nodded no.

"No tips; they don't ever direct you what to do to help combat it?" She was truly shocked.

"No, of course not," a female on the back row offered up. "That's the girl's job. It's our lack of modest dress that causes the problem. We are the ones that must be in control of premarital sex. Wait till you've been here a while, Doc, the 'purity' talks are all about how important it is for you to save your virginity for your husband. Your husband! Do you hear that? What about saving it for your wife? Trust us; that never enters the discussion."

"Why do you suppose that is?" she asked them.

"Genesis 3:16," the girls said in near unison. "Women are to be led—not lead," was the general consensus. Adiel shifted uneasily. This discussion made her feel sick inside.

Puzzled, Aegeus gently shook his head. He could not figure out how a verse about the curse of man related to sexual purity. It just wasn't coming together for him.

"That argument doesn't make sense. Besides, the Bible is full of women who were leaders," the Twelfth noted, taking the conversation in a slightly different direction.

"Not in the important parts," a boy murmured under his breath. A few people around him chuckled.

"What about Athaliah?" she questioned.

"Who?" they asked.

"Athaliah," she repeated. "She was a monarch who ruled over Israel/Judah. Note that I said monarch. She was the ruling queen. There was no king—she was it. Now she was considered evil, so let's be clear on that. But it wasn't because she was a woman. It was because she worshipped other gods, as did most of the male monarchs. She ruled for seven years."

The class sat quietly for a minute. Apparently, they had never heard of Athaliah.

"That doesn't mean God approved of her being in charge," a boisterous boy in the back threw out.

"If you believe the Bible, it does." She stated it matter-of-factly and then waited for just a beat before going on. "The Bible says we are not to revolt against our leaders since there is no one in leadership that God did not put there. So, if you believe that, then you must believe that God put Athaliah in as the queen to rule over his chosen people—women and men alike."

"So, if Bowlinger is elected, we have to honor him as president?" a student from the left of the room questioned.

The class laughed. The Twelfth laughed too.

"Yes, whoever our president is, we are to respect that person. God says that he appointed them himself."

"There are lots of examples," the Ninth offered. "Lydia owned her own business; Phoebe was a deacon in the early church. Acts refers to women prophesying. Galatians says we are neither male nor female."

"But all of that seems to get lost because Paul also said that he didn't let women instruct—never mind that he qualified it as his practice and did not offer it as a command or even condemn those who did it differently. None of that matters. His one statement is enough to keep us wily women in our place—the kitchen. Stay here long enough, Prof, and you'll figure it out," the Ninth finished. Her pain was evident but worse, her spiritual struggle was great.

The Twelfth was a little stunned, but she did not want these students to walk away from her thinking that women had no purpose. There were many stay-at-home moms. Women who wanted it that way and the Twelfth had the highest admiration for them. It was a hard job, much harder than hers. There was indeed great honor in that. There was also great honor in being a mother. It was a thankless job—at least for the first twenty years or so—but it was a beautiful responsibility.

The Twelfth loved being a wife; she loved her husband. But there were also many women who had neither a husband nor children. Were they not just as valuable as the women who had children or husbands?

And what about the role of the father? Wasn't the father just as important? Was a mother to be valued over or above a father? Having a loving father in the home was invaluable. The world was full of examples of the damage an unloving man could do in the life of a child. She believed her value was from being a child of God—that was who she was.

Despite the difficult topic, the Twelfth was impressed with the students' knowledge of the facts of the Bible. But she feared that while they knew a lot about God, they did not seem to know God. Class time was quickly evaporating, and she doubted she would be able to cover all that she had planned. The Twelfth managed to come up with a transition from their discussion to the designated topic, and by abbreviating the activities, she got through the most crucial items before time was up.

The students were surprised to see their glowing hands under the UV light, and she was able to use it to look at their faces and demonstrate how many times they had touched their eyes, noses, and mouths over the course of the class. It proved to be a success, despite the rocky start.

The Ninth, who had started the entire discourse by refusing to pray, came to the Twelfth's office later that day to apologize for her behavior in class.

The Twelfth immediately liked the Ninth. She was a strong young woman who had a great passion for the Lord. But her path was not an easy one, and over the next six months, she spent many hours with the Twelfth, pouring out her heart, sharing her anguish and her struggles. They celebrated her successes, and the Twelfth comforted her when she cried.

On one particularly stressful day, shortly after the Ninth's father died, she looked up into the eyes of the Twelfth and made her promise that she wouldn't leave the town until the Ninth graduated. The Twelfth hesitated. This place was not what she had expected, and she did not plan to stay beyond the year. But the Ninth did not break eye contact, fresh tears in her eyes.

"Please," she pleaded. "Please promise." The Twelfth felt a surge of love for the girl that she could not explain—all that she had endured, all that her young life had brought her way. She took a deep breath, not wanting to make a promise she could not keep. Staying until the girl graduated would be a significant commitment. She reached her hand out and placed it on the Ninth nodding her head slightly.

Chapter 32: The Ninth

She had always known she wanted to be a doctor. As a small child, she had stuck Band-Aids on all her stuffed animals and applied slings to her Barbies. When other little girls talked about being nurses, she dreamed only of being a doctor. She would boss around the nurses, letting them know that as a doctor, she was in charge. Looking back, she realized that the other girls never even considered that they could be doctors. She was grateful to her parents for raising her to believe she could do anything.

Then, of course, all her classmates dreamed of being a teacher. They would play school, with each of them taking turns being the teacher. She never wanted to be the teacher. Instead, she insisted they pretend they were in medical school. Of course, she didn't know to use the term "medical school," so she just said, "doctor school."

When she was five, her uncle bought her her first doctor's kit. She loved it. It came with a doctor's coat, a stethoscope, a thermometer, and a hammer to check reflexes, all packed in a plastic, bright yellow doctor's bag. It became her most precious possession. She wore her stethoscope everywhere.

At church, she would listen to the hearts of anyone who would allow it. Placing the earpieces in her ears and listening to the thump, thump, thump of their hearts was exhilarating. The day she realized it was a prerecorded heartbeat had been devastating. She felt duped.

High school came to her easily, and she graduated at the top of her class. She had volunteered at the local hospital as soon as she was old enough. She wanted to learn all she could about what it was like to be a doctor. She shadowed different types of doctors, spending time in a variety of specialties—some in the hospital, some in private practice. When she headed off to college, she had no doubts about what her goals were.

She planned to attend Johns Hopkins for premed then complete the bridge year before starting medical school. Premed had been challenging, and she spent many long hours studying, but she also found time to be involved in a sorority and serve on the student council. She was well rounded; she was focused, and she had a plan. Everything was going as she had planned.

Two hours after finals in her fourth year, her cell phone rang. She was lounging on the lawn in front of the Eisenhower Library, soaking in the sun with friends before packing up. Emotion choked her sister's voice, her words almost indiscernible. Almost.

Time stood still for one fleeting moment. That moment when everything changes. Those moments that become a time marker in your life and everything else happened either before or after it. This became one of those moments for her. She looked around at everyone else—unaware, unaffected—and she resented that their lives had not just changed in an instant.

The campus swam around her; the words did not make sense. She pieced together that her father, a paramedic, had been on a call when his ambulance was hit by a semi whose driver had fallen asleep at the wheel. He was still alive, but the prognosis was not good.

The drive home was agonizing. The week following even worse. Her family stood vigil in the hospital, praying for a miracle. The days turned into weeks, the weeks into months. Fall semester approached, and her father was still in the hospital. Returning to Johns Hopkins now didn't seem possible. Her father, if he ever woke up, would be paralyzed.

Her mother had gone home to take a shower. The Ninth sat quietly by her father's bed. She thought about her family, about how young her brother still was. Her sister was a senior in high school. Her mom would need her. Her heart settled on the reality that medical school at Johns Hopkins was no longer in her future. But the tragedy of giving up her dream of being a doctor on the same day she gave up the idea of dancing with her dad at her wedding seemed like asking too much.

A team of doctors entered her father's room, and the head physician presented her father's case and asked them questions. While they discussed his situation, one of the physicians, a woman with beautiful red hair pinned back in an unruly, yet professional bun, read his chart.

She smiled at the Ninth, her bright green eyes seeming to pierce through the sadness and heartache. The woman spoke about her father in such a way that made the Ninth feel as if she knew him personally. He was not just a patient on their rounds—he was a person. The woman felt his pulse, smiled brightly, winked at the Ninth, and then led the group of physicians from the room.

When they left, her father stirred. Groaning slightly, he opened his eyes and looked at her; he was groggy. He closed his eyes again. The Ninth jumped from her chair and ran into the hall to find the physicians. They had all moved on to the next room. All but the woman with the wild red hair. She stood in the hallway talking to a young man. The woman looked up and smiled at the Ninth, the kind of smile that is usually reserved for dear friends who you haven't seen in a while.

"He opened his eyes," she offered excitedly!

The woman with the red hair walked purposefully into the room. She called the man's name, and he opened his eyes and looked at her. He smiled at her and then closed his eyes again. The woman placed her hand over his and called his name again very gently. A toothy grin spread across his face, and he once again forced his eyes open. The woman smiled throughout, seeming pleased with what she found.

"Is he okay? Will he be okay?" the Ninth asked, hope streaking her voice for the first time. The woman, stepping slightly away from the hospital bed, turned her attention to the Ninth.

"He is exactly as he should be," she said with a smile. "Are you?" She looked at the Ninth as if gazing into her soul. The Ninth felt a small jolt of electricity as if static-filled carpet had shocked her.

"I . . . I . . ." She wasn't sure how to respond. The woman with the wild red hair waited patiently as if there was nowhere else she needed to be, nothing else in all the world more important than this discussion. "I am supposed to be in medical school at Johns Hopkins," she stammered.

"But you are needed somewhere else?" the woman said as if she understood the predicament. And yet the Ninth couldn't help but feel as if the question were a statement. As if the woman were telling her that she was needed somewhere else—somewhere other than here, somewhere other than Johns Hopkins. It was a statement she would think back on for many years.

"I suppose I am," she said, looking down, tears starting to fill her eyes. Saying it aloud made it seem more real.

"Sometimes, being where you are needed leads you to find what you need," the woman answered. She smiled again and walked from the room. The Ninth stood still trying to digest what the woman had said. It seemed so meaningful, and at the same time, it made no sense at all.

She walked into the hall to find the woman, and she was gone. But the young man she had been speaking to earlier was still there standing near the nurses' station. The Ninth approached him, and they seemed to hit it off right away. He was a PA student from Platitude college not too far from where they were. The Ninth thought that perhaps she might have hope after all.

Chapter 33

Titus and Morax joined the Strongman in his office. The Strongman seemed pleased with how well the last few days had gone. Morax and Titus were equally delighted.

"That was a wonderful opening to the year, sir," offered Morax as he settled on the ornate leather couch positioned in the seating area of the office. He looked around the room and felt a tinge of jealousy that the Strongman's office, including the big windows that overlooked the campus, was so much better than his own.

"I was concerned that you may not be up to the task, but you have done a marvelous job," Morax offered as affirmation. He turned to Titus to ask, "What do you hear from the troops?"

Titus was still standing, recognizing his position in the room. "It is early, my liege, but reports are that the rats left confused and besieged. The males are largely complacent, and the females are anxious. Some of them have swallowed the pill whole while others are struggling. You have created doubt and fear. They do not trust each other."

"Do not grow overly confident," the Strongman warned. His mood melted at the memory of the close encounter with the prophet. "What of the prophet?" he demanded.

"Prophet?" asked Morax, concern evident in his voice.

Titus shifted his weight at this news.

"Yes, the prophet that was in the session with the faculty and staff." The fact that Morax and Titus seemed unaware of the presence of a prophet made him feel more concerned. "How did a prophet slip through?" His anger began to seep out.

"Are you sure?" Morax asked. The idea that there was a prophet among them was so surreal that he was having trouble believing it. Who could this man be? When did he arrive? A prophet among them would be trouble.

"Yes, I am sure!" the Strongman nearly shouted. "I recognize a prophet when I see one."

Morax turned to Titus, who gave a little shrug and a look letting Morax know this was news to him.

"Did he speak to you?" asked Morax to the Strongman.

"She did not."

"A woman?" Morax asked, astounded. The presence of a prophet among them was shocking enough, but the idea that it would be a woman was nearly laughable. Of course, there were women prophets; there always had been.

But in America they barely acknowledged prophets, and they certainly were not going to embrace a female prophet. At least not here—not on this campus. It explained why the Strongman had come out so fiercely about women from the beginning. Morax began to laugh.

The Strongman did not see the humor in it, and his anger burned as sulfur began to pour from him.

"The King sent a prophet—a female prophet." Morax laughed so hard it nearly brought tears to his eyes.

"We have little to fear," suggested Morax. "You have begun the process of demeaning the position of women. You have made it clear that women are not to be listened to or in leadership. We just need to make sure we continue along that line. Hammer it home.

"We can add sermons on how prophecy is no longer a gift, and we can speak about how the women prophets in the Word were not real prophets. Talk about how God only uses women when he is desperate, and there are no available men.

"In fact—" Morax was getting excited about the plan now. "Do an entire series on women in the Word as a way of celebrating their contribution. Share the stories, stay close to the truth, but diminish the effect they have. Be condescending without seeming so."

Morax thought this would work very nicely. A prophet could be trouble, but a female prophet in this environment would be easily dismissed. In fact, the whole issue of the role of women would serve as the perfect distraction. The rats would be so consumed arguing that they would lose sight of what was truly important. Yes, Morax decided this would work out quite nicely. They would refocus on this issue; it would be the perfect distraction.

"Should her voice grow strong," he concluded, "we will label her a Corinthian woman and send her on her way." The plan was wonderful. He didn't know how this woman came to be in the town, but he would destroy her. Listening to them preach lies would eat her soul. She would not be able to stay quiet for long. They would flush her out and crush her.

"Did she recognize you?" he asked.

"I don't think so," answered the Strongman.

"Did she have a warrior with her?"

"No, she was flanked by two guardians."

A prophet with no warrior was even better news to Morax. It was almost too good to be true. He opened the door and yelled down the hall to the Strongman's assistant. She hurried into the room without making eye contact, clearly upset by the Strongman's prior comments. Good, Morax thought. Let her be offended. Let her offended spirit turn her from the Word and the King.

"Bring us a pictorial directory of all the faculty and staff. The president would like to learn their faces and names as soon as possible," he ordered. She nodded her head and left the room, bile rising in her throat and Insecurity clinging to her back and laughing. After she left the room, he closed the door and looked at the Strongman. "Look carefully through the pictures and identify the prophet. We will deal with her."

"Titus, when we find her, we will assign her her very own tormenting demon and a destroyer. Double the warriors we have on standby. If there is a prophet, the King will send warriors. Thicken the dome; they are not to get in. Tell your men to keep an eye out for any prophetic activity."

"Yes, my liege," Titus answered and left quickly. He did not believe the prophet came to be there by accident. If they had missed a prophet, what else was inside the dome that they had missed? But Titus did not see any reason to voice his concerns to Morax or the Strongman.

Chapter 34

Aegeus sent out the message for the angels to convene in the salvage yard. He needed an update on each of the twelve. There were twelve guardians, one for each family. Ayo, Berhanu, and Meir had recently joined the ministering angels to make five in total.

Including Kfir, Adiel, and Aegeus, there were fourteen warriors assigned to the twelve. Undoubtedly, more would be needed when serious combat began, but keeping the ones here hidden had been difficult.

The new demon dome would make it more difficult to get others in, but the angels had never been afraid of difficult. Eventually, all the angels in the town would need to attend the updates. But for now, just those directly assigned to the twelve were included in the meeting.

The increased size of the team necessitated a larger meeting space. In the back of the salvage yard, nearly hidden from sight and long ago forgotten by human eyes, was an old shed. The shed was sufficient size for the current group and allowed some room for growth, so Aegeus moved the meeting there.

ChiBreeze was the guardian assigned to the Eighth, and Aegeus decided to start with him. "Chi, how is the Eighth?"

Chi stood before the group to give his report. "Not well. Meeting and befriending the Twelfth has given him someone to talk to and some support, but the enemy is attacking him heavily. I fear that he may not survive much more.

"A destroyer named Kali has been working day and night to undo him. He has had two car accidents, a cancer scare, and possibly a pregnant daughter. The situation with his wife has not improved, and he is slowly losing steam. He has not mastered his gift and, therefore, carries the burden of all those around him. As the town crumbles, he crumbles. He currently is depressed. I fear we may lose him." Chi sat down to signify he was done.

"Ayo, spend a few days with him and see if we can get him better positioned."

"As the King commands, so shall I do," responded Ayo.

"As the battle nears, we will need more ministering angels; they are on the way. With prayer cover, as you know, we will get resources faster. I trust the ministering angels are encouraging that," Aegeus reminded them.

"Haywood, an update on the Fifth?"

"The Fifth does not sleep," started Haywood. "She was distraught by the Strongman's speech to the students. She carries their burden on her very body. Her heart has remained tender, and she has gone nearly unnoticed by the enemy. My concerns for her are all physical. It has been many months since she slept more than a few hours a night. The lack of sleep is taking a toll." Haywood finished and sat.

Aegeus seemed puzzled by this update. "Why isn't she sleeping?" he asked.

"I believe she is overextended, sir. She will not ever say no. As a result, it is not until the rest of the world sleeps that she can attend to her own needs. She does not dream, nor does she have trouble falling asleep. No tormenting demons are living in her home. She just seems overextended," he replied.

"Berhanu, perhaps you could tackle that?" Aegeus suggested.

But even as he asked, he knew it would take much more than a ministering angel to deter an over-provider. The Fifth had the gift of service, but it sounded like she still had not yet learned to hear the call of the Spirit regarding which acts of service to perform and which to leave for others. "Remind her that his yoke is easy and his burden light." Aegeus wasn't so sure that her only concerns were physical.

"As the King commands, so shall I do," responded Berhanu.

"Voog, what of the Second?" Aegeus asked. But before the answer came, the door flew open and an angel burst in.

"I'm sorry, Aegeus, but I thought you would want to know. The demons are going home to home in search of the prophet."

The angels did not wait for more; they took to the skies.

"Adiel, Kfir, go to the Twelfth. Protect her," Aegeus ordered.

"The rest of you, find the horde, slow them! Report back as soon as you find them."

Each of the warriors flew over a section of the town, looking for the horde. It was late, and most of the homes in town were dark and quiet.

Chapter 35

The house of the Twelfth was dark except for one small sitting room where her husband was doing a jigsaw puzzle. Aegeus flew upstairs and found her looking in the full-length mirror in her room. The two tormenting demons were still clinging to her tightly and were startled by the sudden entrance of an angel. Intuitively, Aegeus drew his sword.

"What is this?" one of them asked with a snarl. "A guardian draws his sword?" hissed the demon as he dismounted from the Twelfth to face Aegeus. Aegeus's hesitation convinced the demon that he would not attack.

A tormenting demon would never win in one-on-one combat with a guardian. But guardians did not engage in battle unless absolutely necessary—they were protectors of their charge, not warriors. They fought only as required to protect their charge. Tormenting demons knew this. The demon walked closer to Aegeus, but not close enough for Aegeus to easily reach him.

"There is something about you," the demon said as he circled Aegeus, scrutinizing him to detect just what it was that was not right.

He strained to see Aegeus better in the dim light. Aegeus turned his attention back to the demon that was still latched to the woman. The Twelfth stood before the mirror looking at herself in disgust. She was randomly pinching and poking areas on her body with a sense of disgust and hostility that only a demon could invoke. From her mouth, she spewed hate speech to herself. The demon laughed in glee as the Twelfth became increasingly discouraged, finding fault with her body.

Aegeus put his sword away angrily and flew from the room to the roof to get out of the prying eyes of the tormenting demon and survey the situation. Kfir joined him.

"Is she okay?" he asked.

Aegeus sighed. "She is being taunted by two demons, and she is not fighting it. She embraces their lies and is feeding them. We have not been cleared to defend her from them since this is training for her. She must learn, Kfir," he said, more as a reminder to himself than Kfir.

Kfir and Aegeus waited on the roof, listening to the glee of the demons in the room below. Aegeus was grateful they didn't know she was a prophet. Ezekiel landed on the roof.

"The horde is two streets over; they will be here shortly," he updated Aegeus.

Aegeus knew there was no further hope of disguising themselves. He shed his guardian disguise and once again cloaked himself in the uniform of the warrior. The other warriors did the same. He let out a battle cry to bring all the warriors to the house of the Twelfth. Tonight, they battled.

Chapter 36

A long-haired demon with a scar led the horde. He smiled at Aegeus with a sense of familiarity.

"We are here for the prophet," he said, the smile never leaving his face. He moved as though he were in no hurry to get where he was going.

Aegeus looked at the demons carefully—there were thousands. Only a few of them were warriors; most were destroyers or tormenting demons.

"You cannot have the prophet," he answered, careful not to shift his weight or move too suddenly. He knew the battle would come—and to be honest, he was looking forward to it. Aegeus was a warrior; he was created and well trained to fight for the King. All this waiting had been challenging, and he welcomed the battle. His blood surged as he prepared. But wisdom and strategy were necessary, and so he waited just long enough to give his warriors time to move into position. They were indeed outnumbered, but fortunately, the enemy had sent the wrong type of demons.

"We will take the prophet," said the long-haired demon. "And when we are done destroying her, I will personally come back for you." His eyes were fixed on Aegeus.

"It is unwise for a warrior drawing his sword to boast like one who has already won the battle," Aegeus quoted the Word as he drew his sword.

The long-haired demon swung his sword at Aegeus, and the horde rushed forward. The sheer number of them made the battle difficult. But it felt good to Aegeus to be fighting. He grabbed a destroyer demon and used it as a shield against the more-well-trained warrior. Then he threw its body to the side as it dissipated into black smoke. This seemed to amuse the long-haired demon.

Aegeus looked over his shoulder and saw Adiel and Kfir both in battle. Kfir had a massive smile on his face as he slashed at tormenting demons and threw them from the roof of the house. A human walked by with his dog. The dog barked at the battle ensuing, but the human was oblivious and tugged the dog along, shushing him for fear the barking would disrupt the quiet evening. For some reason, this struck Aegeus as funny, and he chuckled as a blade sliced into his arm.

The pain of the cut brought his attention back to the battle. The long-haired demon stood still watching him, a grin on his face.

"Come now, Aegeus; don't make it so easy for me," he taunted.

"Who are you?" Aegeus inquired.

"I am the one who will destroy the great protector," he said, once again swinging his sword at Aegeus.

Their swords clanked together, and the demon threw his weight into Aegeus, knocking him through the roof and into the house. They landed with a crash in the room of the Twelfth. The long-haired demon was on top of Aegeus, pinning him to the ground, the sulfur pouring from him almost imperceptible in the room. The smoke of hundreds of demons had nearly blacked out the room. Aegeus had not seen them entering the house. He turned his head, desperate to find the Twelfth.

His eyes locked on her. She was on her knees on the floor, her head touching the ground. Sobs shook her body as hundreds of demons piled on top of her.

They clawed and bit at her in a near frenzy. Her Light was dim, flickering from the effort. There were too many for her. Aegeus's eyes met the eyes of a taunting demon as it leaned over and licked her face and then dug its talons deep into her. She wailed as the talon sank into her.

"Would you like to watch her die?" the long-haired demon hissed into his ear, sulfur filling Aegeus's lungs. More demons poured into the room, piling onto the Twelfth, biting, scratching, and cutting their way to her.

Aegeus struggled under the weight of the demon. He reached for a small dagger he kept in his boot just for such occasions and stabbed the demon in the side. The demon let out a raging scream and shifted his weight enough that Aegeus could free himself. He knew the injury was only enough to anger the demon, but it bought him time and leverage.

"Aegeus!" Kfir yelled as he entered the room. He pointed to the Twelfth.

"I know. Go for Meir; we will need her!"

Aegeus rose to his feet and grabbed the demon closest to him, throwing it from the house and fighting his way to the Twelfth. Meir would be close, waiting for the call, but she would not be engaged in battle.

With the long-haired warrior demon gone, Aegeus continued slicing and flinging demons as he worked his way to the Twelfth. There were so many on her. As he got closer, they began to tear at him, leaping onto him and ripping at him, slicing him with their talons. He fought on, slashing, and tearing them from his body as he inched closer to her.

Adiel crashed through the floor on top of two demons. She stabbed through them both at the same time and smiled at Aegeus when their eyes met.

"Need help?" she asked, winking at Aegeus. The two of them began to make their way through the demons, but more poured in. And then Aegeus heard it, the ram's horn blast. The reinforcements had arrived. Soon the room was filled with warriors, and many of the demons became streaks of black smoke as they were tossed from the home or dissipated. But the Twelfth was still covered.

Kfir arrived with Meir. The demons would need to be removed from the Twelfth before Meir could minister to her. Ministering angels were more delicate than other angels. They did not carry any weapon other than the Light of God. They were not defenseless, but their role required something different—something more tender that the humans could relate to.

Aegeus and the other warriors worked to clear the remaining demons from the Twelfth, her soul was tattered from their attack. They formed a circle around her and Meir. She covered over the Twelfth, whispering truth to her. The Light of the Twelfth began to flicker more brightly.

The demons, realizing their position was lost, flooded into the town to find other souls they could torment.

"Kfir, check the others; report back," Aegeus ordered.

"Adiel, get a team of warriors and secure the perimeter; I don't want any more demons getting in here!"

"How is she?" he asked as he turned back to Meir. She waved him away. Her hair was a crisp blue today, a peaceful, quiet hue. It was cropped short and wispy. She wore a flowing top of a light material Aegeus could not quite place—it may have been something new the King had created.

Paki arrived to get an update.

"You're bleeding," he said matter-of-factly. Aegeus looked down at the gash on his arm. He had forgotten about it. Paki walked over and touched it, healing the wound.

Aegeus nodded a thank-you.

"How is she?" Paki asked.

"I don't know," was the only answer that was honest. Hundreds of demons piling on a person could do much to destroy them.

Meir curled around the Twelfth on the floor, wrapping her wings around her and quoting scripture and song lyrics. She filled her mind with encouraging things her husband had said to her, things she had read in her daily devotional, memories of things the Spirit had told her. She soothed her, and her spirit began to settle.

After some time, the Twelfth got up from the floor and moved to her bed. Meir followed her, wrapping herself around the Twelfth, offering her comfort and peace. In time, when she felt the Twelfth was stable, Meir rose from the bed and laid her hand on the alarm clock. Aegeus looked at her with a question in his eyes.

"She is strong, and the Spirit is strong within her. Worthlessness and Doubt had the strongest hold on her so she will need reassurance over the next few days. They convinced her that she was not good enough, not thin enough, not smart enough to be here.

"They filled her with lies about her husband not loving her, not wanting her. Her husband is her earthly stronghold, the one person here that keeps her grounded, the person who makes her feel loved, so attacks that cause her to question her marriage are particularly vicious."

"The clock?" Aegeus asked.

"She wakes up to NPR every day and listens to the news. Tomorrow she will wake up to songs of praise and worship on the Christian station that reaches here. She won't be able to find NPR on the dial, at least for a little while."

She smiled a sly smile and winked at Aegeus. She paused as if unsure whether to continue.

"What is it?" Aegeus asked, sensing her hesitation.

"She has always been able to feel the angels. She doesn't normally realize that is what it is—she just knows she senses heaven, her connection to Sanyi was real, and she could feel his presence. She cannot feel you, and so she fears that she is somehow farther from the King."

"I don't understand that." Aegeus shook his head. "I am a different type of angel than Sanyi. Humans can't normally feel any of us," he said as if in his own defense.

"I know that Aegeus," Meir said, laying her hand gently on his arm. "But she doesn't. It is not a criticism; it is simply what is happening. Paired with the conditions in the town, she is very unsure of herself. I will stay with her for a day or two to make sure things are back on track."

Meir started to leave the room and then stopped. Aegeus looked at her expectantly.

"Aegeus, you have more in common with her than you think." Meir paused.

Aegeus looked puzzled. He stood silent, waiting for her to go on.

"She is a warrior, Aegeus." Meir met his eye briefly before leaving.

Aegeus looked at the Twelfth and tried to see her as a warrior, but he could not.

Chapter 37

Titus pulled open the heavy door of the old church. The door creaked loudly as it swung outward on its hinge. The smell of mothballs wafted out to meet him. Wooden pews with red velvet bench cushions filled the sanctuary. Stained glass windows lined the room. The windows had no particular pattern, no scenes from the earthly life of the Lamb.

Titus preferred them plain. The hues were mostly blues, purples, and greens. Titus loved old churches. He smiled at the irony of a demon enjoying entering a church building, but it held some nostalgia for him. The wooden floors announced his arrival. The sun was streaming in through the stained-glass windows, giving the church a glorious light.

Morax sat in the front of the sanctuary with another demon. Based on the long black hair and size, Titus assumed it was Seneca. If Seneca was here, it was not a good sign.

Morax stood as soon as he heard Titus approaching. Seneca stood with the lazy confidence of one who knows he is in charge and that their very presence brings trembling. He smiled a slow smile at Titus. They did not offer the traditional greetings of the hairless rats. There was no need; they were alone.

"You have failed in battle." Seneca was not one to mince words.

"I was not in the battle," Titus offered, trying to sound more confident than he felt.

"Your demons cannot kill a simple woman," Seneca snarled.

"Yes, I am disappointed in that. Tell me, Seneca, what did happen in the battle. I understand you were there—in the very room with the prophet. The battle must have been intense indeed. What went wrong? I will find the guilty party and make sure they are punished."

Titus knew he was risking his life by goading Seneca, but he could not resist. He began to sweat slightly from his boldness.

Seneca walked confidently toward Titus, his smile never wavering. Titus stood tall and still. Seneca approached until they were face-to-face.

"You reek of fear," he said quietly into Titus's face.

Titus did not flinch, but his insides trembled, and he was sure that he did indeed reek of fear.

"Seneca," Morax spoke only his name, but it was enough. Seneca was a warrior; he lived for nothing more than to kill. He was a great warrior and had seen many battles. But he respected Morax. He stood motionless glaring at Titus, and then his mouth softened into a snarl, but his eyes remained fixed in hate.

Morax put his hands in his pockets and looked at the ground for a moment. Titus was struck by how well Morax could emulate the hairless rats.

Morax spoke calmly, but the ice in his tone was evident. "The prophet is proving to be a problem, Titus. Your demons have failed in overcoming her. Warriors of the King protect her. How did they get in?"

"They were already in Platitude, my liege. Reports are that they have been here for some time disguised as guardians." Titus stood unmoving.

Seneca leaned against a church pew, looking at Titus as if he were a junior demon.

"Kill the prophet," Seneca said softly.

"I assumed you had," Titus began.

Seneca moved with great speed, covering the short distance between them, and grabbed Titus around the throat. His demon breath poured into Titus's nostrils as their noses pressed together. Titus began to feel himself suffocating. But he refused to indicate weakness.

"Seneca," Morax said again. Seneca released Titus begrudgingly.

Seneca spoke softly, but not gently. "Cover the prophet in demons, Titus. Put an entire team of destroying demons on her. Find a way to kill her. She has many weaknesses; send taunting demons." It conveyed a quiet evil that caused Titus to feel a shiver.

"The Strongman will continue to undervalue women and speak lies into the town that will upset them. This will weaken her. Cover many students in taunting demons and send them to her. Overwhelm her with them so she will be exhausted.

"Keep her so preoccupied that she has no time to care for herself, no time to eat or rest or feed her soul. She will tell herself she is doing the King's work. Fill her office with hurting souls until she carries so much of their burden that we can easily destroy her."

Morax smiled at the plan; it would work.

"And what of her warriors?" Titus asked, reminding them all of the obvious.

"Aegeus and Kfir are but two. We will reach her. I have secured the town, and no further warriors will arrive from the enemy without us knowing. More demons arrive daily, and soon the dome will be complete—too thick to be penetrated. I will kill Aegeus personally."

The idea of the dome made Seneca smile; it would block off the entire town from the Light.

"If you cannot cover the prophet with demons, then cover those around her—her friends, her family, her coworkers. Cover her office with them, cover her neighborhood, block out the sun because the demons are so many. Bring in as many as we need." Morax wanted the objective to be clear.

Titus nodded his understanding to Morax. He looked again at Seneca briefly and couldn't help but feel that destroying Aegeus would be personal for him. Understanding that they had said all they had to say to him, Titus left the church to begin the attack.

"Seneca, are you up for this?" Morax turned to him as he asked.

"You forget your place, Morax," Seneca said with the same quiet anger he had been using with Titus.

"This is personal for you. We can't afford to make mistakes." Morax spoke with confidence, almost in a fatherly tone, but he did not overestimate his position. They had mutual respect, but Morax knew that Seneca was dangerous.

"Do you question me, Morax?" Seneca walked closer to Morax, sulfur beginning to ooze from him.

"I have no doubt of your greatness in battle." Morax did not move. He did not fear Seneca the way Titus did. Morax was sure of his position. "What I question is if you will see clearly when it comes to Aegeus."

"I will kill the prophet." Seneca looked directly into Morax's eyes. "And then I will rip the wings from Aegeus and deliver him to the King."

"Our King or his?" Morax asked, unflinching.

"There is but one King, Morax—even the demons acknowledge that. Worry about your job. I will do mine." Seneca flew from the church, leaving Morax alone.

Chapter 38

Titus gathered a group of destroying demons and went to the top of Elpída Mountain. It was late November, and the mountaintops were covered in snow.

He smiled as he thought of the confusion and chaos it would cause in the valley below when the flood poured into the town. But it was not confusion and chaos that he was after. Tonight, he would kill the prophet.

She and the Eleventh had gone to a movie at the small theater in town. Titus had timed it so they would be returning across the small covered bridge at the same time as the flood. What movie was it again? Ah, yes, War Room. The irony of it pleased him. He thought briefly how unappreciated he was. Destroying a human was an art—one he was quite skilled in.

The demons covered the mountaintop and began melting the snow and ice. There was a slow trickle that quickly turned into a rushing river of icy water pouring down the mountain, filling the streams that led to the town.

In preparation, Titus had deflated one of the tires on the Twelfth's car. This would ensure that she would be delayed leaving the movie, giving him ample time. He had plenty of demons along the route. Tonight, he would do what Seneca had failed to do—he would kill the prophet.

The Eleventh and Twelfth exited the movie, walking out into the chilly November air. The Twelfth had not brought a coat. In her mind, it wasn't quite cold enough, and the walk from the theater to her car was short. The Eleventh wore a wraparound sweater that she pulled tighter. They finished their popcorn and chatted about the movie.

"I don't know how they eat this," Kfir said, spitting the popcorn from his mouth. Aegeus just shook his head. Then he felt them. The presence of demons—lots of them. Kfir felt it too and drew his weapon.

"Steady," Aegeus said as he looked around them. Taunting demons and destroyers surrounded them. It was the number of destroyers that concerned Aegeus. So many destroyers were a bad sign. The Twelfth started the car and pulled out of the parking lot.

"Adir, ride in the car with them. Kfir, fly on top, keep anything from entering. I will ride point," Aegeus directed.

But the women hadn't gone far before the Twelfth realized something was wrong. She rounded a corner and pulled to the shoulder of the road. It was an isolated area; about two hundred meters ahead there was a steep drop-off on both sides of the road, just before the bridge. Both women got out.

"You have a flat tire," the Eleventh called from the back-passenger side of the car.

"Oh, great," said the Twelfth as she walked over to join the Eleventh. Suddenly she was regretting the decision not to bring a coat. Demons flew in from every direction, swarming the two women.

A bloodcurdling scream erupted from the Eleventh. Adir flew from the car.

Kfir and Aegeus turned toward her. She was face-to-face with a demon. He had revealed himself to her. She had seen demons before, but she had never seen so many at once. They swarmed around the two women, flying past in swift succession. Adir, sword drawn, fought to keep them at bay.

She watched as they flew past and ran their hands through the hair of the Twelfth. Her hair would fly out as if the wind had blown it. A blaze of Light would flare from the Twelfth, keeping them from attaching to her, but the Eleventh could not see that. She could not see the angels fighting to protect her and the Twelfth. She saw only the demons closing in.

Adir fought to push the demons back keeping them as far from the women as he could. Aegeus and Kfir fought off the hundreds more who were closing in from the woods around them. But, of course, the Eleventh could not see that either.

The Eleventh looked around frantically, taking in the hundreds of demons rushing toward them. She walked backward, putting distance between her, the car, and the demons—or so she thought.

Breaking past Adir, a particularly evil demon spoke to the Eleventh, sulfur pouring from his mouth. "I will destroy you," he said as he stroked her face.

She recoiled from his touch and in her haste, fell backward down an embankment.

Adir broke her fall, preventing her from hitting her head. But her ankle was injured in the process.

The Twelfth stood frozen where she was. The Eleventh began to yell the Word into the night air. More demons poured in from the surrounding woods.

"Get them in the car!" Aegeus yelled to Adir, as he slashed at demons.

The Eleventh was on the ground, yelling out verses into the night, her eyes wide with horror.

The Twelfth stood in shock, trying to understand what was happening. Fear flew in from behind and grabbed the Twelfth, digging his talons into her spine.

Kfir swung his sword at Fear, trying to free the Twelfth. But even as the demon dissipated, the Twelfth did not move. Meir arrived in a swoosh.

"What are you doing here?" Kfir asked.

Meir ignored him. She laid a hand on the Twelfth, whispering to her, and then she flew away from the fray of battle. The Light of the Twelfth flared brightly, putting a circle of protection around her. She ran to the Eleventh.

"Are you okay?" The Eleventh was lying in the ditch, holding her ankle, and staring wide-eyed at the demons that surrounded them. She was shaking from the adrenaline as well as the cold. Adir performed a covering, protecting the Eleventh with his wings.

"Do you see them?" the Eleventh asked, no longer in fear but in shock.

"See who?" the Twelfth asked, looking around her anxiously but seeing nothing. She too had begun to shake from the cold.

"Demons. Hundreds of demons," she whispered. The Eleventh looked around her, concerned for them both but confident of her protection from the King.

The Twelfth saw nothing. She said a silent prayer of thanks that she could not see anything and then helped the Eleventh to her feet. Her ankle was broken from the fall. Adir helped support the weight of the Eleventh.

"Do you hear that?" the Twelfth turned her ear toward the sound, but she couldn't quite place it. The women both stood still, listening.

Kfir heard it too and took to the treetops to find the source.

"Aegeus! A flood, two hundred yards out, coming in hot!" he yelled in warning. Aegeus looked around, the women were in the ditch, vulnerable. The distance between them and the car was too great.

The flood hit with great ferocity. Adir covered the women with his body, but it was not enough. They were washed from their feet and temporarily submerged in the freezing water. The force of the water snatched them like dolls and tossed them about.

Demons roared with laughter as they grabbed the women from under the water and dragged them farther below the surface. The Twelfth gasped for air, clawing desperately for the surface, her body hurting from the cold. Debris rushed past her, banging, and bruising her face and legs.

Adir grabbed the Eleventh, pushing her toward the surface. Her wraparound sweater had come loose and weighed her down. Her lips had already begun to turn blue from the icy water. She coughed and sputtered, gasping for air when her head finally reached above the surface of the water.

Adir looked around for the Twelfth. Kfir and Aegeus were flying toward him, but they raced against the current. Hundreds of demons descended upon them, delaying Kfir and Aegeus as they battled their way forward. Aegeus searched for any sign of the Twelfth.

The Twelfth rammed into Adir under the water. He grabbed for her, just managing to get a handful of her shirt, and shoved her to the surface. She shook visibly from the cold. He brought peace to them both, removing their fear and giving them clarity of mind; he needed them to be able to think.

The freezing water rushed them toward the drop-off. If they went over it, they would both be lost. Adir steered them toward a tall tree. He put himself between the Twelfth and the tree, which slowed their pace, giving her time to reach out and grab it. She could barely feel her hands, but she wrapped her arms around the rough bark of the tree. It ripped at her arms, face, and hands.

The Twelfth clung to the tree, her feet washing out from under her, making her completely horizontal.

The Eleventh held the leg of the Twelfth, and Adir covered her hand, holding tight to secure the bond. The water raged past them, rushing past like slivers of glass piercing their frozen skin.

The Eleventh held fast to the Twelfth. She saw the demons circling them, darting in and out as they yelled taunts. The demons picked up large branches and hurled them at the women, knocking into their hands and faces. But none of the demons could get close enough to touch either woman. The Eleventh prayed; it was all she knew to do.

"I can't hold on," the Twelfth moaned. The sound of the rushing water nearly drowned out her voice.

"You can.; you have to. If you let go, we will go over the edge!" The Eleventh began to panic.

Adir, once again, sent them calm and peace to help them think clearly. He could not reach the hands of the Twelfth from where he was to help secure them. But he held her ankle in one hand and the hand of the Eleventh in the other.

The demons aimed large tree branches at the hands of the Twelfth. They smashed into her frozen, bleeding hands, causing them to slip on the rough bark, digging into them. Pain shot through her. The water, streaked with blood, rushed past the Eleventh.

Adir continued to pour calm feelings into the women. He held tightly to them both. If the Twelfth's grip failed, he worried he would only be able to save one.

He looked at the Eleventh—she was his charge. His mission was to protect her with his very life.

But he also understood the greater mission. Would he let the prophet die? He strained against the rushing water. He might not be able to save them, but he could offer them comfort and peace so they would not die afraid.

The demons swarmed in and began stabbing Adir in the back and in his hands. He yelled out in anguish and frustration. His hands began to slip, blood poured from the stab wounds in his back. His suffering energized the demons, and they swarmed faster and faster into the scene, stabbing his back, neck, and hands, clawing at his wings. He began to feel a fog settle over him.

Chapter 39

"I've got her." The voice was familiar and comforting, but it sounded so far away; Adir couldn't quite place it. "Adir, let go; I've got her," Aegeus repeated.

Adir tried to focus, to make sense of what he was hearing.

"Aegeus?"

"Yes, let go, Adir—you have done well. Kfir has you. You are injured. Let go so he might heal you."

Adir tried to focus; he had to be sure. He turned his head toward the voice. Aegeus's face greeted him, concern showing in his eyes. Adir let go.

The Eleventh was shocked to be lifted from the water and dragged to dry land. The man did not make eye contact; he did not speak to her. He seemed seven feet tall as he grasped her arm in one hand and clutched the back of the Twelfth's shirt in the other.

He walked through the rushing water as if it were a trickle. As he dragged the women along like rag dolls, he did not speak; he did not look at them; he merely walked. When he arrived on dry land, he dropped them to the ground, brushed his hand across their car, and kept walking.

The women sat on the dry land coughing and catching their breath. They were freezing and soaked. The Twelfth's hands were severely cut and bleeding. She could not feel her toes.

They were grateful to be alive but not entirely sure what had just happened. Their phones were ruined by the flood.

The Twelfth told the Eleventh to start the car and get it warmed up while she changed the flat tire— the whole reason for their stop. She opened the trunk and retrieved the jack and tire iron. Shivering, she went around to the passenger side of the car and discovered the tire was not flat. Befuddled, she stood for only a second, her body shivering from the effort. She circled the car checking all four tires. No flats. Aegeus, Kfir, and Adir stood next to the car watching her.

"Nice touch fixing the flat." Kfir nodded to Aegeus, who smiled back. "If I didn't know better, I might think you were worried about her, Aegeus," Kfir added, giving Aegeus a friendly shove.

"We are neither friend nor foe to them, Kfir; we fight for the King," Aegeus declared.

But even as he said it, he knew that in his heart, he struggled. He had indeed been worried about the Twelfth. He silently scolded himself for this weakness.

For thousands of years, he had been careful to protect his heart. He could not bear to ever again have to look into the eyes of someone he loved and know they were now enemies. He could not afford to have feelings for the humans. He reminded himself that he was here to do a job—protect the Twelfth—and caring for her was not part of it. Certainly, he had slipped, but it was not a mistake he intended to make again.

The Twelfth got in the car. The heater was running full blast, but it was not yet warm. The women prayed, thanking the King for sparing their lives and for the stranger who had rescued them.

A strange feeling spread over Aegeus as he heard the women giving thanks for him. He couldn't remember anyone ever praying for him before. He walked in front of the car and laid his hands on the hood. Warm air rushed into the car, warming the women. Shaken and injured, they headed for the hospital as soon as the Twelfth's hands were warm enough to feel the steering wheel.

Chapter 40

Titus stood unflinching, staring into the night. They had again failed to kill the prophet. The rage boiled inside him. He stood unmoving, letting it fill him. He closed his eyes, savoring the essence of it. It had been a long time since he had felt such rage. He knew it would not be long before Seneca heard of his failure.

Demons began to gather around him, waiting anxiously for his orders.

Titus remained still, eyes closed, anger raging.

Finally, one of the demons approached him and spoke. Titus ripped his dagger from its sheath and plunged it into the demon until his hand was deep inside the demon's body. He screamed into the night, and thousands of demons all over the town took flight. The sky blackened from their presence.

Titus, eyes wild with hatred and frustration, yelled out to all who listened, "Swarm the prophet's home! Cover her husband! Cover her office! Cover her students in darkness! Fill her days, have them contact her day and night seeking her counsel! Give her no rest, no peace! Find any family she has and cover them! Torment and destroy as many as you can!"

Thousands of demons flew from his presence to do as he had commanded.

Chapter 41

The semester was winding to an end, and everyone was ready for the Christmas break. Students were getting antsy with the promise of a month-long break calling to them. Faculty and staff were just as ready, the good students had worn themselves out, and the bad students were suddenly very interested in what was needed to get an A. Prayer—prayer for a miracle—was all that would help some of them.

The college was covered in soft white and blue icicle lights on every building. On the first Friday of December, two weeks before the break, as was the long-standing tradition of the college, the students, faculty, and staff gathered to decorate the big evergreen outside the Great Hall.

As was the tradition, the science department provided hot chocolate. Students stood out in the cold night air, clutching the warm mugs of hot cocoa. Little marshmallows, shaped like DNA, floating in the cups would stick to their noses if they weren't careful. Warm snickerdoodle cookies greeted all those who braved the cold.

The Bible department provided a nativity reenactment. The live animals in the stable created an authentic feel. Professors played the part of Mary, Joseph, and the shepherds. They used a doll for Jesus. Some years they included the wise men and some years they did not.

Everyone would join in decorating the tree. Each department brought their own ornaments. After the tree was decorated, there was a tree-lighting ceremony. The tree was spectacular and sparkled like a beacon in the night, the angel on top aglow. They all gathered around the tree and sang Christmas songs. The night was quiet and their voices beautiful.

The angels stood among the humans and turned their faces toward the King as his children sang out classic Christmas carols, but none was as moving to Aegeus as when they sang "Silent Night." Thousands of voices singing to the King on that cold night stirred him. One by one, angels from all over Platitude arrived silently. Together, they joined the King's children in praise.

Snow began to lightly fall as they sang, and before the night was over a soft blanket had covered the town.

The King's children were never quite as full of his Light as at Christmas. There was something about the innocence of a baby, the newness of life, the vulnerability of God incarnate that stirred them. Even the angels remembered that night, all of heaven and earth had paused to watch and celebrate the birth of the Lamb.

Aegeus had been there and remembered well the shock of seeing the Lamb confined to that tiny body, unable to care for himself and yet flowing with the power of heaven itself. Aegeus understood, in one simple moment, what humility looked like. He remembered being breathless as Mary stroked the cheek of her baby, the way her heart swelled with love for her child.

Christmas also brought out the best in Platitude. Lights adorned nearly every home. Carolers filled the streets nightly, and snow was often enough to keep the town white and crisp without overwhelming things.

The presence of so much Light agitated the Strongman. He could barely get himself to speak of the birth of the Lamb. Instead, he used the final service of the semester to discuss the sanctity of marriage. He spoke of the union of Adam and Eve as the model. He reminded everyone that God had created man first, giving him dominion.

Then he spoke of the marriage of Joseph and Mary. The words stuck in his throat as said them. He despised the holy family.

His hatred for Mary was so great that even her name made his skin crawl. If only she had been unwilling to bear the child, the burden of being an unwed mother, or the stigma associated with it.

And Joseph? Joseph being willing to overlook her pregnancy, refusing to send her to the stoning that she deserved. If there was anything the Strongman hated more than a righteous woman, it was a righteous man. A godly man was unstoppable.

But outwardly the Strongman preached with such conviction. He trembled, and to those who watched, he seemed to do so out of overwhelming reverence. He took this opportunity to diminish the role of Mary to nothing more than an incubator. He used the story of the Lamb to rail against abortion and premarital sex—to pour out guilt. He took the beautiful story of how heaven came to earth to bring hope and peace and turned it into an opportunity to offer condemnation and judgment instead.

Over the last six months, the Fifth, Sixth, Seventh, Eleventh, and Twelfth, despite their generational and life experience differences, had become friends. The women had initially met at an art exhibit featuring the Seventh's work, along with the work of her students. They hit it off right away. It was a gritty friendship forged in fire.

It had become their practice to meet once a week and share their struggles, praying together. They had created a safe place where they could admit their doubts and share their collective wisdom on life. They were honest and raw with each other.

But as was usually the case, each of them held her deepest needs close and did not share those. Even in this group of friends, they did not trust enough to lay out their innermost pain—some pain was just too deep to share. And so, the prayers could not ever be as strong as they might have been, and they could never find real freedom.

The woman had chosen the office of the Sixth this week. She had a small Christmas tree in the corner; it was perfectly decorated in purple and gold. She had taken the time to wrap empty boxes and place them underneath it. It was beautiful, like something straight out of Better Homes and Gardens. Soft Christmas music played in the background, and the cinnamon apple cider scent from her diffuser wrapped the room in a warm, lovely smell.

The weeks leading up to Christmas break had been particularly difficult. Students flooded into the women's offices with significant problems—souls that yearned to hear that they were loved. Their students' sadness seemed palpable and affected the women. The husband of the Twelfth became distracted and easily angered. The Fifth had been standoffish.

Their souls were heavy from the burden the Strongman had placed on them over the semester. Every sermon, no matter the topic, seemed to be an opportunity for him to diminish the role of women. Sometimes it was with overtly offensive statements such as his cow statement early on; sometimes it was more-subtle, by choosing words that belittled their contribution.

And it seemed that no matter how many students they saw, there was still a line of them wanting the counsel of these women. Their stories ranged from divorcing parents, unexpected illness, pregnancy scares, or marriage problems. The women were exhausted.

Each of the women had begun to doubt herself, searching her heart and the scripture to find the truth. So much of what he was saying seemed right. His words were taking a toll on them.

Adiel, Kfir, and Haywood stood outside the door of the room where the five women gathered. Aegeus went with them to provide protection in case demons were able to breach the room.

"I had a student crying in my office this week," began the Fifth. "She had decided not to ever marry and broke up with her fiancé. She said she couldn't imagine why she would ever get married just so someone would tell her what to do. She valued her independence and didn't want to have to give that up to be married.

"Her boyfriend was going into the ministry, and she knew that as a physician assistant she would make more money than him. Her Bible professors told her she could not be a good Christian woman and make more than her husband—or even work full-time. So, she has decided to remain unmarried."

"How sad," commented the Eleventh. The other women agreed. Aegeus stood near, astounded by the story.

"How did the boy take it?" asked the Seventh. The Seventh was a natural encourager. People felt better about themselves just from being in her presence.

"He told her he didn't believe she would have to give up her independence. He said her that her independence was one of the things he loved most about her—that he viewed marriage as something they did together and that he believed the Bible told them to submit to each other, meaning he would not rule over her but that they would walk together.

"But it didn't seem to matter. She said that while he might feel that way, if the Bible says she would have to be ruled by him and report to him and that she could not make more money than him, then she would constantly be sinning. And while he might not care, she was not willing to spend the rest of her life violating God's law," the Fifth concluded, sadness and anger evident in her eyes.

The Twelfth stared at the Fifth for just a moment—something about her eyes cried out. They implied that perhaps her anger and pain came from somewhere deeper.

"I think the word 'submission' should be better defined," suggested the Twelfth. "I think the church has messed that up. And honestly, why do we all ignore the verse that says we are to submit to each other? It isn't just about women submitting, husbands are also called to submit to their wives and to God. Submission is meant to be mutual; why do we ignore that?" she asked, feeling her temperature rise.

"My husband likes the dishes to be pre-rinsed before they go in the dishwasher," she started. "I don't care at all about pre-washing, and I think the dishwasher should be able to do that for you—that's its job. But on nights that I do the dishes, I pre-rinse because it makes him happy. That is submission. He does not stand over me and demand I pre-rinse. He does not even mention it. And he doesn't mention it if I don't. I just know that he likes it, and so I do it.

"He knows I hate it when he leaves the toilet seat up. So, he puts it down. That is submission. He quit smoking years ago because he knew I didn't like it. That is submission. We submit to each other daily out of love—not out of fear or demand.

"He does not tell me what to do. I don't tell him what to do. It isn't about that. I hate that we associate submission with the idea that it means one person gets to tell the other one what to do. We aren't dogs.

"Submission is about understanding that marriage is give and take, both of you have to give. It is about harmony, not hierarchy. When you learn to let things go, and you love someone enough to avoid things they don't like and do things they do like, it makes for a more harmonious home. Both people have to submit." The Twelfth stopped there because she feared she was dominating the conversation.

The Eleventh picked up there. "And, of course, when there is something you can't agree on, your husband has the final say."

"I don't agree with that," said the Seventh. "I know I'm not married, but I don't think it works that way.

"When you can't come to an agreement, I think you both should pray about it. And God will give you an answer. But if you still can't agree, then I think you each should think about your motives. Are you doing what you think is in the best interest of the family; are you doing what is in alignment with God; or are you being selfish? I don't think you have to concede to do things your husband's way just because he is a man and you are a woman. Look at Abigail in the Bible. She did not just go along with her husband Nabal—and she was rewarded for it."

"Who was Abigail?" the Eleventh asked. She had become a Christian later in life and was not as familiar with the Bible.

The Fifth provided a quick overview. "Abigail was married to a man named Nabal, who was something of a jerk. Nabal offended David and David was going to kill him. Abigail went to David and smoothed things out behind Nabal's back. Her husband had a stroke and died when he found out what she had done."

"The typical answer to that is always that the exception is if your husband tells you to do something contrary to God's law. Then, and only then, can you disobey him," the Sixth responded.

"But Nabal was just rude, not violating God's law so that argument doesn't stand," offered the Twelfth.

"What I want to know is, if marriage is just about giving a man control of your life—clearing the path so he can accomplish his goals while giving up any goals of your own—and letting him tell you what to do while you wash his clothes, clean his house, and birth his children, what value is there for a woman to get married?" asked the Eleventh.

Aegeus shifted uncomfortably. The King had declared from the beginning that it was not good for man to be alone. He had created a woman so that he wouldn't be. Aegeus thought back to Adam and his search for a companion. The King had created Eve; Adam had been overjoyed. He celebrated her arrival, a day never passed in the garden that Adam did not express that joy to Eve. Aegeus wondered when that had gotten lost.

"He will provide for you financially and guide you spiritually," the Sixth answered, sarcasm dripping from her lips.

"I don't need anyone to provide for me financially or guide me spiritually. So, I guess my student was right—you should only get married if you need someone to take care of you. I guess that is why we see that trend in the country," the Fifth retorted.

"According to our college administration, that would then make you a rebellious woman because a woman's calling is to get married and have children. Not doing so is a sign you are rebellious and selfish," the Sixth fired back.

"What?" the Twelfth asked, baffled by the statement.

"That's what he said." The Sixth let the facts speak for themselves. "Naturally, as a nonmarried woman, I can never fulfill my calling. I suppose I shouldn't have waited for the right one to come along. I should have married for money years ago," she said, causing the group to laugh.

"Apparently, they are telling the students in the Bible classes that if a man doesn't make enough money to support his family, he can't call himself a Christian," the Fifth offered.

"Based on what?" asked the Seventh.

"They are basing it on 1 Timothy 5:8," she offered, pulling up the Bible app on her phone to read the passage to the group.

"That's not what I think that means," offered the Twelfth.

"The students say they are taught that a man's biblical role is to be a provider. In accordance with God's role for him, he must provide for his family, and his wife must bear children—that is her biblical role," offered the Sixth, starting to feel a bit sick to her stomach.

"But what if God gave the woman a job making a lot of money in order to support a husband going into the ministry who won't make anything?"

"Out of alignment with the biblical role of men and women per the current administration."

The Fifth shook her head in disgust, as did Aegeus. He marveled at how little understanding they had about how the King worked if this was what they thought. The King created each of them to be unique. Each of them had a purpose only they could fulfill. Each of them had a path and journey just for them. Certainly, females were designed to be able to bear children, but that didn't mean that was their sole purpose in life.

"So, what if you don't want to have children?" the Seventh asked. She had been thinking for years that she did not want to have children. She felt God calling her to the international mission field—places that could potentially be dangerous—and she had no desire to take children into that setting. It just wasn't a yearning she had.

"Then you are selfish and are rejecting God's gift of children. Of course, there are those women who cannot have children. They can never fulfill the great calling of God. They apparently have no purpose, nor do women who remain unmarried. Or perhaps God will find them a secondary purpose, but their lives will be less important than those married with children." The pain in the Sixth was evident in her comments. The other women shook their heads in disgust at the idea.

"I wonder if Esther realized that saving the entire Israelite civilization was not her 'great calling'?" the Eleventh suggested. "I mean, did she have children that we know of?"

"She did, later. What about Deborah?" the Twelfth offered.

"Oh, well, you should know that Deborah was not a judge over Israel like the other judges—the 'men' judges—and she was only used because there was no man available. Apparently, when God gets desperate, he will resort to using women—at least according to what my students tell me they're being taught," the Fifth said.

The Twelfth shifted in her seat. The conversation had nearly become too much for her. She struggled, and she prayed, and she questioned. She had read the verses over and over, and she just didn't see them the way they were being taught. She wanted to know the truth.

"What about Sheerah?" she asked. Aegeus nodded his head, excited that the Twelfth had thought of Sheerah. He had not thought of her for a long time.

"Shee who?" asked the Sixth.

"Sheerah, from 1 Chronicles. She was a woman, and she built three cities, naming the third one Uzzen Sheerah— 'listen to Sheerah.' Do you think that she didn't command men? Do you think she didn't rule over them as she built her cities? And we know nothing else about her. We don't know if she was married or if she had children. What we do know is that she built three cities—just like the men. Oh, and we know that God used one of her cities to throw hailstones down on the Philistines while time stood still. Read it."

"I've never heard of her." The Eleventh looked puzzled and pulled up her Bible app to look up the passage.

"There are lots of women in the Bible you may not have heard of," noted the Twelfth. "The Old Testament genealogies are full of them. First and Second Kings list the mothers of all the kings except for two, specifically giving the names of both the father and the mother.

"Most scholars believe the queen mother was an actual position of authority within the royal family. We know from Solomon that his mother had a throne right beside him in the throne room—much like Christ is said to sit at the right hand of God.

"Many women are also listed in the genealogies. Pay attention to the ones that say, 'sons' compared to the ones that say 'descendants.' Often the ones that say, 'descendants' list both males and females."

Aegeus looked at the women in the room. They were women with many talents and beautiful souls. They were in various stages of life and relationships, and he hated the idea that even one of them would leave this room feeling as if their life and their future did not have meaning if it did not involve marrying and having children. Those things did not define you or your purpose. Being a child of the one true King was what defined you.

"God himself called Job the most blameless of all men. He was described as a man of great integrity, the finest man on all the earth. If you look at how he managed his family, I think you get a great model of what a father and man should be." The Fifth offered.

"What I find interesting," she continued, "is that at the end of Job, when God once again blessed him, we are told the names of his three daughters but not the names of his sons. We are also told that Job treated his daughters as equals to his sons, including them in his will. If that is how the finest man on the earth behaves, shouldn't that be our model?" she concluded.

The others had never thought of it that way. The Twelfth wondered why she had never heard that pointed out from the pulpit. Aegeus felt proud of the Fifth, despite his best efforts to remain neutral.

The Eleventh looked at the Twelfth and asked, "Do you believe the man is the head of the home?" Certainly, they all recognized how loaded this question had been in the media recently.

"The Bible says the man is the head of the home. I believe he is to be a servant leader, as was Christ. Christ never forced anyone to do what he wanted. He was never selfish in his leadership, and he sacrificed his very life for the church.

"I don't think it means he's 'the boss' in the way that we think of bosses because the Bible also says a husband and wife become one. How can you be one and yet be divided into rank? It is a dichotomy I can't quite explain. Like the trinity. I just have to accept it on faith. I'm pretty sure it also says he should deal with any intruders and/or bugs," she finished with a smile.

The other ladies laughed at the joke, and Aegeus found himself smiling too.

"Perhaps the church should focus more on teaching mean what it means to serve their wife instead of focusing entirely on teaching women to submit to their husbands," Added the Eleventh. The other women nodded in silent agreement.

"A husband has a responsibility to love his wife as Christ loved the church. To care for her, and protect her with his very life. He is responsible for helping her be the best version of her that she can be by loving and supporting her, by not placing any roadblocks before her. But by and walking with her. He has full authority to do that. In that way, he is the head of the wife. But that responsibility, that authority, does not translate into him being the boss of her, or having the authority to command her what to do – that level of authority is reserved for God alone. At least that is how I understand it", the Twelfth said.

The women's Lights burned brightly as they struggled with these ideas and concepts and worked to understand what the Word said. Aegeus tried to remain impartial, but he found himself cheering for them in their success and wishing they could hear him when they had it wrong.

"What about that 'helper' issue?" asked the Seventh, circling back to the conversation.

"Anytime I ever have to call for help, I am ecstatic to have help arrive. I did not see that help as inferior to me but as someone who could do what I could not. Men cannot do it alone. They need women. God said it was not good for man to be alone. Why would you undervalue that? It is a partnership," the Fifth offered.

The Twelfth looked at her and at that moment realized that the Fifth had indeed known great love. She wasn't sure what caused her to think it exactly, but she knew that the Fifth had, at one time, loved a man deeply.

"I heard a great sermon on that once," the Seventh offered. "I'll e-mail the link to everyone." She pulled her phone out and started looking for the link. "I honestly think the issue is one of nomenclature. It is how we define 'submission' and 'helper' and 'head' that brings about the problem. Perhaps it is something that can only truly be defined within the confines of marriage? Perhaps it is personal and will look different for everyone? Perhaps no standard answer will fit every marriage. So much of the Bible is personal."

"And isn't that the whole purpose of the Holy Spirit? To convict us? To teach us? To interpret scripture? Maybe there is no one answer," the Twelfth offered, her Light burning bright.

The others looked at her and considered this possibility. They had indeed had prior conversations about how the Spirit led some people to not drink. For them, drinking was wrong because the Holy Spirit told them not to. Just as in the Bible some had been called to special diets or to not cut their hair, etc. It was not about rules but obedience, and sometimes that looked different for each person. Perhaps submission looked different in every home. But of course, that idea made people uncomfortable.

"Are you suggesting there is no one standard of truth?" the Sixth asked, alarm rising in her.

"Not at all. There is indeed truth, I am just suggesting that in some things, perhaps it is more personal than that. In some things, it is about conviction." The Twelfth stopped because she felt concerned they were going into dangerous territory. She was not trying to imply there were no absolutes.

The ladies' time was over, and they prayed together before each left to get back to work.

"I see their Lights are all burning brightly," observed Kfir as Aegeus exited the room. "I trust it went well?"

Aegeus nodded consent. "They are all in alignment with the Word regarding men being the head of the home. But they are not sure what that means. They have been taught many conflicting ideas, some of which come from the Strongman and are of course designed to demean and hurt them. But they seek the truth, and the King will show them that."

Haywood walked with the Fifth toward her office. She was distraught after the discussion, and her face was flushed. He worried about her. Perhaps he would call in Ayo again tonight to try to minister to her.

"Haven't the Eleventh and Twelfth both been married many years?" asked Adiel, already knowing the answer.

"Indeed." Aegeus nodded, starting down the hall after the Twelfth.

"And aren't they happily married?" Adiel followed.

"Indeed," Aegeus answered again.

"And they have not yet figured this out?" Adiel asked, baffled by the ways of humans.

"Knowing and knowing that you know are not the same thing," Aegeus answered.

Adiel nodded knowingly. That she understood.

"Think of it this way," he went on, "warriors, guardians, and ministering angels are all different. We meet different needs and were designed for different things. Is the warrior better than the guardian or the ministering angel?" Aegeus asked.

"Of course not," Kfir answered. "We are all needed. We are all necessary. We are equals and work together as a team."

"And who is in charge?" Aegeus asked. Kfir laughed at that.

"The King is in charge," Kfir said as if to a child.

"Am I in charge of you, Adiel?" he asked. A look of shock spread over Adiel's face as she tried to comprehend the question.

"None but the King is in charge of me," she replied.

"Am I in charge of you, Kfir?" he asked, turning to Kfir, who roared with laughter.

"None but the King is in charge of me. You are in charge of this mission, but not me. I am free to make my choices and to do what I think is best, and I answer to the King for those choices. Being in charge of the mission and being in charge of me are two different things."

Aegeus nodded. "Exactly."

Chapter 42: The Sixth and Seventh

The Sixth and the Seventh were six months apart. They had grown up together, neighbors and best friends since third grade. The Sixth was the older of the two. She liked to think she was also the more responsible one. She had spent her life playing by the rules. She wore a rough exterior, but it covered over a tender heart—one she was petrified of being broken.

She was tall and beautiful and attracted the attention of many men, but she intimidated most of them. The Sixth liked to take the safe road. She weighed options, considered consequences, and always tried to do the right thing. She feared punishment, and although she would never admit it, she feared the rejection that came from it.

The Seventh was originally from the Dominican Republic, but her family had moved to California when she was young. The Sixth had taught her English and about American culture. She quickly became the protector of the Seventh.

The Seventh was adventurous; she followed her heart and paid little consideration to the consequences. The Sixth bulldozed trouble from her path. But the Seventh rarely noticed. She wasn't much of a rule-follower, but she did have an overactive conscience that kept her from going too far astray.

The girls had grown up knowing the Lord, but each had chosen her own path when committing to becoming His children. They were as close as sisters. They had gone to the same college, the Sixth studying accounting, the Seventh pursuing art. Now they shared an apartment in a bohemian town, just outside Platitude.

The Sixth wore crisp, clean lines, with well-pressed suits and heels, her curly hair always painstakingly straightened and pulled into a tight bun. The Seventh wore flowing fabrics with patterns, and dangling bracelets, wearing her hair loose about her shoulders.

The Sixth was recruited first. She was working in an exhibitor's booth at a conference in Tulsa. A wayward handcart rolled into her display, sending things sprawling across the exhibitors' hall. As she scrambled to pick up the pieces, a woman with wild red hair approached her.

"Let me help you," the woman offered with a smile that was kind and gentle. The Sixth was frazzled from the incident and from working at a job she hadn't liked in years. If she were honest, she would have to admit that she had lost a little respect for herself for even working there. But bills didn't pay themselves, and the Seventh was often late with rent since sculpting did not provide a steady paycheck. She smiled at the woman, accepting the help gracefully.

When the display was back in order and all the materials she had brought with her were once again in neat rows on the table, the woman with the red hair stood quietly looking at the display. The Sixth found herself growing a little uncomfortable. The woman with the wild red hair smiled at her in reassurance.

"You could do better." It was not a question but a statement. The Sixth looked down momentarily, and then a slight fleck of anger sparked inside her. The woman stood firm, not flinching.

"Thank you for your help. I truly appreciate it. But if you will excuse me, I have to get back to work." The Sixth felt unexplainable anger, and yet when she looked at the woman, she couldn't help but feel like the woman's green eyes were looking right into her soul.

"I know you have many talents; I am a talent expert," the woman said. "You are wasting them, and you know it. Leave what is good for what is better." She reached into her jacket pocket and pulled out a small business card with nothing but a logo. Handing the card to the Sixth, she allowed their eyes to lock briefly, and then she walked away.

The Sixth put the card quickly in her pocket with the intention of throwing it away once she was back in her hotel room. She felt flustered by the woman's abruptness. She smoothed down her suit jacket, pasted on a smile, and threw her mind into her work—even if it was work she hated. *How could this woman have known?* She wondered. *Who had put her up to this?* When she returned to her room later that evening, she threw the business card in the trash.

"How was your day?" the Seventh asked as they were chatting by phone.

"Oh, I'm living the dream," the Sixth said with a snicker. She went on to tell her about the encounter with the woman and the odd business card.

"How mysterious! What is the logo?"

The Sixth attempted to explain the design to her, but it just didn't translate well. She fished the card out of the wastebasket and snapped a picture with her phone and sent that instead.

It took the Seventh nearly six weeks to determine that the logo was for a Platitude College hidden in the mountains, in the middle of nowhere. At her encouragement, the Sixth reviewed their job site. They had an opening in the accounting department that was perfect for her.

After she had been working there for just over a year, the art department had an opening, and she recommended the Seventh.

Chapter 43

The last day of the semester finally came, and the Twelfth was looking forward to the long break. Christmas was in two weeks, and she had not done any of her shopping. She had been so busy with students and grades that she had let things at home go.

Her Wednesday night group was planning a progressive Christmas party, and she had lots of cleaning to do to be ready. She was thankful for a few weeks to focus on her family. She bundled up, put Christmas music on her iPod, and started to lock up her office to begin the walk home.

Just as she was walking out the door, a young man from her afternoon class asked if she had a minute.

Aegeus immediately noticed the demons that clung to him—demons that had been with him for a long time. Most tormenting demons were opportunistic. They tormented their charge for a season, but they did not remain long term.

But just as the King had knitted each human together, providing them with all the gifts they would need to find him and fulfill his perfect plan for their life, Satan too took a great interest in the birth of a human child. Each human would be assessed shortly after birth, and Satan would determine the sin that would work best for that individual. He would assign tormenting demons to them based on his findings.

For some, it was lying. Certainly, all humans lied. But some people lied for no reason. They lied about everything. Some people lied just because lying was their default setting. They justified their actions by calling them "white lies" because they didn't hurt anyone. Once the sin became part of you, it was easy to convince yourself that it wasn't a sin at all.

For some, it was gossip. They lived for a juicy bit of gossip. If there wasn't any, they made some up. You could hardly tell a gossip that they were gossiping. They would tell you they were just telling you what was happening. Often, gossip was disguised as prayer requests, which somehow justified it.

For others, it was gluttony, or jealousy, or lust, or selfishness, or pride. Ah, pride, that was one of Satan's favorites and one of the hardest to overcome. Those demons dug deep. Their talons sank deep into the person's heart and would fester if the human did not ever remove the demon.

When the person accepted the Spirit, things got more complicated. The Spirit would rail against those sins and burn and scorch the demon. The demon would cry out in pain, but cling tightly, anxious to keep its charge.

The Spirit would be grieved that the person clung so tightly to the demon. Often the person would wail and beg the King to deliver them from this sin, and yet they would cling to it desperately—perhaps even unknowingly because it was so much a part of who they were. This young man had one of those demons dug deep into his chest.

The Twelfth invited the young man in, and they sat together in the small seating area. She offered him some water, but he declined. She could see immediately that he was uncomfortable. He shifted uneasily and didn't make eye contact.

She said a quick prayer, asking God to give her wisdom regarding whatever the young man wanted to talk about. She asked that God give him courage and help him feel comfortable.

Meir entered the room silently. She looked at Aegeus and smiled. He smiled back. If the Twelfth had summoned Meir, it meant she was making progress. Meir positioned herself between the Twelfth and the boy and laid a hand on each of them.

The Twelfth gently prompted the boy. He looked down at the floor and unknowingly placed one hand across his chest, pinning the demon to his body. A single tear ran down his face. He remained silent as he struggled to control his voice. The Twelfth prayed for him.

"I have a secret that I have carried for many, many years," he started. "I have carried it alone, but now I am afraid it has gotten too heavy. I have been praying, and I feel like God has directed me to share it with someone. And after praying about it for a while more—well, here I am." He paused as the Twelfth waited.

She continued to pray silently while she listened. Her Light blazed brightly within her. The red-haired woman arrived and placed her hand on the back of the Twelfth. Power filled the room. Kfir saw the Lights and came to stand guard at the door.

"It is important to me that you know that I love the Lord," he went on. "I was raised in a Christian home by good Christian parents. I go to church, I pray, I read my Bible daily. But as long as I can remember, I have been gay." He stopped there. His heart laid out bare and unprotected—his vulnerability palpable. The demon clinging to him hissed in anger that he had told anyone. He looked down at the floor, not daring to meet the eyes of the Twelfth.

"Am I the first person you have ever told?" she asked him gently. He nodded yes in response.

"Thank you for trusting me with something so big." She felt honored that he had come to her and petrified that she might say the wrong thing.

She ached for him and longed to hug him as a mother. She thought about her own son and what she would want someone to say to him if he confided such a significant secret in them.

"Do you think your sin is any different than mine?" she asked him.

He looked up then, a puzzled look on his face. She waited.

"What is yours?" he asked, genuinely interested. Her sin was self-centeredness. She tended to lose track of what was going on around her and just focus on her own needs, her own life, and struggles. She shared this with him.

"But you are always listening to people. You are always asking how we are and investing in us?" He said it as a question since what she was describing was not how he saw her.

Aegeus listened closely, his own heart breaking for the boy. Shaking the sin that Satan had assigned you was difficult. Few humans ever fully rid themselves of it. Most faced a lifelong struggle against it. All of heaven grieved over it.

"It is an everyday battle. I have to remind myself every day to look outside myself—because honestly, I am happiest when I am not focused on me. I am happiest in moments like this when I am sharing in your life and helping others face their struggles. But I have to work at it because when I am not careful, I lose sight of those around me and get overwhelmed by my own needs and my own issues. And when that happens, I find myself sinking into a quagmire.

"Our sins are the same. In God's eyes, our sins are equal. I sit here before you broken over my sin. But there are moments when I embrace it. I soak in it, I rub it all over me, breathing it in and justifying my own self-absorption. I have battled it as long as I can remember."

She smiled at him. He smiled back. More angels flocked to the office, surrounding it, protecting it, for this was a holy conversation, one in which all of heaven was invested.

"I don't want to die an old man alone," he blurted out, emotion strangling him.

Aegeus yearned for the final battle. He longed to see Satan defeated and humanity restored and free from the pain and anguish of sin. He did not think the humans understood how much heaven grieved for them—how intricately involved heaven was with their daily lives and their development.

Did the humans understand that all of heaven cried out for every young man and young woman like this one? Did they know how much it grieved all of them to see the King's children struggle so much? Did they understand that the King did not cast blame for the temptation that Satan laid before them? Aegeus found himself a bit surprised by his own reaction to the boy.

The Twelfth and the boy sat for more than an hour discussing his fears, his struggles, and his courage. Carrying his secret had been a heavy burden, and every day he was overcome with the fear that someone would find out and he would be dismissed from school. It was a lot for a person to shoulder alone. Now, she would help carry it. She would pray for him daily and serve as someone he could come to when he struggled.

She encouraged him to share with his parents what he had shared with her. She again thought of her own son and said a little prayer for the man he would one day become. She asked God to place people in his path that he too could confide in if he ever needed to. She prayed that they would have the wisdom to encourage him to come to her with his struggles, and she prayed that she would handle whatever it was well when he did. She reassured the boy that he was not alone—something he desperately needed to hear.

His struggle was no different than her own or that of any other Christian on the planet. As much as we like to rank our sins, there is no rank, no hierarchy; they are the same. She reassured him that he was loved and valued for who he was and that he didn't have to be anyone other than that. He did not have to earn love; God gave that freely. She assured him that his secret was safe with her. When they were done, they prayed together, and the boy left.

The Twelfth sat for some time, praying over the conversation, and that she had said the right things—things that allowed the young man to see and hear God, things that would encourage and build him up.

Chapter 44

The walk home was long and cold. The streets were slippery, and after falling twice, her clothes were wet, and she was bruised. She knew she was going to be late for the progressive dinner. She was sure her husband would be frustrated that she hadn't gotten home in time to help prepare. Her porch light glowed an inviting color, and the sounds of Christmas spilled out to the street. She loved the group and felt a surge of joy as she stepped in to join them.

Her appearance from slipping and falling must have been worse than she thought because she attracted immediate attention. The Third, after having a good laugh, directed the Twelfth to head upstairs and change; they would wait for her.

She pulled off her clothes and quickly changed into something warm and comfortable, then rejoined her friends in the living room. She looked around at these faces: the First and his wife, the Second and Third, the Fifth, the Eighth and his wife, the Eleventh and her husband. They were a source of support and encouragement to her. She would not have made it without them.

The First and his wife had done well in the town before the arrival of the Strongman. But the Strongman's comments about the role of women had ripped open old wounds in his wife. The First had avoided sharing the Strongman's opinions with his wife, but of course, it came up often in the group. She never spoke of it, but he could see her slipping into old ways, the sadness starting to creep back into her eyes.

He often wondered if she regretted marrying him. If her purpose truly was to be a mother, then he had kept her from achieving her God-assigned role. The First knew, intellectually, that a woman's sole purpose was not just to have children. He could reflect on the women of the Bible where it was clear that women served in many other valuable roles—all of them equal.

He looked over at his wife, and he knew that if the Strongman stayed, he and his wife could not. But in the meantime, they would speak truth and encouragement to as many college students as they could. The counseling office had overflowed with students in the last six months. Suicide attempts were up, depression was up, and self-loathing was at an all-time high. He prayed for the students at the college and for God's protection of them. Aegeus was pleased to see that the First had fulfilled his purpose in the mission.

The Second and the Third regaled the group with stories of their days on the mission field. Aegeus found himself mesmerized every time the Third told a story—she had a great gift for it. Completely captivated, he would listen intently.

The Second and Third wore a crown of splendor and served as a source of wisdom to the group. They also opened their home to host the weekly meetings. The Second was polished and wise without being stuffy; he brought a great perspective to the discussions. The Second and Third both knew God well and ignored the

Strongman and his comments. They had a solid marriage, and his comments had no bearing on them at all. The Second dismissed them immediately and encouraged his wife to do the same.

The Fifth and the Twelfth had become good friends at work. They worked in the same building and often had lunch together, swapping stories of classroom debacles, workplace politics, or just life. They confided in each other and leaned on each other.

But the Twelfth often felt that the Fifth was holding something back. On occasion, she would stop the conversation abruptly or get a faraway look in her eye. The Twelfth did not press the issue.

The Fifth did not sleep. She ate sporadically. She refused all ministering by Ayo. She had a thick wall around her. The words of the Strongman would send her into a spiral of frantic activity—anything to distract her mind, anything but sleep. Others saw her excessive service activities and were amazed by how dedicated she was. Some resented her for what they viewed as over-achieving. Haywood saw it for what it is was, a way to silence the pain. He continued to express concern about her to Aegeus.

The Eighth and his wife had faced many struggles since arriving in the town. The Eighth's research partner was a vindictive and jealous man. Jealousy was his sin from birth, and Satan had chosen well. Jealousy was a powerful tormenting demon, and the man had long ago embraced it.

The Eighth was a great researcher. He arrived at the college and made suggestions for improvements in the department that were implemented and praised.

Instead of being pleased with his success, his research partner became jealous and set out to undermine the Eighth. Most of those efforts failed, but his anger and eventual hatred of the Eighth were strong, and the Eighth could barely breathe under the weight of it. Initially, he thought he could win over the man, so he worked longer and harder, ignoring his family in the process. Depression clung to him, sapping his energy.

His marriage had suffered as well, and his wife's disappointment was added to the disappointment, confusion, and fear of all the others. He carried all of it as if it were his own. If not for Adir and Chi Breeze, the marriage would not have survived.

The angels had fought hard battling the demons that swarmed both the Eighth and his wife. Tormenting demons urged them both to leave, to abandon their marriage, and his wife had left briefly.

But Adir had fought for them. He had called in support from warriors and ministers. Berhanu and Ayo had been ministering to them for several months.

Through it all, the Eighth and his wife faithfully attended the group. It was where they found encouragement, drawing strength from the prayers and support. It was important to the Eighth that his wife did not feel ostracized or judged, and in the group, she was loved.

The group recognized the seriousness of her actions when she left home and celebrated her return to her family. They also understood the need to love her and support the efforts to mend the marriage. She had never been mistreated here, and the Eighth treasured that fact.

The Eleventh also worked in the same building as the Twelfth. They had weekly meetings with the Fifth, the Sixth, and the Seventh in which they shared prayer requests, updates about what God was doing in their lives, and just hanging out as women. It was something they all needed. The Eleventh had come to the King later in life, and she had a passion and zeal for God that often encouraged the others. Her friendship had been a critical support for the Twelfth.

The humans mingled about, walking from home to home, enjoying a time of fellowship and comradery. The angels guarding, protecting, and ministering to them did the same. The Twelfth seemed to have two left feet on the snow, and she repeatedly slipped as they walked from home to home. The rest of the group could not help but laugh at her misfortune. The angels also laughed and worked to keep her upright, or at least from breaking anything. It was a nice way to start the Christmas break.

Chapter 45

Christmas had not been as restful for the twelve as Aegeus had hoped. The demons had swarmed the town, their cover so consuming that the residents of Platitude had not seen the sun in weeks. The husband of the Twelfth had been covered in demons, and although he fought against them, there were so many that when he shot one from himself, another replaced it.

Eventually, no one could withstand that. Discouragement seemed to have the strongest hold. Aegeus, Kfir, and Adiel had been fighting non-stop, but even that had only kept the demons to a minimum. Several times the Twelfth had smelled the sulfur, but no one else had smelled it, so she had dismissed it as her imagination.

Demons knew no holidays, and they often worked even harder to discourage the King's children on holy days. They believed that if they could bring strife and sadness to these holy celebrations, they could stop the King's children from celebrating. They would be so consumed with their own discouragement and despair they would forget the King. The twelve did at least have time to rest, to be free from the messages of the Strongman.

The Wednesday night group continued to meet over the Christmas break. Things were going well. Aegeus looked forward to their gathering each week. He found it fascinating to listen to them wrestle with the Word, and he particularly liked the way the angels would listen in and join in the conversation even though the King's children could not hear them.

They cheered when one of them got something right after a long struggle and sighed when they had it wrong. It got exciting at times, but the energy and power of the King that always came from those gatherings was something Aegeus had never experienced before. It had become his favorite thing about earth because it created a feeling he knew nowhere else but in heaven.

There was only one week of the Christmas break left before the students returned, and Aegeus wanted an update on the twelve. He entered the meeting location in the salvage yard and was pleased to see the other angels were all there. The angels milled about chatting, laughing, and sharing a meal. Aegeus stood and just soaked it in.

Haywood approached him, bringing with him a full wineskin. He poured some into a small wooden tumbler and handed it to Aegeus along with a piece of aina, a tender plant similar to pineapple, its flavor a bit more savory.

Kfir stood in the back with a steaming cup in his hand. This puzzled Aegeus. There was only one hot drink in heaven, something similar to apple cider, but it was made from the fruit on the trees, which often varied, so the drink itself was different every time you tried it.

Aegeus closed his eyes to concentrate, then took a long deep breath in to smell what Kfir had. His eyes flew open in surprise as the smell of coffee hit him. He sniffed again. Coffee? From the smell of it, robust coffee. He walked toward Kfir. The smell of the coffee growing stronger as he approached.

"Kfir, are you drinking coffee?" Aegeus couldn't help but laugh at the idea of it.

Kfir looked up with a big smile on his face, excitement in his eyes.

"I thought I might try it; it smells so good." His smile was infectious, and Aegeus laughed despite himself. "It's called, Death Wish coffee and is trendy at Perks."

Berhanu and Emeka goaded Kfir, daring him to try it. For as long as Aegeus had walked the earth, angels had dared each other to try the food. Before the fall, the angels had eaten freely from the garden. But Eden had been destroyed during the flood.

Food on earth was different from the food in heaven. Eating the things on earth that had been made by the King was reasonably safe, but it was eating the items made in factories that became the angel equivalent of a triple-dog dare.

By far, Kfir had tried the most things. This was impressive considering how much more time guardians and ministering angels spent on earth. He had many stories of mishaps. He once ate something called a hot dog at a stadium in 1974. No one was quite sure what it was, but Kfir spit it from his mouth so far that it hit a spectator in the back of the head. The man convinced himself that it was a fan from the opposing team. And before the angels knew what was happening, a riot broke out in the stadium. The assignment had been simple, and the riot was not part of it.

Kfir's food tasting led to another riot at another stadium the next week—one of the most significant riots in baseball history. As a result, the warriors had to spend three additional weeks on earth sorting it all out. The angels referred to it as the debacle of 1974.

Kfir put the cup to his lips and breathed in the overpowering scent of the Death Wish coffee, which was covered in whipped cream. The other angels gathered round and chanted his name, encouraging him. Kfir took a sip. His face elongated and his right eye squinted shut; his tongue poked through his lips just a little. Whipped cream clung to his nose. He declared it delicious but a bit on the chemical side. The other angels erupted into laughter.

Aegeus called the meeting to order. He wanted to get an update on what had been happening with the twelve. He saw some of them regularly, so he wanted to start with those he knew less about. He began with the Fourth. The angel of the Fourth stood and gave an update.

"The Fourth is the direct supervisor of the Twelfth. His son was in prison for four years on a drug-related charge, but he was recently released. The boy was too ashamed to face his parents, so he was living on the streets.

"Somehow the boy's mother found out, and she called the Fourth, asking him to find the boy and take him in. The Fourth told no one; he merely took a few days off and went in search of his son.

"He found the young man hungry and dirty, but otherwise unharmed. The Fourth brought his twenty-four-year-old ex-convict, recovering addict son home, and celebrated his homecoming but told no one in the town. He felt it best to keep personal matters private.

"This burden has proven to be heavy. Demons swarm his home, trying desperately to get to his son. But the Fourth has prayed a hedge of protection around the young man that is so thick with heaven's power that only the son himself can fail.

"The Fourth and the Twelfth are getting along very well. The Twelfth trusts him. He values her and her contribution to the department, and he has made sure she knows it. The King selected the Fourth because the King knew that it would take a very particular type of man to manage the environment that the Strongman would create.

"The King knew that the Twelfth's first reaction would be to leave since this was not a battle she wants. It is a topic that makes her very uncomfortable. And he knew that she would need to be surrounded by people that would encourage her to stay.

"The Fourth was uniquely positioned to do that, but he also has broad shoulders that will not stoop under the pressure of the Strongman—he will lead the department well."

"Berhanu, make sure you are making regular trips to both the Fourth and his son. Let's get a couple of warriors on them as well." Aegeus did not want to risk it. "What of the Tenth?" he asked.

"The Tenth works in Human Resources. He has a lust demon that clings to him from his youth, and though he battles daily, he has not yet been able to break free. Since moving to the town, he has done well resisting temptation. His wife is covered in tormenting demons, and in this environment, she is sinking into depression. Ayo comes to minister to her often but freeing her from the demons enough to receive ministering has proven a challenge.

"The Tenth has a great deal of knowledge regarding the Word and is passionate about the Spirit. He fears the Twelfth and, therefore, avoids her. His avoidance is evident, although the Twelfth does not understand it. She has incorrectly interpreted it to mean that he is concerned with her performance and regrets allowing her to be hired.

"It causes her concern, and if left unchecked, it will develop into distaste and then disdain. He is, however, fascinated by her in a way he cannot explain, and he monitors how she is doing. He respects her, but he fears her greatly because he can see that she is a prophet."

Aegeus was concerned about this development. The Tenth would be the one to finally challenge the Strongman, but he would never fulfill that role if he continued to avoid the Twelfth.

"Meir, see if you can get the Fourth and the Tenth in the same room for a discussion regarding the Twelfth. Perhaps the Fourth can ease the Tenth's concerns about her," Aegeus suggested.

Meir nodded in agreement.

"What of the Sixth and Seventh?" Aegeus continued.

"The Sixth is very distressed over the Strongman's statements. Worthlessness has found her a willing host and has dug talons deep into the girl. She is actively seeking a way out of the town. I fear she may not last through the year.

"The Seventh is doing well. She and the Twelfth are friends, and they encourage each other. But the call to her from the mission field is strong. Her time here is not long."

Aegeus nodded in understanding—this mission was taking a toll on them all. He asked Amitiel, the researching angel, to share any insights he may have that could help the angels better serve their charges. Amitiel provided additional insights about each. He did not rattle through them as if they were the mere numbers by which they were called but told their stories as children of the King. The passion by which he told their stories made Aegeus question his own clinical approach to the humans.

Chapter 46

The spring semester started without considerable fanfare. Like the fall semester, the first day of classes included a noon service that everyone attended. The Strongman made his way to the podium. He smiled at the students and then began.

"Welcome back. I hope that you spent some quality time with God over the break. It is so vital to your walk that you pray and read your Bible every day. Some people would tell you that you don't have to do that, that it is something nice to have but not a required thing. But we know that isn't true.

"We know that you cannot know the Father if you do not spend time in prayer and studying his Word. One of the signs of a good Christian is a daily quiet time. Giving in to the temptation to skip it will destroy you.

"We see evidence of this all over our country—all over the world —but let's focus on our own little town. I got a report over the break from the counseling department that I found troubling. My heart breaks to hear such reports, and I have been praying diligently for you over the last few weeks. We have a real issue on our campus, and I would like to spend this semester addressing it. Will you let me do that?"

He waited for the congregation to offer affirmation. The Twelfth was sitting with some of the people from her department. They exchanged concerned glances. The Eleventh's eyes grew wide, and she began to pray urgently. The Twelfth looked at her and mouthed, "demons?" and the Eleventh nodded. She could see thousands of demons soaring through the room, touching, and brushing against students, faculty, and staff. The room filled with their smoke. The angels stood stoically around the perimeter. Now was not the time for battle.

"The problem we have here is a lack of faith," the Strongman continued. "This is evident in the fact that we had a record number of students in the counseling department last semester for depression. We had numerous suicide attempts on campus. We even got a report from our insurance that faculty visits for depression were up. How can this happen on a Christian campus?"

He let the question linger in the air with a look of consternation.

"I mean, the joy of the Lord is our strength. If we do not have the joy of the Lord, we need to spend more time in prayer and Bible study. Some people turn to drugs for depression and anxiety, but I am here to tell you that you just need to turn to God. God is your anti-depressant. God will take away your anxiety.

"What I see here is a sin issue. The Bible is sufficient for all your needs. We don't need to medicate; we need to meditate! If you are here today and you are depressed or anxious, you lack faith. You have a sin problem, and we need to get to the heart of it.

"I am going to be working with the counseling department to make sure they are using Christ-centered counseling and not relying on secular wisdom to solve spiritual problems. Because I have to tell you that you can't have the Spirit of God inside you and be depressed!" He nearly shouted the last part.

The room was silent except for the jubilant cheers of the demons. They watched as Lights dimmed and flickered. The demons swarmed the students, filling them with doubt, deepening their depression and anxiety and pouring on guilt.

"I am going to make a promise to you. I want you to listen; I want you to hear what I am about to say because I am going to make you a very important promise. If you let me challenge you spiritually over the next fifteen weeks, I promise you that you will leave here free from depression, free from anxiety, free from mental health issues.

"Those are the work of the evil one. I will give you the verses you need to free yourself from them. I will arm you with the spiritual tools for you to walk away from depression and anxiety. Is that okay?

"Can I walk this journey with you? Can I help you free yourself from these demons? My goal for us—listen close—my goal is for us to not need a counseling center anymore! I want to arm you with everything you need so that when depression comes knocking on your door, you will know exactly how to rid yourself of it.

"You will declare the promises of the Lord, and you will be free! There will be no more depression; there will be no more anxiety; there will be no more mental illness!" He shouted it out to the group.

The demons roared with glee, and many in the crowd cheered as well.

The Fifth looked as if she might throw up.

The Fifth, Eighth, Eleventh, and Twelfth walked out of the Great Hall together. The Twelfth couldn't help but wonder what the First must be thinking about this. When they were away from the student's ears, the Fifth opened the topic for discussion.

"How many people do you think he damaged today?" she asked.

"Too many," said the Eighth, a sadness settling over him.

"Did he just say that you couldn't be a Christian and be depressed?" the Twelfth asked, unsure that she had heard correctly.

"That's what I heard," the Fifth agreed. They all muttered agreement. It was indeed what they had heard. As they walked back to their building, they explored the idea that depression could be a sin issue.

The Twelfth felt so shocked she could not even be angry yet. "Can you even imagine how you would feel if you were in that room and suffering from depression?" she asked. "Do you know how dangerous it is to suggest that medication is unnecessary? Can you even imagine the ripple effect of the things he just said?"

As she finished her questions, the Twelfth did not notice the quiet resolve that had taken over the Fifth, but she did notice the Eighth who had grown quiet.

When they got to their office building, the Twelfth separated from the others and began the long walk to her own office. The Eleventh walked with her.

"There were thousands of demons in that room," she whispered to the Twelfth. The Twelfth stopped walking and turned to look at her.

"Thousands?"

"Thousands," she confirmed. "They were jubilant. I wonder if he did it on purpose. Do you think he is evil, or do you think he is clueless?"

They had not had this conversation before, and the Twelfth was slightly hesitant to say what she thought. She paused, subconsciously pressing her lips together as they paused in the seating area outside the Twelfth's office. The Eleventh noticed.

"You think he is evil?" she said half as a statement and half as a question. Panic streaked her voice just enough to make the Twelfth nervous.

"I do. But that doesn't mean he is. I have tried to think he is just clueless or insensitive. I have even tried to believe he was right and I was the issue. But I keep coming back to the same conclusion: he is evil. He is not a good man who is confused. He is an evil man who is intentional. He is trying to destroy our campus for some reason." There, she had said it. And in many ways, it felt good to lay it out there.

"Oh no," the Eleventh shook her head in dismay, concern covering her face. Her Light flared brightly, filling the area with light. Aegeus and Kfir basked in its power, wondering what the Spirit was telling her.

"Well, I could be wrong; I mean just because I think it, doesn't make it right," the Twelfth said.

"No, you're not wrong. You're a prophet—you would know."

"What?" The Twelfth was genuinely shocked. She stared at the Eleventh, not believing what she had just heard. "I am not a prophet." She emphatically stressed each word individually. She shook her head and took a step back.

"Of course, you are. You didn't know?" the Eleventh said with a smile. Then she turned and walked away.

Kfir shouted for joy, and Aegeus laughed despite himself. The seed had been planted; she had been exposed to the truth. She would reject it, of course. The question was for how long. But now that the seed was there; the Spirit would take over and water it until the Twelfth accepted the truth. Now they could make real progress.

The angels celebrated—it was the only good to come from the Strongman's speech. Kfir danced about the hall, looping his arm with Aegeus's and swinging him about. They both laughed and celebrated; it was a wonderful moment. Students filed by as they rushed to class, unaware of the angels celebrating the birth of a prophet.

The Twelfth stood stunned for a moment and then tried to put the entire conversation out of her mind. She had a class to teach. She dashed into her office, grabbed her lab coat, and rushed to class.

Chapter 47

The students appeared downtrodden, and she knew that they too must be reeling from the comments of the Strongman. She wished she could reverse it or say something that would help them, but instead, she focused on the day's lesson.

She was covering how to perform pelvic exams. She required the male students to get in the stirrups, so they could have a better appreciation for the procedure and develop empathy for the patient. They remained dressed, of course.

Because this was the introductory day for this skill, she had them divide into groups of three. One person took the role of the patient and climbed into the stirrups. One of them performed the mock procedure. They were required to know the names of the instruments and equipment and to go through the steps in the proper order.

The third person was responsible for documentation and assisting. Each person would do a walk-through in each role. Tomorrow they would use manikins and perform the procedure, getting a sample that would then be analyzed for them to read, interpret, report, and document. For today they just needed to get comfortable with instructing the patient in a way that was professional and make sure they knew the steps and equipment.

While they were working, a female student tried to slip into the class late. The school had a strict late policy, and typically the doors to the classes were locked when class started. The Twelfth had locked the door as required, but Aegeus had unlocked it when he saw the young woman coming.

Her hair was dripping wet and in disarray. Her uniform was also wet and had large white bleach stains covering what should be emerald green scrubs. She smelled strongly of bleach, and just under the edge of her long-sleeve undershirt, well-formed bruises were visible. Her eyes were red and wild. She had her hair hanging over her face, but the signs of trauma were evident near her left eye. Her late entrance caused considerable disruption, and the entire class stopped to see who had come in.

The Twelfth's Light burst forth from her, shooting the straggler demons from the room. She looked to the Ninth and asked her to take over monitoring the class. Then she looked at the young woman and said, "Come with me." She spoke authoritatively and professionally with no signs of emotion on her face.

The young woman walked behind her down the hall. She began to panic as the Twelfth walked briskly toward another lab. She knew the penalty for being late, and this was not her first offense. Fear that she would be dismissed flooded her. They walked through the hall and entered another lab. Without speaking, the Twelfth opened a cabinet and searched through it.

"Professor, I am so sorry," the student offered. "My husband got angry. He didn't want me to come to school today. He threw my uniform in the toilet and poured bleach on it. When I tried to get it out, he hit me. He shoved my head in the toilet and poured bleach on me. He knew I couldn't come to school without my uniform. I know I am a mess. I am so sorry, please. Please….I…I can't be kicked out"

The words poured from her mouth. Fear and panic strained her voice; her plea was heart-wrenching. The Twelfth, rage coursing through her, turned to face the student. She held a fresh uniform in her hands and offered it to the girl.

"He doesn't get to win—not today," she said as she looked the young lady directly in the eyes and handed her the uniform. She walked from the room before the girl could speak. Once outside the room, she stopped and leaned against the wall. Her hands were shaking. She took a few deep, steadying breaths to compose herself, pushing back tears. Then she rejoined her class already in progress.

The young woman rejoined the class in time to get through one rotation. The Twelfth did not see her again until classes were done for the day. The young woman walked into her office once again in her bleach-stained clothes and handed the Twelfth the new scrubs neatly folded. The Twelfth stood when she entered the room.

"You can keep those," the Twelfth answered, sorry that she hadn't made that clear earlier.

"No, I can't. If I take these home, he will destroy them too." She held them out to the Twelfth. She spoke without sadness—she was past sad. She accepted that this was her new life.

"Then I will keep them in my office," the Twelfth said, taking the scrubs from her. "And each day you will come in and get them. You can change here at school and leave them here at the end of the day. I will take them home and launder them for you as needed." She too spoke without emotion, without any illusion of options. This simply was how it would be. The student nodded.

"I suppose you want to know," the girl started, looking a little uncomfortable.

"Only if you want to tell," the Twelfth replied.

"Perhaps another day," the young woman said. "I don't think I am up for it today."

The Twelfth reassured her that she was always happy to help. She made sure the girl knew the resources available to her before she left. As she was leaving, the student paused and looked back.

"Professor? Do you think he hits me because I am not submissive enough?"

The question nearly undid her. Her heart jumped into her throat, her knees nearly buckled, and she again fought against emotion. There were so many things she wanted to say, but she settled on just one.

"No. He hits you because he has control issues and needs help; it has nothing to do with you." After the student left, the Twelfth closed her office door and cried out to the King.

Chapter 48

The weekly meeting was in the Twelfth's office this week, and the Sixth, the Seventh, the Eleventh, and the Fifth came in with their lunches and sat down. The women were discouraged, and it showed. The conversation was a little forced at first—no one seemed to want to speak.

The Eleventh eventually got them started by blurting out that the Twelfth thought the Strongman was evil. She went on to say that she had told the Twelfth that she trusted her judgment as a prophet.

"I am not a prophet," the Twelfth protested, rolling her eyes. She felt slightly embarrassed that the Eleventh had said such a thing in front of the others.

"Of course, you are," the Seventh said, looking surprised that the Twelfth denied it. The Twelfth looked at her, stunned, and shook her head no.

"You didn't know?" the Seventh asked, astounded.

"Prophets are old men from the Bible. No one does that anymore, and certainly not me." She felt embarrassed to even be having this conversation.

"It makes sense," the Fifth offered, looking as if she had just considered it. She too was completely ignoring the Twelfth's protests.

"No," the Twelfth said, looking from woman to woman. "No," she repeated as if by saying it twice it was settled. "First, that isn't true; second, saying things like that here will get me fired. Let's talk about something else. Let's talk about the idea that depression is a sin issue and we don't need anything but the right Bible verses to resolve it."

They all groaned at being reminded. The conversation quickly became serious. The women began by expressing heartbreak that such a thing had even been said. They were in agreement that it would isolate those who were depressed even more. The Fifth pointed out the obvious: all the people in the Bible who suffered from depression—Abraham, Jonah, Job, Elijah, King Saul, Jeremiah the prophet, and of course the most famous, King David. In fact, a great number of the Psalms were written by a depressed King David.

"And what about Proverbs when King Solomon, the wisest of all people to ever walk the earth, asked who could bear a broken spirit?" the Eleventh asked.

"Certainly not Elijah. He was so depressed he wanted to die. God had to send angels to attend to him," the Sixth added. "But of course, that doesn't happen anymore. I wonder why he doesn't send angels anymore."

Aegeus and Kfir exchanged a look, shaking their heads in dismay. Aegeus exhaled.

"I think he does," the Twelfth ventured.

Aegeus and Kfir leaned in as she went on to share the story of when her son saw the angel on the roof. The story of Sanyi. Aegeus was interested to hear the story from her perspective. She had been gardening in the yard with her children. Her youngest, under the care of Lavi, had asked her who the men on the roof were.

The Twelfth had looked and seen no one. Her son had described a warrior with a sword fighting against two bad guys. She told him she didn't see anyone.

Aegeus, of course, knew Sanyi was a guardian, not a warrior, but the child did not know this. He also knew that Sanyi reported that on another occasion she had seen him herself, but Aegeus noted she did not share that story. He couldn't help but hope she would since he would like to hear it. The other women listened to the story about her son and were mesmerized.

While they trusted the Twelfth, it was still hard to believe in something you could not see. The Sixth shifted uneasily in her seat; her Light burned brightly, but Aegeus could see that she struggled against it.

"And," the Twelfth went on cautiously, "I believe that when we were in that flood"—she gestured toward the Eleventh— "I believe that was an angel that saved us. I can't explain it any other way."

The room was quiet except for Kfir. "Did you hear that?" he asked, jubilant.

Aegeus stood stunned. It was a strange sensation to hear her talk about him—for her to recognize that he was an angel. Even to think that she had seen him and knew he existed. It caused a stir in his soul he couldn't quite explain.

"Then why do they let terrible things happen? If angels are here, why don't they protect us? Why do they let children get hurt? How do you explain that?" The Sixth spit out the words. She tried to hide her anger and hurt, but she had failed.

The Twelfth's Light suddenly erupted, and she knew—she just suddenly knew—that the Sixth had been sexually abused as a child, by someone close to her family, someone she trusted. She had kept that secret from everyone but the Seventh. She suppressed the pain. If you had asked her about it, she would say that she had dealt with it. But in reality, she feared men because of it.

She wouldn't say she feared men—she may not even know it. But she feared them and found fault in every man who tried to get close to her. She did not trust them, none but her own father. She put on a brave front—a hard front—but in her heart, she longed to marry but knew she could never do so because she could never trust a man. Not just for herself, but for her future children.

She certainly was not willing to ever again let anyone have complete authority over her—male or female. God alone had that position. To hear the Strongman say that this was a faith issue—that it was a sin issue, that she just needed to read more Bible verses—left her feeling sick.

It was not a lack of faith in God, but a lack of faith in men. Was it sinful for her to feel hurt and betrayed? She read her Bible, she prayed, she was active in her church, she loved the Lord, but she had wounds deep in her soul. And per the Strongman, she had nothing to offer a husband anyway since her virginity, her most prized offering according to the Strongman, was stolen when she was only eight years old.

Aegeus wanted to be able to explain. He wanted her to understand. It wasn't just about the angels. There were demons too. And prayer, why did so few of the King's children pray? Did they not understand the power of prayer? Aegeus wanted to ask his own questions.

The King had promised tranquility and paradise in Eden. But Adam and Eve had opted out. Was that the Angels' fault? Adam and Eve had let evil on to the earth. And now, there is evil. Paradise will one day be restored, but in the meantime, evil will happen. It is not because the King sleeps, or the angels have taken a vacation. It is because evil came to dwell among them.

Did they not realize that it grieved the angels too? Did they not realize that it changed everything for the angels, that before the fall the angels did not spend their days fighting for the King's children? They had other jobs. Everything had changed—everything, not just things on the earth.

He doubted they ever gave much consideration to how the fall had impacted the angels. He doubted they gave much consideration to how the angels watched over them every day, how they grieved and celebrated with them. How they fought so that the King's children would always have a way out of temptation, only to see them choose what was evil over and over again.

Did the humans ever think about the sacrifices that were made by heaven itself to care for them, to protect them? The angels fought against those who had once been their comrades-in-arms. Those they had called friend. And while they hated the evil that now consumed those who had fallen, it still grieved all of heaven to see someone once so holy and pure now so covered in evil, with no hope of restoration. To watch them change from a holy, heavenly being to a demon was agonizing.

For just a moment, Aegeus let Seneca enter his mind. It had been many years since he had allowed himself to think of Seneca. The look in his eyes when he had fallen. The terror he experienced almost immediately once separated from the King. The sight of seeing the Light of God removed from him. Looking into Seneca's eyes and knowing that someone he loved as a brother would become his mortal enemy.

The memory was so powerful. He had to shake it from his mind. He tried to tune back in to what the women were saying. They had moved on from the Sixth's comments. Aegeus had missed what was said. He felt himself start reconstructing walls that he had begun taking down.

"Of course, King Saul was depressed because God himself sent a tormenting spirit to him," the Twelfth was saying. "That is actually a little scary. But what I find fascinating is that the demons still seem to have access to God."

Aegeus understood why people wondered about this, but of course, he also had stood in the throne room with the King. He understood that everything in all of creation had access to the King.

There would come a time when that was no longer true, but during this age, there was nothing that did not have access to the King. Separation from the King was separation from all hope, all Light, all that was good, replaced by suffocating in darkness, evil, and hopelessness. Eternal torment. The real question was if they took advantage of having access to him or not.

The women ended their time with prayer, and each of them headed back to her respective office. The Eleventh and Twelfth walked down to the faculty lounge to get a cup of coffee. The lounge was a spacious area. Three walls were solid glass, letting in lots of natural light. Two couches sat in an L shape on one wall with a large coffee table. A lush rug filled the space, creating a relaxing area to sit. The other side of the room had a large table with chairs around it. It was an industrial-style table with folding chairs, a stark contrast to the couch area.

Several faculty and staff sat in the room eating a late lunch and talking when the Eleventh and Twelfth came in. A tall, thin woman was saying, "I just don't think you can be an alcoholic and be a Christian."

The Twelfth felt a rage she had never known course through her. She willed herself to stay silent. Her hands began to tremble. She went to the coffee kiosk and selected a light roast from the cabinet.

A stocky man sitting next to the woman added, "I know what you mean. I am always amazed when people claim to be Christians, but you can tell from their lives that they aren't. Like you said, alcoholics, drug addicts, Democrats." The group all laughed at that.

The Twelfth's rage grew even stronger. She willed the coffeemaker to brew faster. What was wrong with it? The Eleventh stood beside her, frozen in place. Water, it must be out of water. The Twelfth took the tank off and went to the sink to fill it. The group at the table continued.

"I mean, how can you call yourself a Christian if you're having an affair?"

"Or if you are gay," another added.

"Do you think you can be a Christian if you are a gossip?" The Twelfth swung around and said it before she even realized what was happening.

The group looked at her a little stunned. "Or what about if you're judgmental? Can you be a Christian and be judgmental? What about liars? Are they excluded? Can you be a Christian and be a liar? How about sinners? Surely, you can't be a Christian and still be a sinner." The words poured from her mouth. Her hands shook at her sides. Her Light blazed from her and filled the room. The air crackled from the power of the King.

"You know those are different," the stocky man said.

"How?" she shot back.

"It's just different. Telling a lie is different from having an affair. You can't say it isn't." He felt secure and justified in his position.

"It is different to us, as humans, but to God, it is sin. All of it. And sin is a separator. But how dare you be one too? How dare you put a hurdle between anyone and the cross? How dare you tell anyone that they must remove all sin from their life before they can approach God?

"Who are you to say what struggle they will have? Just because you become a Christian, you don't stop sinning. You don't suddenly get over it. The only difference between them and us is that we have hope. God fights for us. We have stepped out of the darkness and into the light. But our struggle does not end.

"There is no sin on this earth that a Christian hasn't committed. None. We are just as evil as anyone. And you have no right to say that anyone can't be a Christian because of their sin. There are plenty of Christians who struggle, and you should be ashamed for putting barriers between them and God.

"It is only with God's help that they have any chance of ever winning against their struggle, and that is true no matter if their struggle is greed, lust, alcoholism, addiction, or pride."

She left the room without her coffee. The Eleventh caught up with her in the hall. Kfir and Aegeus high-fived each other before going after her.

"Hey, are you okay?" The Twelfth stopped and turned back toward her. She let out an exasperated sigh.

"Can you believe that? There is no way to finish that sentence that is correct. You can't be a Christian if? Seriously? There is nothing that can finish that sentence that would be correct. Nothing." Her anger had started to subside, but it had not left her.

"I'm a Democrat," the Eleventh blurted out. The Twelfth gave her a confused look.

"What?"

"I'm a Democrat." She said it again as if it were a confession.

"What does that have to do with anything?"

"One of the things he said was you can't be a Christian and be a Democrat. But I'm a Democrat." She said it with such simplicity, such purity.

The anger evaporated from the Twelfth. She smiled at the Eleventh.

"Well . . . I guess I can overlook that." She smiled wider. She couldn't care less what political affiliation someone had. The Eleventh was her friend; the idea that they could not be friends, or that she would judge the Eleventh based on political affiliation was ludicrous.

"I'm serious, some people do tell me that—that I can't be a Christian if I'm a Democrat." She looked a little anxious.

The Twelfth just shook her head. "You know that's crazy, right?"

"Of course, it's the Republicans who aren't Christian." The Eleventh winked as she said it.

Chapter 49

The Wednesday group had gathered once again in the home of the Second and the Third. The evening was a little cool and damp, so the Second had started the fireplace. The fireplace was a large stone one with a simple wooden mantel. The hearth was raised off the ground so someone could sit comfortably by the fire if they wanted to. It was a gas fireplace with remote control.

Kfir was mesmerized that a push of a button on a remote control could render a fire, so each time the Second and the Third left the room, he pushed the button, turning the fireplace off and on. He was completely enthralled by it. Once the rest of the group arrived, Aegeus insisted he stop. The fire took the chill out of the air and created an inviting setting.

The group had decided on stone soup for dinner. Each of them brought items to put in the soup. The broth was already on the stove, and as each one arrived, they added their ingredient. The Twelfth had brought chicken that she had shredded and sautéed with olive oil and her favorite spice. The Eleventh added small red potatoes. The Third added celery and carrots. The First added onion and green beans. The Eighth brought garlic, basil, and oregano along with a beautiful loaf of French bread that filled the air with the aroma of fresh-baked bread.

The house had an open floor plan between the kitchen and living room. The group members mingled between the rooms as they chatted about life in the town. They had been together nearly a year, and in that time, they had grown close; in fact, most of them were surprised by how quickly they had bonded.

They met every week on Wednesday, but they also had a special gathering every month. The events varied each month and included things like a backyard barbecue, a bike ride and picnic lunch, movie night, a Christmas party, the progressive dinner, game night, and billiards.

They also volunteered together one Saturday a month. They had served at the homeless shelter, the women's shelter, and a soup kitchen. In those places, the prayers were so raw, so honest that the angels found great strength.

Each time the group gathered, the angels also communed together, they looked forward to it. They used the time to share updates on their charges and discuss strategy. They listened to the King's children as they talked about their jobs, their passions, their histories, and their families.

The angels listened closely to gather their collective knowledge about the college and the impact of the Strongman's messages. The group had established a rotation to determine who would attend his weekly service. The one who went filled in the rest of the group each Wednesday.

But their discussions of the Word were the ones that the angels most enjoyed. The angels had started bringing their own snacks, and they would also eat and discuss the Word, but of course, the angels had the advantage of having stood face-to-face with the King.

Seeing them struggle with understanding the Word helped Aegeus to better understand them. He had never considered there were so many ways to interpret what they called a verse. He knew only one way—the King's way. But of course, the Word had not been written for the angels; it had been written for the King's children.

After the fall, when the children could no longer see the King, they needed a way to do so. The Word gave them that way. But the King had never intended them to use it to beat each other—a weapon they wielded against each other. And he certainly never intended it to replace the Spirit. It was a looking glass through which they could be introduced to him and their desperate need for him.

Aegeus found that many in the town worshipped the Word above the King. They prized it over the Spirit.

Each member of the group got a bowl of soup and some bread and then found their way to a seat in the living room. The angels had noticed from the early meetings that they seemed to sit in the same spots every week. This amused the angels—the King's children were creatures of habit. It made them more predictable, and that was one of the things that made it easier for the enemy. As they chatted about the soup and shared anecdotes from their week, Aegeus got an update from the other angels.

The attacks over the last few months had been intense. Demons swarmed everyone associated with the Twelfth, but the demon presence was so intense in the town that it had become hard to distinguish.

The Eighth's wife had left him. She told him via text before she jumped on the back of a motorcycle and sped out of the town to start a new life—one free from all the sadness and sorrow that filled the town. But the farther she got from the town, fewer and fewer demons covered her until finally, she was alone with her own thoughts.

Berhanu had gone along with her, and as soon as the demons left her, he went to work. At the first stop, she called the Eighth and sobbed into the phone, asking his forgiveness. Ayo was with him when the call came in, but she had not been needed. The Eighth could feel his wife's anguish and shame through the phone. He went to her and brought her home. She had not been gone more than four hours. Since then, they had been going to counseling outside the town, and while things certainly were not perfect, they had begun to repair their marriage.

The demons could not touch the Second and the Third, so they focused on their students instead. They sent overwhelming numbers of them to the Second and the Third, who found themselves working extraordinary numbers of hours.

The extra hours caused them to have less time together, less time with the King, and less rest. They soon found they were too tired to do much other than work, and the Third began to seriously plan their formal retirement. But during prayer, the Spirit revealed to her the real issue, and she went to the Second about it. Together, they made a plan to put aside what was good and focus on what was best.

The Eleventh and her husband had also faced many trials over the months. The Strongman's words brought back many memories of her youth, and she found herself struggling with depression. She feared that if anyone learned of her rape and attempted abortion, they would ostracize her. She began to tell herself that she was not good enough, not pure enough, and if anyone ever saw who she was, they would reject her.

It seemed to be something that all of them struggled with—the feeling of not being good enough. Aegeus wondered what it was they weren't good enough for. They were good enough that the Lamb died for them. What more was there?

The Eleventh's struggle with depression was only made worse by the Strongman's declaration that depression was a lack of faith. The Eleventh sank even deeper into depression until she did not want to get out of bed. For many weeks, Meir went to the Eleventh morning after morning and prompted her from the bed, but it became harder and harder to accomplish.

The angels coordinated encounters for the Eleventh to assure that her soul was getting fed and that Meir would continue to have something to work with. Eventually, her husband, with considerable help from the angels and the First, had convinced her to seek help. She had been prescribed an antidepressant, and, she had gotten better. The combination of medication and counseling had served her well, and she seemed to be well on the way to recovery.

The Fifth remained a mystery. The demons came to her at night. They swarmed her home night after night, filling it with memories. The Strongman's words tore at her soul, yet outwardly she gave no true indication of the sorrow that was within. She wore a smile, she laughed at jokes, she complained very little.

But at night the demons brought her nightmares, and after months of nightmares, she gave up sleeping. Ayo and Berhanu had been there several times to minister to her, but she refused their help. When she stopped sleeping, the demons stopped coming. But Haywood worried what impact not sleeping would have.

The Twelfth, like the Fifth, did not need the demons' help to torment herself. They swarmed her husband, her children, and her students anyway. Her days at work were long and filled with anguished students fighting the demons they could not see. A day did not go by that a student wasn't in her office crying.

She shared in their anguish and helped carry their burdens, but it left her so emotionally empty that she had little to offer her own children when she got home. Her husband saw her exhaustion and picked up more and more of the responsibilities at home.

But instead of seeing this for what it was, a loving act of kindness, she interpreted it through the lens the Strongman had taught her to use. She began to see it as evidence of her failings as a mother and wife. She convinced herself that her husband was not happy because she was not the right kind of wife. She tried desperately to put aside her own opinions and do whatever he suggested, but it made them both miserable.

Once tensions were high in her marriage, she began to crumble a bit around the edges. She ramped up her own self-loathing—no demons required. She tried so hard to fit into a mold she didn't believe in and didn't agree with, all the while counseling student after student not to do that.

Because of all the discussion on the role of women, women who did desire to be stay-at-home moms felt as if they were doing something wrong. The Twelfth encouraged all of them to follow the passions the King had given them, to seek first his will for their lives, and to listen for his voice.

The Tenth continued to avoid the Twelfth and resisted all efforts to help him see her as an ally. His avoidance of her was intentional and comprehensive. Partnered with his resistance to both the angels and the Spirit regarding her, he was weakened, which made him more vulnerable to demon attacks.

Temptation was high, and he began to seek out women who would fill that need. Preventing that took many angels, but so far, they had been able to prevent anyone from succumbing to his advances.

The Twelfth had eventually realized the condition of the Tenth. Watching him flirt with young women turned her stomach—and yet she also felt a great sadness for him. The Fourth also noticed what was happening to the Tenth and his treatment of the Twelfth and began to pray diligently for him while trying to encourage the Twelfth.

It was an encounter with the Ninth that had finally helped the Twelfth find her way out. The Ninth had become a regular in the Twelfth's office. The Ninth met a young man, fell madly in love, and they were engaged. The Ninth wanted to keep her maiden name, an act of respect and honor for her father, but she struggled with if that was disrespectful to her husband, something the Strongman had taught her.

The Twelfth challenged the idea that it was disrespectful. After all, wasn't there an example in the Bible? There was a story in Ezra chapter two of a man taking his wife's family name, so this was not a new concept.

The Ninth had looked up the verse on the spot. Barzillai was the name. That settled the matter in the mind of the Ninth.

For some reason, that breakthrough with the Ninth helped the Twelfth regain perspective. That night, she and her husband had a long talk, and things were starting to improve at home. But the Strongman's poison had burrowed under her skin and getting rid of it would take time.

The First was perhaps the most impacted by the latest messages from the Strongman. Every service of the spring semester was on the topic of counseling. The Strongman declared over and over that there was no need for science-based counseling. There was only a need for more prayer, the right Bible verses, and repentance. It was such a simplistic view of mental health.

The First went into his office the day after the Strongman's speech to find a new directive. All mental health issues should now include counseling, and it should be based on a list of approved Bible verses that were attached to the directive.

Counseling sessions should be based on finding the sin issue and counseling the student through it. Should the sin issue be something in violation of the code of conduct, like smoking, drinking, or sex, the student should be referred to Student Services for appropriate disciplinary action.

Medication should be used only as a last resort for extreme cases. The First was stunned; there were so many issues with the directive, he was not sure where to start his protests. So, he hit the delete button and directed his staff to do the same.

Chapter 50

Students quickly adjusted to this new threat and the number of students going to the counseling center dropped dramatically. Only the most severe cases continued. The First spent his days helping students with eating disorders, addictions, and the trauma of childhood abuse among other issues.

Many of them had lost faith that God was paying attention. The First prayed for them before and after each session, and when he felt the Spirit led him, he started to help them rebuild their faith along with their tattered souls. He prescribed medications when medically warranted.

The Strongman reported the great success of his counseling plan week after week by sharing with the campus that the number of students needing counseling was down. This, he told them, was evidence that his approach worked.

He did not mention that the number of suicide attempts was up or that across campus grades were down. He did not mention that morale was eroding or that enrollment for the next year was dropping. But in the Great Hall, he celebrated how well his plan was working.

The First worried that eventually, the mental health department would close, but he was wrong. It was not the Strongman's intention to close the center but to replace the licensed counselors and psychiatrists with nouthetic counselors. Nouthetic counseling rejects traditional psychology and psychiatry and instead insists that the church should be the source of all counseling. No special certification or licensing required.

The First was filling the rest of the group in on what was happening. The Strongman had terminated several psychiatrists in the center and replaced them with nouthetic counselors with no prior experience. The Strongman also asserted that because counseling was now based on biblical principles and not psychology, women could no longer counsel males in the center.

Aegeus looked around at the small group of friends. Not quite a year ago, they had been strangers. Aegeus had gotten to know each of them well over the last year; in some ways, he knew them better than they knew themselves. They were all so magnificently flawed, so deficient. Their journey was so full of bumps and failures.

And yet, they were all perfect. Each of them covered by the Lamb, filled with the Spirit, and a reflection of the handiwork of the King. He marveled at the beauty of it. The power of their imperfection and their need for each other. They had found their own brotherhood.

He looked around at his brothers, those he went into battle with every day, and he realized that they were not so different. The King's children also went into battle together every day, and they too needed a brotherhood to support them in that battle.

In some ways, their battle was more difficult than Aegeus's because they could not see their enemy. Aegeus found himself wishing that he could become like them and teach them how to use the most powerful weapon they had, the Light of God. If for just a short time they could see him, hear him, he felt sure he could prepare them for the battle ahead.

The group spent the evening discussing all these things and praying over them. They spent time discussing what the Word said about each of these issues and searched their hearts to see if it was their own pride or ignorance that kept them from the truth.

Chapter 51

"How was work?" the Twelfth's husband asked, kissing her lightly and handing her a knife intended for the fresh vegetables on the counter. She sat her workbag down and began chopping vegetables while he cooked lamb and made what appeared to be Tzatziki sauce.

"Gyros?" She wasn't sure why she asked. What else would it be? But she asked.

"It just sounded good to me."

"Cook's choice." Long ago they had agreed that whoever was cooking could decide what they were having. The non-cook did not get to complain. Often, whichever one was cooking still asked the other what they wanted, but on nights like tonight when cooking began with only one of them in the house, the cook picked. She loved gyros.

"How was work?" he repeated. Lowering the heat on the lamb, so it didn't cook too fast.

"Interesting. Always interesting. I honestly love that I work somewhere where I can pull my Bible out during a meeting to reference it. I love that I can pray with my students and speak freely of my faith. But wow. Sometimes I just want off the crazy train."

She shredded cabbage and carrots for gyros while she talked. How could she even explain what it was like?

"Something happen today?" he asked, reaching around her for another cucumber. He enjoyed chatting about their day while they cooked. Something about pairing the intellectual with the tactile resonated with him.

"My day was full of the same story a million different ways. Everyone that came through my door thought they were the only one who didn't have it all together. They all carried some great burden they were afraid to tell anyone for fear of judgment.

"This female/male thing is out of control. Girls telling me they have no hope of a successful marriage because they're not virgins. It's just ludicrous.

"Girls telling me their husband of three weeks is more interested in porn than them. Or that their husband never spends time with them because he is too busy with video games. And if she says anything, he tells her he is in charge, and she needs to submit to his authority. Females rejecting marriage altogether because they have been told it is about them giving up their dreams to help their husband fulfill his." She sighed as she thought through all the hurting people who had walked the path with her today. She said a quick prayer of thanks that God had seen fit to send them to her, and she prayed for each of their situations even as she recapped the general ideas to her husband.

"They tell them that a woman's job is to help a man accomplish his goals?" Her husband stopped cooking and stared at her, baffled. She nodded her head. "What about her own goals? And what about unmarried women?"

"Precisely." She appreciated that he understood.

"What about women married to horrible, horrible men or women married to men who aren't Christians, or widows? Have they no more purpose?" he went on.

His mind could not wrap itself around what type of man would need to make a woman believe she had no purpose but to cater to him. "As I recall," he went on, "there were three curses in the garden. Work would become actual work, there would be increased pain in childbirth, and woman would desire man, but he would rule over her, indicating there would be a power struggle. Now correct me if I am wrong here, but we have medication to help ease the pains of childbirth. Does anyone at your work say using that medication is sinful?" He had stopped cooking to look at her.

"Not that I know of," she said with a smile.

"Do any of them claim that having a job you are passionate about—one that does not seem like 'work'—is sinful?"

"No."

"What about if you have a job that doesn't actually require you to do work that is all that hard. Is that sinful?"

"No. I haven't heard that."

"Why then have we picked the one saying men will rule over women and decided that men not ruling over women would be sinful and somehow in violation of God's plan?" He paused for a moment and then had to turn back to the lamb that was now filling the house with its aroma.

"Oh, I can explain that. The punishment was the woman desiring her husband. See, God created man first, so that made man in charge. Woman accepted this completely until the fall." She sliced the vegetables a bit more aggressively than was necessary.

"First, I don't see that anywhere in the Bible. Second, I don't think anyone mentioned that to Eve. If she were clear about the fact that Adam was in charge, then she would have consulted with him before eating the fruit. He was standing right there with her. And part of her sin would also have been that she usurped her husband's authority.

"And if he were supposed to rule over her, wouldn't the first sin truly have been his failure in leadership? I mean, if he was in charge, shouldn't he have stopped her from eating the fruit, making a leadership fail the first sin? Where, before Genesis 3:16 does God mention man ruling over woman?"

He saw her pain over the whole topic.

"The idea is that man was created first, and thus he has dominion over woman. And of course, he named her, further solidifying his dominion over her." She sounded exhausted even as she said it. He could sense her exhaustion, and knowing her well, he understood how trying this must be for her. He turned her toward him and looked into her eyes.

"Tell me the problem with that," he pressed.

"The problem is that animals were created before Adam. So, creation order seems meaningless. Someone had to be first. And, as far as naming, Hagar named God when she was in the wilderness. This did not give her dominion over him. And of course, Adam didn't actually name her until after the fall. It is a silly theory." Moving it from her head to her heart was the issue.

"I wish I could convey how stressful it can be," she lamented. "The women are so subjugated and yet so strong at the same time." She paused.

"Isn't that the way of women?" He asked, stroking her cheek. In her eyes, he could see the pain that she felt for these women, for the students, for the young men who would one day be husbands and fathers. "I am exhausted from it, and this issue comes up every day. Every day. I wish they would just quit talking about it already. Like I said, some days I just want off the crazy train." She looked down at her shoes. She was tired.

"What does the Father tell you?"

"Honestly?" she hesitated, ashamed of her answer. Her husband smiled back, waiting. "I haven't talked to him about it too much. The whole topic makes me so upset I just want to walk away from all of it." There, she had said it.

"From God?" He knew the answer already, but he asked anyway. Aegeus leaned in closer; he did not know the answer, and he was eager to hear.

"No. From the church. I love God. I love being with God. I love feeling him and hearing him. But this whole 'women's role' conversation makes me feel like less. It makes me angry and hurt. God tells me what he wants me to do. God directs my path—not some man in a pulpit. Did God just create me so I could have babies and take care of you?"

The pain in her eyes was evident. Her questions did not upset or offend him in any way. To the contrary, he felt offended for her.

"If I were a woman," he began, "and I was told that getting married meant I had to be in the background for the rest of my life, I would stay single. If I were a single woman and were told that my purpose in life was to get married and have children, I would feel purposeless. If I were a woman who could not have children, I would feel purposeless. If I were a woman whose husband could not give me children, I would wonder how I made such a poor choice in a spouse. If I were a widow, I would wonder what point there was in me still living. So I ask you this: who would benefit from silencing women? God or Satan?"

He kissed her gently on her forehead and then walked away, leaving her alone with that thought.

Aegeus watched as her husband walked away to put the meal on the table. Her face showed an internal struggle. Her Light burned bright, and he hoped she would listen to the Spirit. She hesitated only a moment, turned her face toward heaven, and then joined her husband in setting the table and rounding up the children.

Later, in the cool of the evening, when dinner was over, and the dishes were put away, the Twelfth put on a light sweater and walked out on the deck. Aegeus followed her outside. She stood for a moment, soaking in the night air.

It was a particularly beautiful night. The crickets chirped, and the lightning bugs made everything seem magical. She thought for a moment about the crickets. Their sound was comforting, and yet, it was a desperate cry for companionship or an angry warning to aggressors. Despite that, it sounded beautiful to her. It made her wonder if her own desperate cries sounded beautiful to the King.

She looked up to the stars, and tears began to well in her eyes, but she fought them back—she was too worn to cry.

"Where are you?" she whispered into the night. "You brought me to this place. I feel like you have given me an impossible task and abandoned me here." She wrapped her sweater more tightly around her. Aegeus stood motionless as he watched her. Prayer was a holy thing.

"They think I am a rebel," she continued. "They have labeled me a feminist. A feminist!" The word seemed to stick in her throat. She shook her head gently.

"I don't want this battle. I am too tired to fight, and I am not even sure I am fighting on the right side. I just know that they are destroying these women. They are doing so much damage in your name. Where are you? Why have you given me this task? I am not right for this—I can't be objective and passive. I can't remain silent like they keep telling me women should be."

She paused for a moment, and Aegeus thought perhaps she was done. The air crackled from the prayer, and he remained still, not wanting to move. It was so raw, so honest. It caused a stirring in him he did not quite understand.

"God, why this? Why this issue? Why me? I went from being the most conservative person in the room to the most liberal. What changed? Not me. You moved me.; you brought me here. I expected it to be different. I don't want to be in the middle of this. Who am I? I have no authority to speak on this topic. I am no expert. These people have years of biblical training; they have been to seminary. Who am I? Why won't you help me keep my mouth shut? God. Please."

She dropped her head for a moment and was still. "Please, God. I can't." It came out as a whispered plea. She sank into a chair and sat silently for quite some time, her head resting in her hands. Aegeus stood, unmoving, mesmerized. Finally, after some time, she stood and walked to the edge of the deck to look out over the yard.

"Not my will but thine. I will do whatever you tell me. I will pay whatever the price. I ask only that you give me courage, strength, and wisdom and that you stop me from speaking anything other than the truth."

She was resolved; she was sincere. The power of the Spirit-filled the night. Her prayer to the King concluded, Aegeus walked toward her until he was standing directly in front of her. He knelt, so they were eye to eye. Emotion overwhelmed him.

"I am Aegeus, warrior of the King, and I will fight for you."

Neither of them moved. Aegeus stared into her eyes, aware that she could not see him but wishing that she could. The night was silent except for the chirping of crickets.

Chapter 52

God was walking in the meadow when Michael joined him. He was under the great tree with his hand resting against its trunk. Light flowed from him into the tree, causing the bark to glow. He smiled as the light made its way up the tree across the branches and into the leaves. The leaves began to change colors and new fruit sprouted. A wide array of colors, shapes, and sizes of fruit adorned the tree. Michael stood at a distance, watching.

"Michael, you bring me news of Aegeus," the King said without turning around.

"I do," Michael answered as he joined the King under the tree, excitement tinging his voice. The King looked out over the meadow toward the city.

"Which of all the flowers is your favorite, Michael?" the King asked.

"The M. longipetala," Michael answered, eager to tell the King about Aegeus but knowing not to rush.

"Ahh, the Evening Stock—that is a fragrant one," the King acknowledged. Before he had finished saying it, the meadow was filled with them. Michael took a long, deep breath and savored the aromatic scent.

"They are beautiful," Michael said.

"There is beauty in all that is not evil if you know how to look," the King responded. He walked away from the tree, which seemed to cry out for him as he stepped away. The King stopped for a moment and smiled as if listening to a message from the tree.

Then he continued with a slow, easy walk back toward the city. The King was never in a hurry. He was never late, and never early; his timing was always perfect. When you walked beside him, your timing also became perfect.

"What news do you bring of Aegeus?" the King asked.

"He understands your love for your children." Michael was excited to make the report. The King stopped walking and looked at Michael, a smile spreading across his face in celebration of Aegeus's progress.

"I knew the Twelfth could reach him." He smiled. "Aegeus would make an excellent Archangel. And how does she fare?" he asked, referring to the Twelfth.

"The seed has been planted. And she wrestles with it."

"When the time is right, Michael, she will discover her true self, what I created her to be, and it will be glorious."

Chapter 53

The Twelfth stood at the sink looking out at the evening. The sky was clear, the stars bright. Summer was just around the corner. She was washing the dinner dishes. She liked hand-washing the dishes sometimes; the warm water on her hands, soft music in the background, and the gentle scent of the dish soap were comforting to her.

Dinner had been difficult, the kids were riled up, her husband was a little cranky, and her patience was long since gone. She had lost her fortitude with one of the kids and fussed at them more harshly than she intended. As a result, no one else had spoken the rest of the meal.

As she finished the dishes, she thought about the papers that needed to be graded and the e-mails still in her inbox. She had a full night of work ahead of her; grading was definitely one of the disadvantages of being a college professor. She poured herself a cup of decaf, got her workbag, and settled into her favorite chair with a stack of papers.

Reading the third paper, she felt certain it was plagiarized. She let out a deep sigh and opened her laptop—a quick Google search would indicate if further investigation was warranted.

The woman with the wild red hair silently entered the room, her face serious. She sat down beside the Twelfth and laid her hand on the laptop. A Facebook notification popped up; the Seventh had shared a photo. The Twelfth, avoiding the issue with the paper, clicked the notification. Facebook was a great distractor. The picture was of the Seventh and the Fifth outside a Mexican restaurant.

The Twelfth leaned in to study the picture. It had been taken about a week ago when they had all gone to lunch at Sombrero's, a Mexican restaurant in the next town over. The restaurant was having a trivia contest; the winner got free sopaipillas. The Fifth had won by a wide margin, and the Seventh had the lowest score, so they had taken a picture together. But in the photo, the opposite seemed true. The Seventh's smile covered her face, while the Fifth had sadness in her eyes.

The Twelfth "liked" the photo, closed Facebook and went back to investigating the student paper. But the look in the eyes of the Fifth haunted her. She found herself distracted by it, trying to think of the last time a smile had reached the Fifth's eyes. She couldn't remember.

"Focus," she said aloud, trying to get back to grading; students could be vicious on evaluations if you took too long returning their papers. But she couldn't shake the feeling that something was wrong. She decided to Facebook stalk the Fifth and searched her name, but the Fifth didn't have a Facebook page.

Again, she redirected herself back to her work. She typed in the phrase she was questioning from the student's paper and immediately got a hit. She wrote down the name of the journal and the title of the article and then put a zero on the paper. She would do a more thorough check in the morning, using the plagiarism software they had on campus.

She started working on the next paper, but her mind kept returning to the Fifth—that look in her eyes. The Twelfth Googled the name of the Fifth. But all the results pertained to a reality TV star with the same name. She jumped to the third page of results, but again all the results related to the reality TV star. She tried the seventh page of results—nothing. The woman with the red hair gripped her shoulder. At the bottom of the page, there were related search results, one of which caught her eye—an obituary.

The Twelfth clicked on the obituary. It was for a soldier who had died in Iraq. He had been killed when a roadside bomb exploded. Then she saw it—a simple phrase that carried considerable weight. He was survived by his wife and unborn child. His wife just happened to have the same name as the Fifth.

The Twelfth sat stunned for a moment, not believing what she had just read. She explained it away as a coincidence. But something about it whispered to her, reaching deep into her heart, and telling her she had stumbled upon something.

She thought back to the moment when they had been sitting together, and she had suddenly known that the Fifth had indeed experienced the deep love of a man. Her mind flooded with little moments, with looks and comments over the last year that told her that this man—this story—was the story of the Fifth.

She stared at the screen for a long time, letting her mind work out the details, linger over memories that supported the theory that this man had once been married to the Fifth. Guilt began to slide over her. Why didn't I pay more attention?

She looked back at the article, searching it for additional hints or clues. What about the child? Was it possible the Fifth had had a child? She put the man's name into Google. Articles about his death filled the page. She waded through them, searching for information about the Fifth or her child.

As she searched, she found more and more information until she finally stumbled upon a picture of the Fifth and her daughter. Several hours of searching passed before she saw the article on the fire. She continued to tell herself it was a coincidence. Who could carry such a secret?

The Twelfth sat motionless, her mind racing. She felt such grief and sorrow for the Fifth. How could she have had carried this alone? Why didn't she tell anyone? And then, with a sudden surge of nausea, she thought of all the things the Strongman had said over the last year. She remembered how the Fifth often went off by herself after hearing him speak. Suddenly she felt sick.

She looked at the clock; it was after eleven. The Fifth did not sleep but calling her this late seemed rude. She sent a quick text to the Fifth to check on her. There was no response.

The Twelfth looked at the long-since-forgotten papers and started to stack them up and put them back in her bag. The woman with the red hair stood and placed both hands on the Twelfth. Light filled the room. A sudden and unexplained sense of urgency filled the Twelfth.

"Go," the woman with the red hair said emphatically into the ear of the Twelfth.

The Twelfth got her keys and headed to the Fifth's house. What could it hurt to drive by? She needed gas anyway, so she decided to go by the gas station and then drive by the Fifth's just to make sure everything was okay.

The Fifth's car was not in her driveway. The town was small, and everything in it closed by ten; it wouldn't take long to check the entire thing. The streets were empty, and things were quiet. Storm clouds were forming over the woods; she hoped to be home before the rain started. The Twelfth tried calling the Fifth—no answer. Panic began to set in. She made her way around the town, checking parking lots for the Fifth's car. On the side of the road at the edge of the woods, she found the Fifth's car. Suddenly, the unexplained urgency overwhelmed her.

Chapter 54

The Twelfth ran through the woods, terror ripping through her body. Aegeus flew beside her, leading the small army of angels, and scanning the woods for the Fifth. The smell of demons reached his senses, and he knew they were getting closer. The Twelfth ran, tripping over small roots; tree branches ripped at her clothes and tore the flesh on her face. She yelled out the name of the Fifth but got no answer.

"Aegeus!" The cry came loud with a hint of desperation. It was Meir. Aegeus turned toward the sound and rushed forward. The Light inside the Twelfth shone brightly, and she too turned toward the cry of Meir.

In his hurry, Aegeus did not see the destroyer demon drop from the tree, but he felt the blow as the sword sliced through his arm. He drew his sword and found that the destroyer was not alone. Swords drawn, the angels began to battle their way toward Meir and the Fifth.

The Twelfth stopped suddenly and stood still, looking about with uncertainty. Her eyes were wide with fear, and for a moment Aegeus wondered if she could see the battle that raged around her. She yelled out the name of the Fifth, looking around wildly.

Destroyer demons began running toward the Twelfth, teeth bared and sulfur pouring from them. They left a thick dark smoke that soon blotted out what little light remained. Panic filled the Twelfth, and she screamed out.

Aegeus sliced his sword through the demons surrounding him. He ducked just as a demon warrior delivered a blow that smashed into a tree causing a loud thunderous sound to shake the woods.

The destroyers reached the Twelfth, and Aegeus could no longer see her well. He swung his sword with all his might, hitting a large warrior and leaving a gash across his chest. Black blood gushed from the wound.

He looked around him and saw his small army fighting their way toward where they last saw the Twelfth. He heard Meir cry out his name again—this time more desperate.

The first Light blast was so quick that Aegeus was not sure he had seen it. But the scream was undeniable. Then came another blast of Light, brighter than the first. A demon screamed out in agony, and then another and another.

Demons were blasting over the tops of the trees as they tried to grab the Twelfth. The smell of blistered demon filled the woods, and Aegeus could not help but smile. He could not reach her, but the Spirit was strong within her. He saw her running again, demons surrounding her but unable to touch her. He felt proud of her.

The Fifth was on her knees in the woods. Tears streamed down her cheeks, the gun shook in her hand. Meir could not reach her. Her guardian, Haywood, was covered in destroyers as he battled to keep her protected. He could no longer fight properly—there were too many of them. He covered her body with his, wrapping his wings around her to keep the destroyers from touching her. Her Light burned so dimly it was almost unnoticeable.

Haywood grabbed a destroyer and tossed it from him, but it merely scrambled back as more joined in, slashing and biting him. Meir watched helplessly as more and more demons entered the fight. Haywood's blood began to splatter their demon faces; his wings became tattered and torn. Meir stepped out from her position, unnoticed by the demons, and ran toward him.

"No!" he yelled, warning her back.

They both knew that the only hope the Fifth had was Meir. But Meir could not get to her—the demon cover was too thick. Ministering angels were not warriors. Meir was not trained in combat.

Her eyes met Haywood's, and she froze. He knew. He knew this would be his last battle, and his eyes pleaded with her to save his charge. Meir nodded slightly to let him know she would do all she could, then she stepped back from the fray and tried not to hear the sound of the demons tearing him apart.

A scream escaped Haywood's lips as a destroyer bit down on his neck. He grabbed the demon and threw him far from the pile. He felt the sharp pain of a sword piercing through his back. He felt his strength begin to leave him, and yet he knew that he had to hold on a little longer. There were many demons still emerging from the woods, piling on to him. If he acted too soon, the Fifth would have no hope. He had to protect her until Aegeus arrived and Meir could minister to her.

A cry of pain erupted from Haywood as the demons ripped a hole in his wing. Pain seared through him. A demon reached through the hole and grabbed onto the Fifth. Haywood could not remove the demon without uncovering the Fifth. He was pledged to her, and he would not uncover her. He bent lower, his body even closer to hers.

Aegeus heard the cry. The battle raged on, and he pushed his way toward the Fifth. The demons around Aegeus started to pull back, but Aegeus noticed it was not out of fear or retreat. They were rushing to the sound of the angel cry. Aegeus flew with all his might toward Haywood.

The sight of his brother covered in demons was enough to stop Aegeus short. Blood poured from Haywood's neck and back. His wings were both broken, one had a wide gaping hole; the demons were reaching through it, tearing at the hole like wild beasts. Haywood fought for the life of his charge and for his own life.

Aegeus was still too far to reach them, but he propelled himself forward with a newfound ferocity. Haywood looked up, and their eyes met; he looked deep into Aegeus's eyes, his own pleading with him, not for his own life, but the life of the Fifth.

Haywood mustered all his strength and started to uncurl his broken wings. The pain of the task registered on his face. He began to stand, revealing the Fifth, who huddled on her knees beneath him. He knew that this was her only chance. He would destroy the demons and give Meir and Aegeus enough time to save her.

As he stood up, the demons rushed to cover the Fifth, filling her with lies. Despondence and Guilt dug their talons deep into her, sulfur pouring from them in their frenzy. Haywood raised his body, strong and tall, and mustering all his energy, he used the Light of God to blast the demons from the woods. For just a moment the woods were still and quiet.

Aegeus rushed forward as the blast sent demons flying by him. Haywood collapsed to the ground. The Fifth stopped crying. She lifted the gun to her head. Meir ran to the Fifth and wrapped her body around the Fifth, searching for anything she could use to comfort her.

Demons began to fill the woods once again. The angels formed a circle around Meir and the Fifth. Swords drawn, they served as a barrier.

"Don't let them through," Aegeus yelled. "Meir, help her!" he yelled over his shoulder.

"I'm trying!" Meir shouted, sounding panicked. "She doesn't have much to work with; she has not been feeding her soul well." Meir dug deep within the Fifth. The pain was so raw, so overwhelming. Finding anything she could use was difficult. She waded past the pain, past the self-hate and loathing. There was so much blame, such sorrow.

The Fifth had been feeding her soul guilt and shame for many years. She had worked to punish herself for the death of her daughter. She had buried it so deep and refused to even speak of her daughter. She had kept the secret, and it had been killing her.

Meir brought thoughts of the Fifth's family to her. She flooded her with words of encouragement, words from her youth, favorite Bible verses, and words from the eleven. Meir dug deep to find anything that would save her.

"Meir!" Aegeus yelled as he battled the demons, pushing them back to buy Meir time. More angels flooded to the woods. The clash of swords sounded like thunder throughout the town. The Twelfth ran through the woods and into the battle just as the Fifth pulled the trigger.

Time seemed to freeze. Meir felt the spray of blood cover her, but the reality of what had happened took longer. The body of the Fifth slumped to the ground next to Haywood. The demons roared in triumph, taking to the skies to celebrate.

Aegeus spread his arms and wings wide, and lifting his head to heaven, he dropped to his knees and yelled out a cry of anguish to the King. All those with him did the same—all except for Meir. Meir knelt beside the Fifth, cradling her lifeless body. Tears dripped down Meir's face, splashing onto the Fifth, whose blood she now wore. The cry of the warriors rose above the trees and filled the air.

Chapter 55

The demons took to the skies in celebration of the death of the Fifth. Titus sat atop the church steeple watching, pleased with himself. It had not been easy for the destroyers and taunting demons to reach her; Haywood was a formidable guardian. But the Eighth had seemed the higher priority, so the angels had focused on him, which allowed Titus and his demons to focus on the Fifth. It was easy once he learned about her husband and daughter.

On a foggy day in April, during her junior year in college, the Fifth had been in a fairly minor car accident. The fog had reduced visibility, and as a result, she did not have enough time to avoid hitting the small gray truck crossing the road in front of her.

The sound of crashing metal had filled the air, and her airbag smashed into her face, breaking her nose. She was otherwise uninjured. She had hit an Army man. He was uninjured.

She was whisked away from the accident with little contact with him, but he sought her out at the hospital to make sure she was okay. They had dated three years and married during her time in graduate school. They were happy when after five years of marriage, she learned she was pregnant. In the third month of her pregnancy, her husband received orders to Iraq. He was killed in action five months later.

The Fifth gave birth to their daughter three days before her due date, less than a month after burying her husband. She loved her child more than she could ever have imagined—she was all that the Fifth had of her husband. The girl grew and served as a great source of joy to her mother. She had her father's eyes and his smile, and each day the Fifth felt as if she could still see just a small hint of her husband.

When her daughter was seven years old, the Fifth went on a date with a man she had known for some time. She had not been on a date since her husband had died and had no real desire to go, but her friends had encouraged her to do so. And so, she had agreed. She made arrangements for a friend to come over to watch her daughter, who begged her not to go.

The Fifth arrived home to find her home in flames, her daughter and friend lost to the fire. She shattered that day, fracturing into a million pieces. She poured herself into her work, never discussing the fire or her daughter. She simply could not face it. She could not say it out loud. When she moved to Platitude, she told no one that she had been married. No one knew of her daughter. No one knew of the pain that she carried so deeply inside of her—pain that had erased who she was, leaving only broken pieces of a person.

Day after day, as she listened to the Strongman make comments about how a woman's only purpose was to raise a family and serve her husband, she felt each shard of her broken soul stab deeper into her. What purpose did she have now? She had failed. What use was she to God? She covered herself in guilt and shame.

Ministering angels had attended to her almost daily, but she resisted them. She wanted to punish herself. She had nothing left but the shame and guilt. What must her husband think of her as he looked down from heaven? How disappointed he must be that the only thing he left with her—the only piece of him left on this earth, their beautiful daughter—was no more because she had been so selfish to want a night away.

Now she had every night away. What she would give to have the worst day with her daughter back. Being in Platitude, she had not told anyone about her daughter or husband because she thought it would be easier not to have to discuss it. But it also meant that she couldn't discuss it. Over time, that too seemed like a horrible injustice that she should be punished for. So, she robbed herself of anything that eased her guilt. She could not forgive herself.

Titus rubbed his left arm gently. A sword had grazed him in the battle. *Merely a flesh wound and well worth it,* he thought.

Chapter 56

"Beautiful, isn't it?" Morax asked, joining Titus on the church roof overlooking the town.

Titus was not pleased to have his moment interrupted. He had won a great victory, and his demons were celebrating in the town. He wanted nothing more than to sit atop this church and watch.

"The town or the celebration?" Hopeful that his displeasure at being interrupted wasn't obvious.

Morax smiled then took time to ponder the question before answering.

"Both, but I was referring to the town. The mountains are glorious."

For just a moment Morax forgot that he was a demon. He forgot that long ago he had made a decision that changed his course. He had chosen the Prince over the King. It had proven to be a mistake, one he would pay for for all of eternity.

But for a minute, he forgot all that and just soaked in the glory and majesty of creation. The mountains reached for the heavens, the stream running through the town bubbled praise to the King. For just a moment he forgot why he hated the hairless rats so much. Titus watched, intrigued to see Morax this way.

A crash rang out from the street below, bringing them both back to the present. Morax looked down to see a truck wrapped around a light pole. Demons covered the truck and the bystanders so that no one did anything to help the driver. They pulled phones from their pockets and bags and recorded the last breaths of the driver—it would make a great post on social media. All those phones and no one called for help, no one reached out to help, no one prayed. Titus looked at the scene and smiled. Oh, yes, he had done very well here indeed.

Morax watched, too. It was going to be a very good night for the demons. His earlier sense of nostalgia forgotten, he patted Titus on the back.

"You have done well, Titus. A promotion may be in store for you." It was a promise Titus longed for.

"Thank you, my liege. But the prophet still lives. Do we have plans?" Titus wanted to see the mission through, and he wanted to be the one responsible for destroying the prophet, if for no other reason than to gloat over Seneca.

"Seneca and Aegeus will meet in battle tomorrow. Once the angels are gone, we will have no problems destroying the prophet." Morax smiled at the thought of it.

What was the King thinking, sending a female prophet to this place? He laughed out loud. He knew the King rooted for the underdog, but a female prophet? Preposterous. Even without the demons, that was unlikely to work in Platitude.

"Where is the battle?" Titus asked, surprised by the news.

"Seneca has chosen the barley field on the backside of the campus." Morax laughed gently and shook his head in disbelief. "You should be impressed, Titus; you aren't the only one with artistic flair." Titus wasn't sure if he should be pleased that Morax had noticed his creativity or insulted by the comparison.

"I'm not sure I understand." The reference confused Titus.

"Many years ago, before Seneca lost the Light, he and Aegeus were friends. One might even say best friends. They were, along with others, assigned to fight alongside King David. Over time, each warrior fought with a specific warrior of David's. Seneca was assigned Jashobeam, and Aegeus was assigned Eleazar."

"Aren't they two of David's mightiest three?" Titus asked, his interest piqued.

"Indeed. Your history serves you well, Titus. Having Seneca and Aegeus was what propelled them to be among the three. Things were going very well for them, and their victories were many. Seneca and Aegeus are both great warriors. But the battle of Pas-Dammim would change everything.

"The Philistines and Israelites had met for battle in a field of barley. It was a sunny day with no clouds in the sky, and a cool breeze blew in from the north. The Philistines grossly outnumbered the Israelites. The battle was in their favor. The Israelite army fled. All except David and Eleazar. They stood their ground to battle, the two of them against the entire Philistine army." Morax smiled, remembering it.

"David never was one for standing down." Titus couldn't help but be impressed.

"Aegeus and Seneca remained in the battle—hundreds of angels did. As you can imagine, the fighting was intense. David and Eleazar fought back to back with the Philistines pouring in from every direction. They swung their swords with the might of ten men.

"Angels fought alongside them, slaying the Philistines. A young Philistine boy, just able to swing his sword, rushed onto the battlefield. He was young, but he was already a mighty warrior. He pushed and shoved his way toward David.

"Today would be the day the boy earned his stripes. He would kill King David. But he was a boy, and his resolve was not quite as strong as he wanted the others to believe. He hesitated for a moment—just a moment. Seneca stood between the boy and David. The word from the King was to kill the boy. Like the boy, Seneca hesitated as the boy raised his sword.

"Aegeus stepped in and killed the boy. Instantly, Seneca lost the Light of God for his disobedience. The battle raged on around them, but Seneca dropped his sword, disbelief registering in his eyes. Aegeus stood before him. His best friend, his brother-in-arms, now his mortal enemy. Aegeus cried out to the King, but Seneca's choice had been made."

"Why didn't Aegeus kill him right there?" Titus asked, unable to fully understand the bond of that type of friendship.

"You would have to ask Aegeus that, but I suppose it isn't that easy to kill your friend," Morax spoke as one who knew.

"Seneca left the battlefield that day and retreated to a cave where he spent hundreds of years alone. Each day the darkness took more of him. Without the Light of God, evil began to overtake him. Hatred filled him; anger, pride, and self-justification consumed him. He emerged from that cave a demon."

"Seneca hates the demons," Titus stated matter-of-factly.

"Seneca hates that he is a demon," Morax corrected. "Seneca hates everyone now. He is one of our mightiest warriors. He fights with great hatred, destined to never again show mercy to anyone. He has convinced himself that Aegeus cost him his Light. He has deceived himself into thinking his punishment was unjust and that if Aegeus had not stepped in, he would have killed the boy."

"So, he has chosen a barley field for their final encounter." The significance finally settled on Titus. The field would surely cause Aegeus to recognize his old friend.

"Do you think Seneca will be able to kill Aegeus?" Titus had his doubts.

"Yes, Titus, I do. I think Seneca could have killed him many times, I believe he is playing with Aegeus as a cat toys with a mouse. He has waited many years to exact his revenge, and when Seneca sinks his sword deep into Aegeus, he wants to be sure Aegeus knows who it is that is killing him."

The two were silent for some time as they watched the demon revelry in the town. Car alarms rang out in the night, the sound of arguing muffled by the thunder of the angels' cries. The sound of the angels made the night perfect for Morax. The demons flew about in jubilation. Lies, Distrust, and Fear made their way from home to home.

"Titus, how did you know about the Fifth?" Morax could not help but be impressed.

"She was so filled with regret and guilt it was obvious she had something hidden. The Strongman's words affected her in a way that was different than the others. I sent Grigori to research her past. He is a great researcher and finally found her secret." Titus smiled again to be reminded of his success.

"We will maximize on this. I will have the Strongman speak to the college about the sin of suicide. I will have him say that it is unforgivable. We will use the Word to prove it. If we can make them believe she will join us in hell, it will make their grief even greater. It will make them fear the King. They will recoil from him. They will feel guilty in mourning her and become unsure of their own position."

Ah, yes, the rats were so predictable.

Chapter 57

Word of the Fifth's death flooded through the campus. Meir returned to the King. Social media was flooded with opinions on the matter—most of them uninformed, too many of them hurtful. The story of real people was rarely as simple as a Facebook post made it seem. Despite the significant lack of details surrounding the death of the Fifth, there were plenty of opinions on the matter.

The Wednesday night group was shaken to their foundations. The Twelfth was devastated. Visions of the Fifth lying dead in the woods filled her mind, choking her with "if only." A sense of helplessness seeped in.

The Strongman called an early-morning prayer meeting in the barley field behind the campus and required all students, faculty, and staff to attend. The group met early in the morning to pray together before going to the field. They traveled together to the field for the sunrise service, but the Third stayed behind. She needed time alone with the King.

A hundred years before, the college had agreed to grow barley for the local farmers to use as feed. Agricultural students had plowed the field and planted the crops. For many generations, the fields had served the farmers in the area and created a cooperative situation between them.

But time had marched on, and farming had died out in the town. The field had long been allowed to grow wild. The Strongman positioned himself on a small platform in the middle of the field. Thousands of demons lined up behind him. Thousands more took to the sky to secure the demon dome, sealing the entrance to the town. The sky grew dark and ominous, blocking out the sunrise. The smell of sulfur, the smell the King had given the demons as a constant reminder of the fate that awaited them, hung thick in the air.

Aegeus and his team stood opposite the Strongman and his demons. Hundreds of angels arrived and stood beside them. The Twelfth stood on the right side of Aegeus. She was trembling slightly, and Aegeus found himself wishing for Meir or Lavi so that she could be comforted.

He unwrapped his wings and put his right wing around her. He knew it would not help her, but it made him feel better to do it. The Eleventh stood wide-eyed, staring at the Strongman. For the first time, she could see his demon and all those who stood behind him. She leaned toward the Twelfth and whispered, "He is a demon."

"I know." Although she could not see them, the Twelfth could feel them.

"There are thousands of them," the Eleventh whispered again, fear infecting her voice. The Twelfth looked at the Eleventh, and a flare of Light shot from the Twelfth, lighting up the otherwise dark sky.

The demons snarled and hissed at the presence of the prophet and the Light. The Twelfth glanced quickly around; concern and uncertainty filled her eyes. Aegeus leaned close to her, and although he knew she could not hear him, he spoke to her.

"You are a prophet of the King Most High. You have the power to call his army. You have the strength to defeat the enemy. Draw on the Light of God." He straightened up and readied for battle. The Strongman began to speak.

The Twelfth leaned toward the Eleventh. "Text the group; ask them all to pray." The Eleventh nodded and pulled out her phone. She sent the text and began to pray.

"We have experienced a great tragedy on our campus. We have lost a faculty member, and our hearts ache for her family and friends. All year we have discussed the devastating effects of sin on our lives. We have now seen, firsthand, the might of the evil one. Depression is a mighty tool, but you don't have to let him take over your life. You don't have to fight that battle alone. This tragedy reminds us that we wake up every day and we fight a great battle not against flesh and blood but against the principalities of darkness!"

Some in the crowd cheered his comments; some cheered the excited way he yelled them out with authority. Thousands of tormenting and destroying demons encircled the field, eager for the opportunity to bring confusion and chaos to those in the field. The Strongman continued.

"There are those that would have you give up your religious freedom and replace it with lies. They would tell you that it is okay for a woman to pass up marriage and children for her career. Do you hear that? Her career? That is selfish and rebellious; it is all about her and not about the Word.

"Acts that are selfish and rebellious lead to separation and uncertainty. You can see the results of such sinful thinking in this tragic situation. This poor woman had no leadership, no one to spiritually guide her through poor choices, selfishness, and sin. Look around you! Look around you and see who is standing beside you that wants to lead you into unrighteousness, who stands among you that is rebelling against leadership? Who among you is wading in the wages of sin? We must cleanse ourselves of the unrighteous; we must purge them from our midst; we must free ourselves from the clutches of death!" the Strongman's voice yelled out into the field.

Demons rushed into the midst of the crowd while he was still speaking. Confusion and Chaos weaved in and out of the crowd, touching the people as they passed. A thick black fog suddenly rolled into the field so that the people could not see each other. They could only hear the words of the Strongman—lies intended to deceive and destroy them. Fear and Distrust joined Confusion and Chaos, shoving, and pushing the humans, each of the eleven began to storm the gates of heaven in prayer.

Tormenting demons took to the sky and began to fly throughout the crowd, shoving and pushing the people. The thick smoke added to the confusion, causing them to blame each other. Their eyes, blinded by the demons, searched the crowd to find the unrighteous that the Strongman spoke about, to purge them from their midst.

Fear choked them as they clutched at their throats. Confusion flew low through the field, causing them to trip and fall. Panic ripped through them. Poisonous lies continued to pour from the Strongman, encouraging them to seek out the lost among them—the rebellious—and to bring them forward for redemption. His lies caused the fog to grow thicker and darker. Destroying demons flashed through the field, starting fights among the people.

Aegeus and the angels, unaffected by the demons, began to battle toward the Strongman. If they could stop him, the battle would be over. The smell of burnt demon filled the air. Aegeus battled his way toward the Strongman, who continued to spew his lies into the crowd. The Twelfth stood frozen in place. The Eleventh prayed fervently. The Seventh had arrived late and stood on the far left of the field. As emotions began to rise and the people began to respond with a mob mentality, she soon found herself surrounded by a group of young college men.

"Purge the unrighteous among you; drag them to the cross; bring them forward so that we can be free of all sin! Search for them among you and bring them to me so that we will have life!" the Strongman screamed into the crowd.

The young men surrounding the Seventh began to converge on her. They recognized her as a friend of the Fifth. One of the men grabbed her arm. Confusion dug his talons deep into him. Anger latched onto his back and stabbed into his spine.

"You were friends with that professor—the one who killed herself. You must be among the unrighteous!" he shouted, dragging her toward the Strongman.

Heartbroken over what was happening and terrified of their intentions, the Seventh struggled to pull her arm free. The boys closed in on her.

Chapter 58

The Twelfth heard the scream and searched the crowd. Chaos was everywhere. People were running and screaming. Fights broke out all around her. About two hundred yards to her left she saw the Seventh, who was surrounded by a group of males. The men were swarmed with demons, but neither the Twelfth nor the Seventh could see that. All they could see was the men dragging the Seventh to the Strongman. The Seventh fought with all she had. Without thinking, the Twelfth and the Eleventh ran toward them.

Adrenaline coursed through the Twelfth's body, helping her push past her burning lungs and pounding heart. Now was not the time to think; she prayed instead.

She tripped and fell over someone and soon found herself being trampled. She struggled to get up, but she continued to get stepped on and pushed back to the ground. She could see the Seventh just a few yards in front of her, blood pouring from the Seventh's mouth. Her shirt had been ripped and was hanging from her left shoulder.

The Eleventh prayed even more fervently. She reached the Twelfth just as a large man fell over her. The Eleventh reached down and pulled her friend from the ground.

"There are thousands of demons," she shouted over the massive noise that filled the field. She looked desperately at the Twelfth. "You are a prophet! You have to do something!"

"I am not a prophet. And even if I were, I don't know what to do!" She met the eyes of the Eleventh briefly and then turned and continued toward the Seventh. Blood ran from her mouth, bruises already forming on her face and hands.

The boys had knocked the Seventh to the ground. One of them was on top of her trying to pin her arms to the ground. The Seventh fought. The Twelfth ran up behind the young man, and with all her strength, she kicked him in the back, right where she estimated his kidney to be. The boy fell over enough that the Eleventh could reach the Seventh and help her to her feet.

The Twelfth did not see the fist until it struck her on the side of the face. Lights danced before her eyes, and for just a moment she went deaf. Pain shot through her face, and she stumbled sideways, nearly falling. She instinctively touched her face, and pain shot through her. He had hit her on the cheek just below her temple. She could feel it swelling, causing her eye to start to swell shut.

She turned to face the man who had hit her. She was not foolish enough to think she could win in a fair fight; he was considerably bigger than her and half her age. But she did not intend to fight fair. She put up her fists, and he laughed at her. With all her might, she kicked him in the groin. He dropped to the ground and began to vomit.

The demon that had been attached to him let go and laughed at his misfortune. He quickly found another host and headed back toward the prophet. The prayers of the eleven that remained continued, and Light slowly began to seep into the field.

Titus had been watching from a distance, but when he saw the prophet, unprotected, he directed hundreds of demons toward her. He would see the prophet destroyed. The demons rushed at her, some in their spirit form, some attached to humans.

Chapter 59

"Aegeus!" The call came out clear and full of panic. The battlefield was loud, but above the noise, above the chaos, Aegeus heard the call. His eyes scanned the field. He did not recognize the voice.

"Aegeus!" it came again, this time more panicked. Then he saw the Twelfth, surrounded by demons. Their eyes met. He knew she could not see him, and yet she seemed to be looking straight at him. Aegeus stood stunned for a moment, then abandoned his pursuit of the Strongman and headed toward the Twelfth.

"Kfir! The prophet!" he yelled as he passed Kfir deep in battle with four demons. Aegeus fought his way to the prophet, slashing through demons as he went. He reached her just as a man, covered in destroying demons clutched her by the throat. Aegeus grabbed the man and threw him across the field.

The Twelfth held her throat. "Thank you," she managed as she struggled to regain her breathing. Aegeus stepped back in shock.

"You can see me?" He asked her, the battle raging around them. She nodded yes in response, rubbing her throat, and trying to reclaim her voice. "How long have you been able to see me?" he asked, completely overcome by this discovery. He felt as if he needed to sit down. Never in all his time on earth had a human ever been able to see him. He had never spoken to a human outside of heaven. Never had he been thanked by one.

"Since the woods," she managed, her voice gruff.

Suddenly, while Aegeus was still trying to process what was happening, a great warrior dropped to the ground behind him. The long-haired demon with the scar, his eyes calm amid the chaos. He smiled, not wanting to forget a moment of this—their last encounter.

"Aegeus, we meet again," he said in greeting. Aegeus felt a rush of familiarity—the feeling that you know someone, but you just can't quite place them. He turned to face the demon, putting himself between the warrior and the Twelfth.

His eyes searched, and suddenly realization settled over him. He was immediately reminded of another barley field thousands of years ago. He had watched as his best friend had fallen from grace. Aegeus had not realized what had happened until it was too late. He had been deep in the throes of battle and saw a boy swing his sword to kill King David. Aegeus had done his duty and protected the King.

As soon as the boy's body fell to the ground, time seemed to stand still for Aegeus. He realized what had happened. His eyes met Seneca's for the last time. He watched as the Light of God was withdrawn from Seneca. It was a horrible sight to behold.

They stood there looking at each other for what seemed like a lifetime. And then, in the blink of an eye, it was over. Seneca dropped his sword and walked away, disbelief washing over him. Aegeus watched him go, knowing there was nothing he could do. Eventually, he had turned back to the battle trying to focus, trying to tell himself it wasn't real. But angels do not lie—not even to themselves. Aegeus slew thousands of Philistines that day along with ten thousand demons.

Seneca waited patiently for Aegeus to remember, wanting to be sure that Aegeus felt the full effect of the memory. When Aegeus's eyes told Seneca he had returned to the present, Seneca drew his sword.

"Seneca," Aegeus nearly whispered it. His sorrow over seeing his friend this way was suffocating.

"I have waited many years for this Aegeus," Seneca said, a snarl on his face. He twirled his sword in front of him. It had taken hundreds of years for Seneca to become completely evil with no hint of the angel he used to be. His love for Aegeus had been completely replaced with hate and blame. He longed for nothing more than to plunge his sword deep into Aegeus's stomach. He wanted to rip the wings from Aegeus's body so that like Seneca, Aegeus could never fight for the King again.

"Seneca, I do not wish to kill you. But I will defend the prophet." Aegeus stood firm. Kfir arrived and stood by him. Kfir understood this battle was Aegeus's and positioned himself between Aegeus and the prophet.

Seneca swung his sword at Aegeus. He was in no rush. There was no sense of urgency, only finality. Their swords slammed together, the sound of it blasting through the field. The voice of the Strongman grew louder and more ominous. Seneca clipped the side of Aegeus's face with his sword before Aegeus could dodge it. Golden blood gushed from the wound.

Aegeus dropped low to the ground to avoid another blow and swung his sword toward Seneca, which caused him to jump. Aegeus shot into the sky after him, each of them slashing and swinging at the other. Aegeus missed a shot with his sword but connected his elbow to Seneca's face, sending him flying backward out of Aegeus's sight.

No longer seeing Seneca, and knowing that Kfir protected the Twelfth, Aegeus headed for the Strongman. If they could kill the Strongman, the fight would be over.

He battled his way to the Strongman then shoved his sword through the Strongman's chest just as Seneca thrust his sword through Aegeus's back.

Aegeus let out a yell as his knees buckled, and he sank down, causing the sword to slice farther through him. Seneca withdrew his sword and wiped it across his own chest, covering himself in Aegeus's blood.

The sword removed, Aegeus stumbled forward, golden blood pouring from his wound.

"The mighty Aegeus has failed," Titus gloated. "Your effort is futile." Titus walked slowly to the Strongman and laid his hand on him, healing him from his wounds.

Aegeus turned toward Seneca, staggering forward, barely able to stand. His eyes met the demon he had once called brother and he saw no hint of the angel Seneca had once been. He saw only pride and contempt. Aegeus took a deep breath, and summoning his remaining strength, in one swift move he shoved his sword through Seneca's chin and out the top of his head. Seneca fell to the ground; Aegeus collapsing beside him.

"Aegeus!" He could hear the Twelfth calling his name from a distance. The sound of running footsteps drew nearer until they stopped. The Twelfth dropped to her knees on the ground beside him. Tears filled her eyes, blood was crusted to her lip and flowing from near her eye. Bruises covered her neck and face. She took his hand in hers, her tears dripping onto his face.

"Aegeus," she repeated his name, a pleading in her voice.

"You are a prophet," he whispered. She nodded her head in response, emotion strangling her voice and leaving her unable to speak. She leaned her head against his chest and cried. Aegeus placed his right hand on her head, wanting to give her comfort. The battle raged on, the smell of impending doom all around them.

"Is this my fault?" She lifted her head and choked out the words. The question pained Aegeus.

"No." He felt the life dwindling from his body, and emotion choked his voice. Aegeus was not sure how to handle the emotions that overwhelmed him. He knew he should say something to her, something to comfort her, something she could hold on to in the days to come, but he could think of nothing worthy of the moment.

"How sweet," Titus said as he approached. Aegeus looked up into his eyes. Titus drew his weapon and grabbed one of Aegeus's wings. Aegeus tried to pull them in and protect them, but he lacked the strength. Titus pulled the wing, wrenching it awkwardly out of place. He raised his sword to cut it off.

"I will finish what Seneca could not," Titus said to Aegeus. Because Titus wore a human body, the eleven could see him clearly.

The Eleventh knelt in the field where she was, each of the others joined her. Gradually others in the field joined in, kneeling in prayer amid the chaos, amid the fear. As one voice, they called out to the King. The Third stormed the gates of heaven, her prayers pouring over those in the field.

The Twelfth's eyes met Aegeus's and the Spirit overwhelmed her. Power coursed through her body, a feeling of electricity filling her—all fear removed. The Light of God poured from her.

Titus could not cross the barrier to touch her. She rose from the ground and stood with her arms out to her sides, putting herself between Titus and Aegeus. "I am a child of God," she said with great force. She wasn't sure what else to say.

The Light caused Titus to turn his head slightly.

The mark of the warrior on Aegeus's chest began to shine, and swords flashed with fire, signifying the presence of the King. The sound of marching resounded throughout Platitude. The fog and darkness cleared. The King's arrival blasted the demons from his presence.

Chapter 60

Aegeus strolled toward the meeting spot. He walked as one who had eternity on his side. He let his hands drop to his sides and brush across the field of wheat he was ambling through. Wheat was one of his favorites. The heads of grain on the stalks felt soft on his fingers, he closed his eyes and continued to walk forward savoring the delicate brush of the plant across his hands. The gentle touch of them reminded him of the frailty of the King's children and the tenderness of their hearts.

His senses soaked in the glory that was heaven. Light warmed his olive skin; the sweet smell of lilac filled the air. Aegeus loved the scent of lilac. He breathed in deeply, letting it soak through him. He turned his face toward the throne room, allowing the Light and power of the King to wash over him and beckon to him.

Standing in the middle of the field, he closed his eyes and listened to the voices of heaven singing the praise of the King. He stood straighter, reaching his full height of seven feet two inches. His wings were tucked into the compartments on his back, where they fit when he did not need them. His hair, the color of chestnut, blew gently in the breeze. His brown eyes were the color of toasted almonds. Aegeus felt the rush of love and overwhelming joy that could only come from the King. He felt the light brush of power caress his skin as if every particle of his being was getting charged.

In the distance, he could see the glimmer of the city. He headed in the opposite direction, toward the large tree in the center of the field. As he walked, he took in every scent, every color, and every texture along the way. The tree stood tall and proud where it had stood for all time. The bark of the tree was rough and cracked in a way that was beautiful.

If you took the time to look closely, you could see subtle carvings in the bark just below the surface. It whispered secrets of the past and the beauty of the future. Its limbs extended in every direction, long sturdy branches. The leaves fluttered in the breeze making a sound like ocean waves. They called out their praise to the King.

Far to the east, he saw a new arrival. She stood near the gate, being welcomed by her husband and child. Aegeus smiled. He hoped Kfir was near enough to see it.

As he reached the tree, he was pleased to see the others were not yet there. Aegeus had seen two passes of fruit on the tree since he'd returned from Platitude. Today he would stand under this tree and be honored by the King. Today, he would become an archangel.

He looked carefully at the trunk of the tree, its carvings beautiful and ornate. He ran his hand gently over them until his hand touched an area that felt warm to the touch. When his fingers touched it, a little shiver ran through him. Aegeus leaned closer.

The carving seemed fresh—new—and it was in the shape of the ancient symbol called the horn. The horn represented the King's power, triumph, fierceness, and strength. He rubbed his hand over it again, and as he did, two things seemed to happen simultaneously. He was sure he heard the tree whisper his name and the name of the Twelfth. And he felt a sting on the back of his left shoulder. When he looked, the symbol had appeared on the back of his left shoulder. Aegeus stepped back from the tree and turned to face the wheat. He closed his eyes and stood quietly, letting the gentle breeze blow over him.

"You look like you're in heaven," the King said, joining him under the tree. The tree reacted to the King's presence. The King walked to the tree and placed his hand gently against the trunk. Golden, sparkling light filled the tree, radiating from it like glitter. Aegeus knelt on the lush green grass before the King.

"I see you have received the mark of the horn.," the King smiled, his hand still on the tree. "The Twelfth now carries the mark as well," he said, stepping away from the tree. The King placed his hand on Aegeus's shoulder, filling him with the Light.

"Aegeus, your heart is heavy. Rise and tell me what troubles you," the King said gently.

Aegeus stood. "What became of the Strongman?" he asked.

"The Strongman fled the battlefield as soon as he saw that the mark of the warriors was glowing. He will eventually resign from the college and go to Washington, D.C. to provide spiritual guidance to the rulers of the nation."

The King waited patiently. He understood this was not what troubled Aegeus, but it was not in the King's nature to rush an issue.

"So, we lost?" Aegeus asked.

The King smiled. While he knew this was important to Aegeus, he also knew that it was not what was truly in his heart. "What was your mission, Aegeus?"

"To protect the Twelfth," he answered confidently.

"Did you do that?"

"I did. But . . . .." Aegeus reflected on the final moments of the battle when Titus was positioned over him, poised to remove his wings. But the prayers of the King's children brought Light into the darkness. The Twelfth discovered her true self, emitting the Light of God and protecting Aegeus until the King arrived.

"Protecting you was the only way the Twelfth could ever discover who she truly was. And knowing who she is is critical to the next phase of her assignment. You did well, Aegeus. We did not lose." The King beamed with pride.

He knew it had been close, waiting for the Twelfth to truly accept who she was, watching as Titus threatened to cut off Aegeus's wings. The army had been anxious as they waited. But the King had known; he understood the importance of the timing.

"But what about the Strongman?" Aegeus hesitated not understanding how letting the Strongman escape was winning.

"Aegeus, many of my daughters have felt rejected by the church. The Strongman and others like him have persecuted them and twisted my words for their own selfish purposes. Through their persecution, my children have started many home churches, and word of me has spread. What the Strongman intended for evil, I have used for good.

"My daughters have clung to me, but they cry out for deliverance. I have heard their cry, Aegeus, and I can bear it no longer. I have sent them a prophet. They must understand how much I love them. The eleven in the town will serve as a voice for my daughters. The battle has only begun."

"But the Tenth failed," Aegeus said, sadness seeping into him as he remembered the death of the Fifth. The King smiled.

"Yes, Aegeus, he did fail. But even that can be used for good. The Tenth will never forget what his cowardice cost. He is my child, Aegeus, and he has come to me for forgiveness, which I freely give. He will find his courage—in time."

The King understood how important timing was. Even as he waited now, understanding that the next question was the one that was dearest to Aegeus's heart. The next question was the one that mattered—the one that had transformed Aegeus into who he truly was. The King waited with anticipation for Aegeus to ask.

Raising his eyes to the King, Aegeus asked what was truly in his heart. "And the Twelfth—what becomes of her?"

The King smiled. Now they could have the conversation he had been waiting for.

Chapter 61

Morax, Titus, and the Strongman gathered at the old church. Titus, full of rage and covered in burns from the arrival of the King, looked around the church. He would miss it. Being in the presence of the King reminded him, if only for a moment, just how far he had fallen.

For just a twinkling, he let his mind wander back to a time when he had walked the streets of gold. At one time, the King's presence would not have burned him, but instead, it would have filled him with power. The memory of it was too painful; there was no greater torment than separation from the King. Without the King, there was no true hope.

Instead, Titus clung to his anger. He comforted himself with assurances of revenge.

The Strongman stalked to the front of the church and grabbed the Bible from the communion table in front. He threw it across the small room, roaring out in protest. His anger consumed him. How had they lost? How could this have happened? They had planned so carefully; they had been patient.

The Strongman had been sure that this battle belonged to the demons. He knew that ultimately the King always won, but this battle should have been theirs.

Morax sighed heavily. He too needed a moment to recover from being in the King's presence. He looked at the Strongman. A fresh scar covered his chest, serving as a reminder of how close things had been. Morax took one more moment, allowing the Strongman to rage and Titus to smolder.

When they were done, he spoke. "We have lost a great warrior today. Seneca was mighty, and we will surely feel his loss to our mission. But we are not defeated. This battle may not have gone our way, but our prince is relentless. He knows the King's children well.

"Certainly, the next stage of the war would have been easier if we had claimed the college. We are not done here. When we go, we will leave behind many demons and much carnage. We will bring in another of our own to continue our work. You have seen how easily we can distract the hairless rats. They will destroy each other over minor things, keeping them distracted from what the King called them to do: love one another."

Titus shivered at the very idea of loving one another. It disgusted him, and yet he knew that if the King's children ever truly got it right, nothing else would matter. He also knew that as long as he had breath left in him, he would never stop fighting against them—his hatred for them was that deep.

He conceded that Morax was right; distracting the humans with theological differences would keep them powerless. Oh, certainly there were some exceptions. There were those who had learned to hear the King's voice. They understood it was about falling in love with the King, not following a list of rules, not passing judgment, not condemning each other. Those were the powerful ones, but fortunately, their numbers were few, and it was easy to turn the right fighters against them.

Morax looked at the Strongman and continued, "When your contract expires, you will move into the next phase of our plan. Washington is primed and ready. We already have your replacement at hand. He will continue our work. Little has been lost here. We have poisoned an entire generation of the King's children. The lies we have taught will remain with them, serving as fodder for the tormenting demons to use against them. They will perpetuate those lies for several generations. Regret and Guilt will flood this place tomorrow, overwhelming them. The messages we have instilled will cause them to rot inside.

"We now know of the prophet. We know of her weaknesses, of which there are many. We will not relent.; we will destroy her. We will work in the minds of all who hear her, and we will distract them with superficial things so that they dismiss her. We will choose the things we know work well—distractions about her being a woman, her looks, how she dresses, her hair, any little criticism will do to keep people from truly hearing her message.

"We have uncovered the others as well. We have set the First and his wife back a decade. We ripped open their scars, and that will not soon be forgotten.

"The Second and Third are deeply entrenched with the King. We can do little to impact them, but we knew that soon after discovering them.

"The Fourth will continue to question his worth as a parent, partially disabling him.

"We killed the Fifth, preventing her from accomplishing the goals the King set out for her.

"The Sixth retains her secret, which will eat away at her soul.

"The Seventh has not yet come out from under the Sixth's wing. She is destined for mighty things, but we can stall that if we keep her filled with self-doubt and incapable of silencing all voices but the King's.

"The Eighth has sunk into depression and is headed down a path of burying his gift. We can make him view it as a curse. If we are wise, we can prevent him from ever using it as the King intended.

"The Ninth is still developing and questioning, and we have a great opportunity to influence and frustrate her.

"We have castrated the Tenth, filling him with pride and ambition. He will not soon forget his shame. We can use that to keep him silent.

"The Eleventh can see us, which poses a significant risk, but we can easily discredit her. However, these are not the only ones."

Morax pulled out the folder he had been carrying. "The King has many children—some more vulnerable than others. We will begin our exit from this place, and Titus will head to Washington, but there are many other targets—teams are already deploying to find the names on this list. None are safe." He held the folder up.

Titus took the folder from Morax and flipped through it. It contained the names of the King's children spread across the nation. A sinister smile spread across his face.

Morax was right. This might not have been the victory they wanted, but it had not been a defeat.

<u>A Note From the Author:</u>

I hope you enjoyed reading The Prophet and that in some small way it changed the way you view spiritual warfare. It was a fun story to write and wrestle with. Log into www.andeedwards.com for additional content related to the book including an angel guide, a study guide and a discussion guide for book clubs.

If you enjoyed this book, I'd be honored if you left a review of it. Reviews help me get more visibility as an author so other readers can find the book. If your review is selected for inclusion on my website, I will send you a signed copy of the next book.

Thanks for reading *The Prophet*, I hope you join me for the next book in the series, *The Seventh Angel*.

Don't miss the next book in the series, *The Seventh Angel*

The Seventh Angel, Prologue

The demon led Titus into the study where Lucifer waited. An overflowing ashtray sat on the desk still smoldering from a cigar freshly extinguished. The room was full of the holiest of all books, it was evident to Titus that Lucifer was searching the Word for something.

"My Liege," Titus offered in greeting kneeling on the expensive Persian rug before his Prince.

"I assume you have a good reason for coming uninvited to my home, for interrupting me, and for usurping your position," Lucifer drilled. But Titus was not concerned by the harsh tone. He knew that what he brought would be pleasing to Lucifer. He would not have taken the risk otherwise.

"Yes, my Liege," he answered humbly. Being confident did not mean he need be arrogant. While Titus understood the value of the gift he brought Lucifer, he also realized he was in a precarious position. Lucifer was the Prince of the earth; he was not to be trifled with. Titus would proceed with deep respect never overtly revealing his betrayal of Morax or his own personal quest for power.

"Get up!" Lucifer snapped at him, irritation, and disgust evident in his voice.

"I bring you news of Platitude," Titus offered as he stood.

"Platitude? The King's college we are taking over?" Lucifer asked as if he didn't already know.

"Yes." He paused briefly observing Lucifer for any signs of anger. He saw only annoyance.

"What is your report then?" Lucifer prompted visibly fighting agitation.

"There was a prophet at the college," Titus once again paused giving Lucifer plenty of time to process the information. He cunningly laid his cards out for Lucifer to see and was instantly rewarded. A small ripple of excitement pulsed through Lucifer chased back by a hint of fear that Titus would never acknowledge seeing. All who were wise feared the King. It was only right that Lucifer should as well, after all, who knew better than Lucifer what the King was capable of?

"Go on," Lucifer asked in a slightly softer tone, his interest piqued.

Lucifer listened as Titus filled him in on the critical elements of the battle in Platitude. Titus did, of course, leave out many key facts, facts he was sure would work against him. He would leave that bit for Morax.

Lucifer listened intently asking only what had become of each of the humans. Titus relayed what he knew which wasn't much.

"Find them and destroy them all. But bring me the prophet alive," Lucifer ordered.

www.ingramcontent.com/pod-product-compliance
Lightning Source LLC
Chambersburg PA
CBHW080819250626
47159CB00011B/3443